THE RELIC

EVELYN ANTHONY

HUTCHINSON
London   Sydney   Auckland   Johannesburg

With grateful thanks to
Denys Simmons and John Pither
for all their invaluable help

© Evelyn Anthony 1991

The right of Evelyn Anthony to be identified as Author of
this work has been asserted by Evelyn Anthony in accordance
with the Copyright, Designs and Patents Act, 1988

This edition first published in 1991 by
Hutchinson

Random Century Group Ltd
20 Vauxhall Bridge Road, London SW1V 2SA

Random Century Australia (Pty) Ltd
20 Alfred Street, Milsons Point, Sydney, NSW 2061, Australia

Random Century New Zealand Ltd
PO Box 40–086, Glenfield, Auckland 10, New Zealand

Random Century South Africa (Pty) Ltd
PO Box 337, Bergvlei, 2012, South Africa

Set in Linotron Bembo by Input Typesetting Ltd, London
Printed and bound in Great Britain by Clays Ltd, St. Ives PLC

To my dear friend
Blanche Kerman,
with love

THE RELIC

PROLOGUE

Prologue

Commissar Gregor Lepkin was working at his desk. It was a handsome desk and it faced the big windows. His office was large and well equipped. He had status. He had been promoted. He was in favour. A beautiful little enamel clock with its matching calendar stood on the desk, flotsam rescued from the bloody tide of revolution. The rich translucence of the green enamel set off the delicate sparkle of diamonds. They gave Lepkin intense pleasure. He liked to wind the clock and change the date card on the calendar. He had done both that morning when he arrived: 20 May 1938. The Imperial cipher twinkled in the sunlight. The clock and the calendar had been looted from the Tsarist Palace of Tszarske Seloe. Years ago he had bought the beautiful little objects from a drunken soldier for a few roubles.

He worked hard; he was a man who prided himself on his attention to detail. Best of all, he had a sixth sense for trouble. On his last three visits to his mother in the devastated Ukraine, he'd discovered that the State security service in Kharkov was rotten with corruption. Old Partymen, grown fat and lazy, bloated like bluebottles on the corpses of Stalin's victims. Five million Ukrainians. Starved, imprisoned, hunted off their lands to die. The punitive forces had gone, their work was completed. The administration left behind had lined its pockets and neglected its duties. Lepkin had been compiling his report for months. It was not his province to question the methods Stalin used. He closed his eyes and hardened his heart in the name of the great cause he had followed since he was a student running from the Tsarist police. The *Cheka*, instrument of terror and repression, had been swept away. The Office of State Security had a new name, NKVD. A new hierarchy composed of dedicated men like himself, career officers, controlling an army of informers and armed enforcers. Even now the Revolution was threatened by foreign powers outside, and by traitors within.

Stalin was right; he had to be. The alternative was unthinkable. Lepkin dared not think it. He wasn't brave like his old friend Alexei Rakovsky. He refused to question, to doubt. Without his beliefs, he was lost; without the party and its leader, there was nothing but chaos. He held fast to that, like a man on a cliff face who knows that to look down is to fall. The little clock had a sweet silvery chime. It was like music. Eleven o'clock.

He got up and went to the window overlooking Dzerjhinsky Square. It was a bright spring day; sunshine struck gold off the cupolas of Saint Basil's Cathedral. A wonder of magnificance and imagination. It pleased his eye every time he looked across at the view. Tsar Ivan the terrible had blinded the architect so he could never build another like it. Lepkin thought sometimes that this was Russia: splendour and cruelty that went hand in hand like lovers. He saw the car sweep into the courtyard below and he sighed.

Memories made him sad. Memories of the old, close comradeship that bound him and Alexei Rakovsky together. The faith, the fierce idealism. How he had admired Alexei, how he had looked up to him! The dangers they shared in those early days! Rakovsky was the elder by two years, and by temperament he was the leader. Lepkin was cautious, Rakovsky gloried in risks.

Lepkin was proud to be Alexei Rakovsky's friend and follower. He had been caught delivering pamphlets and exiled to Gorki for two years. Lepkin was never arrested. He stayed on at university, quietly organizing.

Rakovsky joined the army when the war with Germany broke

out. He was a Russian first and a Bolshevik second when the Motherland was threatened. Lepkin admired his patriotism, but remained in Moscow, co-ordinating workers' movements. When the Tsar's armies faced defeat in 1917, Rakovsky shot the Tsarist officers and led his regiment back to fight for the Revolution. He and Lepkin had stood together in the crowd that welcomed Lenin off the train when he returned from exile.

Now he watched the car draw up, the driver open the door for Rakovsky. Alexei had risen high in the Party. He had been a hero. He was Secretary to the Commissar of Internal Affairs. High office. Power and prestige. He had been chosen by Lenin. That, as Lepkin knew, was the reason for his downfall. All around them, men of the old Bolshevik tradition were toppling into the abyss.

He stepped forward as his door opened and he saw Rakovsky, his old friend. He held out his arms and embraced him.

'Gregor Ivanovitch,' Rakovsky said, 'It's so good to see you.'

'Good to see you, Alexei,' was Lepkin's answer. Rakovsky managed a smile; it was a poor thing that sat uneasily on his mouth. It never reached the eyes. Lepkin knew that look. He'd seen it many times in the eyes of other men.

'Sit down, my friend,' he suggested. 'A cigarette?' Rakovsky took one, lit it and Lepkin noticed how his hand shook. 'Vodka?' he asked.

'Vodka,' Rakovsky repeated. 'Why not? Congratulations on the new office. It goes with the rank, I suppose.'

'I've got more room,' Lepkin said. 'How is the family? It's ages since I've seen them, but I've been so busy with the new job.'

'You asked about the family,' Rakovsky said. 'That's why I've come.'

'But why come here?' Lepkin frowned. He shook his head. Still rash, still taking risks.

'Because I didn't want to compromise you,' Rakovsky answered. 'I'm watched whatever I do, wherever I go. Your people are in my ministry, they're in my offices – everywhere. I've come to see you openly because no one can accuse me of having a secret meeting in the Lubianka. Or suspect you of plotting with an oppositionist.'

He paused. The cigarette had burned down to its cardboard holder. 'My name is on the new list, Gregor. You knew that, didn't you? That's why you've stayed away from us. Not that I blame you.'

Lepkin said quietly, 'That's not the reason, Alexei. But I do know about the list. I've seen your name.'

'It's not just me, but my whole family.' Rakovsky's voice trembled. 'You know what happens – you know what they'll do to them? They came for Rosengoltz's wife and daughter in the middle of the night and they were never seen again.'

He got up, a tall man grown thin, his clothes loose upon him. 'Stalin's a madman, Gregor. A devil. I should have seen it; I should have done something about it. Now it's too late. I did nothing. I stood there and applauded while he slaughtered millions in the name of Lenin. And now it's my turn.'

He dropped back in to his chair. There was a cold sheen of sweat on his face.

Lepkin said quietly, 'We're old friends, but you shouldn't say things like that. Not even to me.'

'Why not? I'm already a dead man. But listen, listen, I've got something to show you. Something to offer you.'

'No,' Lepkin raised his hand to stop him. 'No bribes, Alexei. Don't offer me a bribe.'

Rakovsky came close; he leaned across the desk. He had one hand buried deep in his coat. 'This isn't a bribe,' he said slowly. 'I know money wouldn't buy you. But this hasn't a price. It could save your life one day.'

'Then why can't it save yours?' Lepkin asked him.

'Because Stalin is Stalin,' he said. 'If I gave it to him he'd still kill me and send my family to the Gulag. And it would help to keep his foot on our necks for as long as he lived. I'm giving this to you, Gregor. In return, I want you to save Natalia and the boys.'

He brought out a parcel. It was roughly tied with a frayed cord. He untied the knots; it took time because his hands were shaking. The paper peeled back, splitting with age, and a yellowing cloth with embroidered edges fell away at his touch.

Lepkin couldn't help himself. He stared. He swore an old-fashioned blasphemous oath. 'Holy Christ! It's the Relic!'

He reached out a hand, and Rakovsky said softly, 'Take it. Hold it.'

Lepkin lifted it in his hands. The cross gleamed gold, the great red stones in the body flashed like huge drops of blood in the light. Lepkin shook his head. 'Holy Christ,' he said again. 'I don't believe it. St Vladimir's Cross. Alexei, where did you get it?'

Rakovsky said slowly, 'The Patriarch at Kiev gave it to my mother in 1919. The Reds were winning. He knew they'd take the cross. My mother was only a poor woman, but she was devout.'

'I remember your mother,' Lepkin muttered. An illiterate *matiushka*, with Tartar blood. A figure who served her menfolk and kept in the background. She had been entrusted with the Relic that could give victory to the Whites in the Civil War. Lenin had said publicly that he would grind the hated cross under the heel of his boot.

'My father was ordered to take it from the cathedral,' Alexei went on. Serge Rakovsky was a fanatical Bolshevik, who had suffered the knout and exile to Siberia. Lepkin remembered him only too well. A terrifying man, brutalized by suffering and hate.

'You know what they did to the Patriarch?' Rakovsky said. 'They got nothing out of him. They shot the rest of the priests under the cathedral wall. My father was raging; he said to me, "If the Whites have got it, they'll hold Russia from the Urals to the Black Sea." And all the time it was in a box under his bed, wrapped in my mother's petticoat. He would have killed her with his own hands if he'd known what she'd done.'

Lepkin laid the cross down on the desk. 'How did you find it?' He felt shaken; he couldn't stop staring at the cross. The red stones were full of shifting light. It drew him like a magnet. He thought suddenly, this thing is in my blood. I'm afraid of it.

He heard Alexei say, 'She called me when she was dying. She hated my father, but she loved me. She gave me the cross; and she made me swear on her soul's salvation that I wouldn't give it up. I swore, Gregor. I swore to please her and to let her die in peace. She said to me, "There's goodness in you, my son. One day your soul will be saved because of this." But there's no chance of that.'

He poured himself another vodka, and drank it down. He said, 'It fascinates you, doesn't it? I was the same. I kept looking at it. In the end it troubled me, so I wrapped it up and hid it under the floor in my house. I haven't looked at it for many years, till I knew my name was on the death list. I want you to have it, Gregor. Stalin may not last forever. Then it could be your salvation. And Russia's.'

Slowly, Lepkin re-made the parcel, the paper splitting and the string ravelling up. His hands were unsteady now. He put it in a drawer, closed it and turned the key.

He said, 'I can save Natalia and the boys.'

'And you will?' Rakovsky asked.

'I will. I promise you. I'll get them out of Moscow, to my mother. They'll be safe there.'

Rakovsky nodded. He looked old, and drawn. He took a deep breath that came out as a deeper sigh. 'I'm glad. I know they'll be safe with you. I can try to be calm now. Do you know how long I've got. Is there a date fixed?'

'I wouldn't know,' Lepkin said. 'But it won't be long. There are two Politburo members and eight army commanders on that list.'

'They'll all be murdered,' Alexei said. 'They'll be drugged and tormented till they get up and accuse themselves and ask for death. That's what I fear most, Gregor. I'm afraid of what they'll do to make a broken puppet out of me.'

Lepkin came close. He laid an arm around his shoulder. He looked in to his old friend's face and said, 'Don't be afraid, Alexei. I'm not going to let that happen.'

As they embraced, he slipped his revolver out of its holster and shot Rakovsky dead.

The train to Kharkov was at Moscow station by the time Natalia Rakovsky and her children were hurried through the barrier. But there was no sign of Rakovsky as she leaned out of the window, searching for him on the platform. When the train started moving, she turned back to her husband's driver. He was called Ivan. That's all she knew about him. A big, raw peasant with few words to say for himself.

'My husband,' she shouted at him. 'You said he'd be on the train.'

'Comrade Commissar Lepkin will come to you in Kharkov,' he replied.

Lepkin. The old family friend who was a high officer in the NKVD. It was Lepkin who had put them on the train.

She saw the countryside rush by through a veil of unshed tears. The journey from Moscow to Kharkov would take two days and nights. Viktor, the younger twin, was nestled into her side. He fell asleep. Stefan, always boisterous and active, clambered over the seats. Ivan was showing him how to make paper men out of an old newspaper, folding and tearing with surprising delicacy.

'What's happened to my husband?' she asked in a low voice, when both her sons were sleeping.

'I don't know,' he said. 'Please, it will be better if you sleep.'

She drew the twins closer to her for comfort, and gave way to the rhythm of the train. She knew she would never see Alexei again.

The body of Alexei Rakovsky had been removed from Lepkin's office, the blood stains scrubbed off the floor. His staff had rushed in when they heard the shot. He had dismissed them with calm authority; Rakovsky had been shot resisting arrest. They had heard that explanation before. He'd had time to send Rakovsky's driver on his secret journey. Time to hide the cross. Before the summons came.

He made his way up in the old-fashioned lift to the little room at the top of the building, with its sweeping views over Moscow. He paused by the door and knocked. His hand trembled.

Nikolai Yetzov was a small man; his hair receded and his skin was sallow. He sat like a bird of prey in his eyrie on the top floor. Next to Stalin, he was the most feared man in Russia. He called out, 'Come in,' and watched Lepkin walk towards him. He didn't speak, then looked down at his papers as if there was no one

9

there. He made a note or two, then paused, looking over what he'd written.

The bile of terror rose in Lepkin's throat. He didn't dare cough to clear it.

At last Yetzov said, still looking at his papers, 'I am waiting for your report on the incident this morning, comrade.' He raised his head and stared at Lepkin.

'Why did you shoot the traitor, Rakovsky?'

Lepkin was word perfect. He had rehearsed his story again and again. He said, 'Because he tried to bribe me, comrade. I told him I didn't deal with traitors. Then he abused comrade Stalin. He called him a murderer, a traitor to Lenin.'

'Ah,' the dry voice said. 'Did he . . . What else?'

Lepkin hesitated, as the dark, cruel eyes bored holes into him. He had to be convincing because his life was forfeit if Yetzov didn't believe him. Perhaps even if he did. 'He said he'd be revenged on me because I wouldn't help him. He said he'd name me when he was arrested. "I'll take you to the cellars with me, Lepkin – I'll denounce you".'

'And then what did you do, comrade?'

'I drew my revolver to arrest him,' Lepkin answered. 'He resisted so I shot him.'

There was a long silence. Yetzov played with a pen, twiddling it between his fingers. There was anger in his eyes. He loved to inflict pain and humiliation on his victims. He had been looking forward to bringing Alexei Rakovsky to his knees. Lepkin had cheated him of that pleasure. At last he smiled. It terrified Lepkin to see that smile.

'You did what any loyal Party member would do,' he said slowly. 'You punished him for abusing Comrade Stalin, and you saved your own skin by shutting his mouth. Very sensible. We live in dangerous times.'

'Yes,' Lepkin agreed. 'We do.'

'You have an appointment in Kharkov,' Yetzov's tone changed. It became harsh. 'You'll have an opportunity to prove how loyal you really are, Lepkin. I want that area cleaned of filth. I want every oppositionist, every troublemaker, every enemy of the Party and the State hounded down and brought to me for justice. You mustn't fail, Lepkin. If even one escapes me, you will answer for it. You do understand, don't you?'

Lepkin answered boldly, 'Perfectly, comrade Yetzov. I won't fail.'

'You'd better not,' The voice sank to a whisper. 'You can go now.'

Lepkin went out and closed the door. Very carefully, so as not to make a noise. He had robbed Yetzov of his victim. But he was under a suspended sentence, and he knew it. He went back down to his office, and poured himself a glass of vodka. His hand shook, as his friend's had done that same day. He locked his desk drawers and called in his secretary.

She looked concerned and said, 'Is there anything else you want, Comrade Commissar?' She thought he looked white and shocked. This surprised her. There had been many sudden deaths in the Lubianka.

'Nothing,' he said. 'Thank you. I'm going home now. I have a lot of work to do tomorrow.'

'Of course.' She held the door open for him.

He thought suddenly. *'I need reliable staff. I can take her with me to Kharkov and my clerk Ivanov . . .'*

He had a one-roomed apartment on Ouspenska Prospekt, and he lived there alone. When he needed a woman, he went to a brothel reserved for senior officers in the state security. The women were medically checked every month. He shut and locked the tiny cupboard that served him as a kitchen. The bathroom was communal like the lavatory.

Under the naked bulb hanging from the ceiling he unwrapped the parcel. He whispered the old incantation from the coronation ceremonies of the Tsars. *'Who holds St Vladimir's Cross has Holy Russia in his hand.'* A thousand years of mystic symbolism over the people of Russia.

The concept was like a madman's dream. But without madmen and dreams, there would be no Russia. He lit the stove and burned the cloth. He made a neat package of newspaper and tied it with new string.

He felt cold and sick to his stomach. He sat by the stove and tried to get warm, drinking pepper vodka. It burned his tongue and lit a fire in his chilled body. He drank to his friend, Alexei, and talked aloud to him as he became very drunk.

'I saved you from the cellars. I saved you from the drugs and the stinking hole in the ground where they freeze men to death. A bullet is clean. You used to say that to me when we talked about the war, remember? I'll take care of Natalia and the boys. I'll keep my promise, don't worry. I loved you, Alexei.'

Tears trickled down his cheeks. He struggled up from his chair. It overturned. The bottle rolled across the floor. It was empty. He fell on his bed and slept till the morning. His transfer to Kharkov was granted. By that evening he was on the train. The package was strapped to his body under his shirt.

Lepkin's mother took them in. The apartment was in a converted house; an old babushka came hurrying from the tiny kitchen with cries of excitement at having the children to look after.

Marie Lepkin said, seeing the exhaustion on the young woman's face, 'You leave the little ones to us. We'll feed them and put them to bed. You lie down and sleep.' Knowing the story, she was filled with pity for them.

Natalia lay under the quilt on the bed, staring at the ceiling. Tears filled up and overflowed on to the pillow. '*Alexei, what are they doing to you?*'

She was asleep and didn't hear the outcry from the kitchen. Stefan had kicked the babushka; he wanted to go to his mother. Viktor burst into weary tears. The babushka rubbed her shin and grumbled. Children were devils these days. They had no discipline, no respect. But then the devils were in charge. When the Tsar ruled, Russia was a godly place.

She was waiting for Lepkin when he arrived.

'Tell me the truth,' she said. 'He's been arrested, hasn't he?'

They were alone. His mother had taken the boys to play in the kitchen. Lepkin was shocked by how thin and white she looked. He didn't lie.

He said, 'He's dead, Natalia. I'm sorry.'

She turned away from him, her hands covering her face. After a while she asked him, 'How? How did he die? Did he suffer?'

'No,' Lepkin said gently. 'He was shot. He felt nothing. It was over in a few seconds. I couldn't save him; he came to ask me to look after you and the twins. I could only promise him that.'

She sat down, carefully smoothing her skirt. She was in control now, but as colourless as a dead woman. 'I'm glad,' she said at last. 'He said to me in the last weeks: "I'm not scared of dying. It's what they'll do to make me confess." And you know how brave he was. Tell me how it happened.'

'No,' Lepkin refused. 'You've suffered enough. The details don't matter.'

She looked up at him. She had pale grey eyes the colour of water under a clear summer sky. 'You shot him, didn't you?'

He said simply, 'Yes. It was all I could do for him.'

She stood up. He waited for her condemnation. For tears and reproaches.

'Thank you, Gregor. I can bear it now.'

'What's going to become of them?' Lepkin's mother asked. 'They can't stay here, there isn't room for all of us. I'm so sorry for them, Gregor. The poor girl's been so brave. I'm not being hard-hearted, but the little boys need somewhere to play – the babushka finds them too much to manage. Especially Stefan.'

'I know,' Lepkin said. 'You've been so good to them. So be patient, *matiushka*. Don't worry, I've found a place where they can live. It's in the country. They'll be safe there. I'll leave Ivan with them. You'll visit them, won't you? See they're all right? I'm going to be working so hard and I've got to be careful myself.'

'Don't worry,' his mother said. 'I'll keep my eye on them. You've risked enough to help them. I do know they're grateful. Natalia calls you their saviour.'

He drove the family out to their new home. He helped Natalia out of the car and lifted the twins on to the ground. 'It's the best I could find,' he said. 'It's isolated, but you'll have Ivan to look after you, and it's safe.'

It was an old farmhouse close to a wood. It had stood empty

since Stalin decreed that every small holder in the Ukraine was to be driven off the land. The peasant with a few acres was labelled a *Kulak*, a rich enemy of the Proletariat. The farms were collectivized. The cattle and crops were confiscated and the rebellious Ukrainians left to starve. Millions had died of hunger and disease in the bread basket of Russia. The corpses lay in the gutters of the towns and by the roadsides where they had wandered in their desperate search for food. Those who escaped that fate were herded into the terrible labour camps and worked to death. Stalin's Five-Year Plan for centralizing Russian agriculture was imposed on the Ukraine with merciless severity. The owners of the farmhouse were among the five million who perished.

Lepkin and Natalia walked up the path choked with weeds, and in to the house. It was a single-storey wooden building. It needed paint inside and out; the window shutters were broken, hanging drunkenly on rusty hinges. The patch of garden was a wilderness of brambles.

Lepkin watched her anxiously. She had been living in luxury as the wife of a high Party official. A three-roomed apartment close to the Kremlin. He expected her spirits to sink as she looked round at the stained walls, and the bare earth floors. Instead, he saw a rare smile as she turned to him and called the boys to come to her.

'We can make a home here,' she said. 'I was born in the country, Gregor. We'll be happy here.'

He lifted the boys one after the other. 'You be good,' he admonished. 'Take care of your mother and do what she tells you. Else I'll beat you with a big stick when I come back.'

They giggled at the threat. He set them down and immediately they ran off shouting with excitement to explore outside.

'You've been so good to us,' Natalia said. 'Alexei loved you like a brother. He was right. How can we ever thank you?'

He led her back into the house. 'You can take care of this,' he said. There was a black tin box on the table. 'It's locked, Natalia. One day we'll open it together. But not now. I know I can trust you to keep it safe for me. Nobody is to touch it.'

She took it from him. It wasn't very heavy. Money perhaps.

Rouble notes. Documents. She wasn't curious. Curiosity was a luxury for the idle. She was a woman of her word. 'I'll hide it,' she said.

'And forget about it?' he asked her.

She opened a big box full of clothes and buried the box at the bottom. 'I've already forgotten,' she said. 'When will you come back again?'

'I don't know. I have a lot of work to do. Maybe it won't be too long. My mother will come to see you.'

She watched him leave from the doorway. The car drove off along the path through the pine woods. She heard her sons calling to each other round the back of the house. She went back inside and looked around her. They had shelter, a man to chop wood for the stove, enough to eat.

That night, with her sons curled up beside her, Natalia slept long and peacefully.

It was two months before Lepkin came again. He found Natalia sewing. The sunshine streamed in from the window and her hair shone like a golden halo. She looked up as his step made the floorboard creak. The sewing fell to the ground and she hurried to meet him. There was a high blush in her cheeks.

He embraced her like a brother, kissed her forehead like a brother, and knew that he was in love for the first time in his life.

Natalia had changed from the city girl he'd known. The sun and the clean air had brightened her skin and burnished her fair hair. A little weight had rounded out her thin body. The rooms had been washed down and painted; the stove was blackened and shining clean. There was a bright rug on the floor. Ivan had found it, Natalia said.

Ivan slept on the floor by the door at night in case of intruders.

Natalia cooked for them that night. Gregor had bought vodka and wine, and she made a vegetable stew served with black bread and goats' cheese.

They sat long at the table; the wine was finished and Ivan and the children had gone to bed. At last Gregor was silent. They'd

15

talked of the old days, of Alexei and their memories of evenings spent together talking, getting a little drunk.

'In the last few years Alexei only laughed when he was with you,' she said.

And Gregor said, 'You haven't forgotten him, Natalia?'

'I'll never forget him,' she answered.

He poured some vodka and swallowed it. 'I wish you'd think of me sometimes,' he said.

'I do. I've missed you.'

'That's because you're lonely. I want more than that. I want you to think about me as much as I think about you. You're beautiful, Natalia.'

She smiled at him. 'And you're drunk,' she said.

'Only a little. I love you, you know I love you?' He got up unsteadily. 'I shouldn't say that. Don't worry. I'll sleep outside your door. Like Ivan.'

She hurried to support him, her voice gentle. 'You'll sleep in my bed.'

He let her guide him to the bedroom. She put a finger to her lips.

'Don't wake the children.' She undressed him and helped him in to the bed. She covered him with the quilt. Then she stripped off her blouse and skirt, peeled off her stockings and stood naked.

He groaned at the sight of the full breasts and the shadow between her thighs. 'Natalia . . . I want you . . . I'm so drunk.'

She turned down the lamp and slipped in beside him. He smelt the sweetness of her breath. 'You won't be in the morning.'

Lepkin and Natalia were married in the new wedding palace in the centre of Kharkov.

On their journey home Natalia leaned against Lepkin, warm and submissive to his hands and his mouth in the darkness. 'I wish I were a virgin,' she whispered to him. 'I want to do everything to please you.'

When they had become lovers Lepkin knew that all she felt was gratitude. But now she loved him with a fierce intensity. For a still, quiet woman she was capable of a passion and abandonment

16

that astonished him. And before they fell asleep he asked her the question he had never dared to ask before.

'Alexei . . . Was it like this with him?'

She raised her head and looked at him.

'No,' she said. 'It was different. I loved him, but I would die for you.' She bent and very slowly kissed him on the lips.

When he woke in the morning, she was already up, preparing food to start the day. He lay and listened to her singing. He felt he must be the happiest man in all of Russia.

They had been married for three months when he called her to him, sending the children out to play in the garden. Lepkin took her by the hand. He kissed her. 'You remember the box I gave you – the day I brought you here?'

She liked to tease him, to flirt. 'You told me to forget,' she reminded him.

'I also told you we'd open it together one day,' he countered. 'Husbands and wives shouldn't have secrets. Get it, my darling.'

She came with it in her hands. 'You're so solemn,' she said. 'Is anything wrong? Why do you want the box? I don't care what's inside.'

He didn't answer. He took the key from round his neck and opened it. She saw something wrapped in paper. He laid it on the bed and pulled the covering off. Natalia couldn't help herself. She gasped and stepped back.

'It's a cross! What are you doing with a thing like that?' She hated religion, especially the old orthodox faith.

He had forgotten that. His wife was a true child of her fanatically atheist parents.

'It belonged to Alexei,' he said quietly. 'He gave it to me.'

'Why would Alexei want it? He had no time for all that superstition. It looks old – is it valuable? Where could you sell it? The stones might be worth something.' She looked at it with distaste. She made no move to touch it.

'It is old,' Lepkin said. 'Over a thousand years. And nobody could sell it because it doesn't have a price. It's St Vladimir's Cross, Natalia. The holiest relic in all of Russia.'

17

Now she actually recoiled. 'It can't be. It was destroyed.'

'That's what the Party said when Alexei's father couldn't find it. The Patriarch in Kiev gave it to your mother-in-law. He was roasted over an open fire to make him tell where it was hidden. But he died first.'

She shuddered. 'Don't. I didn't know. I knew they shot the priests.'

'If we'd found this in 1919 half the White armies would have surrendered. Lenin knew what it meant and so did Stalin. To the people it means the God-given right to rule Russia. No Tsar was ever crowned without it in his hand. Even without God, it has centuries of power and mysticism enshrined in it. It's buried deep in the Russian subconscious.'

She said fiercely, 'Not in mine. It's just ignorant superstition – only a peasant like my mother-in-law would believe in such a thing.'

'Russia is made up of ignorant peasants,' he reminded her. 'We've shut the churches and driven out the priests, but there are icons hidden all over Russia. And if some leader were to rise up and show this – there are millions who would follow him. That's why Alexei kept it hidden. He hoped to exchange it for his life if he fell out of favour. But there are no bargains made with Stalin. He knew that at the end.'

'Why do you keep it?' she asked. 'It didn't save Alexei.'

'Alexei said, "Stalin won't last for ever. It could be your salvation." After what's happened he could be right,' he said to her. 'Everything is different now. The Fascist Germans are our allies! Our ideals have been pissed on by Stalin.'

She shushed him in fear, but he shrugged cynically. 'I have a new boss. I work for Beria. Beria is a monster. I don't care. I do whatever is necessary to stay alive, because you and the children are the only things that matter to me.'

She came and put her arms around him. 'We live on borrowed time,' she whispered. 'We have each other, Gregor. I love you so much I couldn't live without you. If we were separated I'd die . . .'

They hadn't heard the door open. The child, Viktor, was standing there, watching them. 'Mama,' his voice quivered, 'why are you going to die?' His dark eyes were brimming with tears.

Natalia gathered him in her arms. 'I'm not,' she insisted. 'I was just telling Gregor how much I loved him. It's the way grown-ups talk, you silly boy!'

'You're not sick, are you?' he asked.

He was the sensitive one, the child haunted by his imagination. Gregor picked him up and swung him on to his shoulder. 'Your Mama's not sick,' he announced. 'We were having a little love talk, that's all. And next time, you knock on the door, eh?'

'I did,' Viktor protested. 'You didn't hear. Stefan hit me and Ivan smacked him on the head. Stefan's very angry. But it wasn't a hard smack.'

'Well,' Gregor set him down. 'One day you won't have Ivan to stand up for you. Then you'll have to hit Stefan yourself, won't you?' He saw Natalia watching them. He patted Viktor kindly. 'You'll be as big as him one day.'

Viktor wasn't listening. He pointed to the bed. 'What's that red thing? That shining red thing?'

Natalia hurried, picked up the cross. Her children had never seen that symbol. It was forbidden. They knew nothing of Christianity or any other religion.

'It's nothing,' she said hastily. 'Just an ornament.'

'Can I see?' he asked.

'No!' She sounded angry. 'Go on, go out and find Ivan and play. And don't let me hear you and Stefan fighting or I'll beat both of you!'

When he had run out she turned to Lepkin. 'Put that away,' she said roughly. 'Lock it up quickly. Did you see him staring at it? Supposing he talks about it at school?'

'He won't,' Gregor assured her. 'It meant nothing to him. He won't remember.' He wrapped the cross in its tattered paper and locked it in the tin box. 'Natalia,' he said. 'We won't talk about it again. We won't think about it. But if ever anything goes wrong, you know what it means and where it is.'

'I know,' she said quietly. 'I just wish it wasn't in this house.'

Religious festivals had been abolished. Instead Russia celebrated the anniversary of the October Revolution. There were parades

19

and speeches in Kharkov and the factories were closed so that the workers could march through the streets. Everybody celebrated and got drunk. Red flags flew from every public building. Bands played, the radio blared rousing Revolutionary songs. It was a day off work. There were huge posters of Lenin and Stalin, head and shoulder side by side. The face of the tyrant watched the people of Kharkov, a slight smile on the lips, an air of avuncular wisdom in the painted eyes.

The next morning, some of the wall posters had been daubed with red paint. It looked like blood streaming over the genial image. The culprit wasn't found, so a token arrest was made of a suspect factory worker. He was given a thorough beating in the police station and sentenced to three months' hard labour.

Lepkin gave his wife the desk set as a present. They were all gathered together, his mother, the babushka, the children and Ivan. There were tears in his eyes as he looked at them all. Natalia was pregnant and her beauty glowed. He was quite drunk and very happy. He laid his treasure before her. The diamonds glittered like frost: the green enamel was as sheer as watered silk.

'Listen,' he said and wound the clock forward. It struck the hour. Viktor stared at it, fascinated by the sweet sounds and the delicate colours.

Natalia said, 'They must be valuable. I don't deserve them.'

'You like them, don't you?' Lepkin insisted.

'They're very pretty,' she said. 'But where can we put them?'

The child Viktor knew she didn't like the lovely things his stepfather had given her. He wondered why.

Lepkin embraced her; they all applauded. He wanted to take her to bed; he squeezed her breast and whispered to her.

She whispered back, reminding him they weren't alone. 'I'll put them away,' she said. 'They might get damaged.' She put the desk set carefully in a drawer. She was embarrassed by the gift. They were pretty toys for some spoiled aristocrat to play with. They had no relevance to her.

*

It was a bitterly cold winter. A time when they hibernated, as the winds and the snow turned the landscape into a frozen wilderness.

Viktor loved the quiet evenings, gathered round the stove with his mother and Lepkin. Stefan preferred to help Ivan with woodwork; he was not a child who liked reading or solitude. Viktor was content; he drew in his book. It was full of pictures. He drew the rabbits he wouldn't see till the spring came and the yellow-eyed cat that had joined them as a kitten, curled up by his mother's feet. He drew the snow and the trees festooned with icicles. He drew the clock and the calendar. His mother had put them on a shelf. She had soon found an excuse to lock them away again. She didn't like them, just as she hated the cross with the red, glowing stones that he'd seen on her bed that day. He knew it was a cross because he'd seen the babushka wearing one round her neck. She'd told him not to say anything or he'd get her in to trouble. He knew his mother hated it because he'd heard her say so to Lepkin.

'I hate having it in the house . . . especially since Viktor saw it.'

He couldn't understand what she was afraid of. Ivan had told him once, people only hate other people because they're afraid of them. It must be the same with things. He went on drawing in his book. Ivan pulling a sled through the snow, Lepkin asleep in the chair, his mouth slightly open.

And he drew the cross with the red stones. He didn't show his book to anyone because he felt his mother would be very angry if she saw that drawing.

The baby was born as the weather turned warm. It was a little girl, and they called her Valeria. Ivan had made a wooden cot, and she lay gurgling happily as the spring turned into early summer. Life was peaceful in their isolated world. But to Lepkin that world was turning upside down. Their Nazi allies were amassing troops along the Polish frontier and Russian armies were on the march. Thousands of people were forcibly evacuated by Soviet forces in the first weeks of the German invasion. The Ukrainians were not to be trusted. Too many were fighting side by side with the advancing Germans. It was the time for revenge.

Captured political commissars or members of the NKVD were shot without trial. Soviet troops were throwing themselves upon the enemy. Soviet planes, slow and underarmed, were ramming the Heinkels and Stukas that commanded the skies. But the German armoured divisions raced ahead: the Luftwaffe bombed and strafed at will. Kharkov itself was being evacuated and was devastated by daylight air raids. Lepkin couldn't persuade Natalia to leave without him. He had already sent his mother on ahead to Moscow. But Natalia wouldn't move. She wouldn't leave so long as he remained at his post in the beleaguered city.

Then, in August, Lepkin came back home unexpectedly. He called Ivan to bring the boys and went to find Natalia. She was holding the baby when she saw him. She looked at his face and cried out, 'No! No!'

He took her in his arms. The child was startled and began to cry. Natalia wept and protested, but Lepkin stayed calm. And firm.

'I'm joining an active service unit,' he said. 'And Ivan will take you and the children to Moscow on the train. Places are reserved for you and you leave tomorrow, as soon as I've gone. The reports coming in are very bad. They're getting closer and closer. I only wish you'd have left sooner.'

He held her closely and then turned, reaching out to his step-sons. They ran into his arms.

Stefan cried out fiercely, 'We'll shoot them. Ivan and me'll kill them.'

Lepkin said gently, 'You'll look after your mother and the little one. You and Viktor will be good boys and take care of them till I get back. You promise?'

They promised. Viktor blinked back tears. Ivan took them out-side. He knew what happened to the political officers if they were captured. His colonel wouldn't surrender. He'd die fighting. He sat the boys down and told them tales of the wonders they would see in Moscow. When he was a lad, he'd queued all night and a whole day to see Lenin lying in his tomb in Red Square. He'd looked just like he was sleeping peacefully. The children began to settle.

Natalia and Lepkin made love that night. They held each other and talked bravely of the future.

'I think I'm pregnant again,' she admitted. 'I've missed twice; I didn't want to tell you because I was frightened you'd make me leave.'

He had laid his hand tenderly upon her stomach. 'It'll be a boy this time,' he said. 'You'll be safe. Ivan will get you to Moscow. We'll beat these swine back in to Germany, don't worry.'

She said, 'If you're caught, they'll murder you, Gregor.'

'They're murdering our people anyway,' he said. 'And you know I have to fight. I'm Russian. I'm not fighting for Stalin. I'm fighting for Russia. Once we've cleared the city, we shall blow up the buildings and the rail heads and leave nothing for them. Nothing.'

'Try not to get killed,' she whispered to him. 'Try to come back to us.'

He kissed her. 'I'll do my best,' he said. He got up and dressed in the dawn light. 'Don't forget to take the box with you,' he said.

'The box?' She sat up, bare-breasted with her hair hanging down over her shoulders.

'The tin box,' he said. 'That cross must never fall in to German hands. And my present to you, Natalia – my clock and the calendar. Wrap them up carefully. Above all, keep that box close to you. Hide it somewhere safe when you get to Moscow. Remember!'

'I'll remember,' she said. 'It's unlucky. I wish we could just smash it to pieces and bury it!'

Lepkin held the battered box in his hands. He had a strange look and it frightened her. 'I think we'd be cursed,' he said.

The terrible separation was coming closer, minute by minute, as he finished dressing. Once more she held him, kissing him and weeping. Then he was gone; the car started up and she couldn't bring herself to go to the door or watch him from the window. Ivan was driving him in to the city. Then he'd return for her and the children. He was armed with a rifle and ammunition. She sat at the table in the kitchen and bowed her head. Then she heard the little girl begin to stir and whimper in her cot. She got up and went to her, soothing her and holding her close.

It was still early, but the sun was up. The boys were making bundles of their clothes for the journey. It kept them occupied. The baby was sitting on the floor in a pool of warm sunshine, playing with a wooden doll Ivan had made for her.

Natalia went into her room to dress. She brushed her long hair. She loved the house and garden, and the cat with the yellow eyes. The children were begging her to take the cat to Moscow. She couldn't bear to tell them that it wasn't possible. Cats wouldn't be allowed on a train. It would be all right, left behind. It would catch birds. It would live.

As if summoned by her thoughts, it strolled into the room and came to rub against her legs. She bent down and stroked the rough fur.

'Silly thing,' she said. 'Why are we all so fond of you?'

And then she heard the noise. It was loud. It throbbed and roared like an animal. Her chair fell over. The cat fled. She ran from her room to the kitchen and saw them through the window. A motorcycle with a sidecar. Painted grey, with the black and white German cross on the side. Soldiers, with bucket helmets and grey uniforms. They were stopped a few yards away. She didn't scream. She couldn't. Fear made her dumb. Her sons had come in to the kitchen. She heard one of them, Stefan – Viktor – say, 'What's that Matiushka? What's that noise?'

Then she seized them, hissing at them to be quiet, silent. 'Don't make a sound. In there, quick,' She thrust the baby in to the cupboard with them. 'Don't let her cry, stay there. *Don't move.*'

She slammed the cupboard shut. As she stepped back, the first of the German soldiers walked in through the open door.

1

'I love this view,' her father said. 'It's the best on the island.' He held out his hand to Lucy. 'Come and sit by me. It's so peaceful up here.'

'The garden is looking lovely,' she said.

He was a keen gardener, and the mild climate made Jersey a plantsman's paradise.

The sea stretched below them at the bottom of a cliff mantled in spring foliage and flowers, girdled by a thin line of yellow sand. Yuri Warren had bought the site twenty-five years ago and built the house. It'd been a minor heart attack that had prompted the move, but the signs had been ominous. He had a wife and two-year-old daughter. He had enough money to retire if he sold the business. Within five years, his wife had died of cancer and he and Lucy were alone. He had lived far longer than anyone expected and he was grateful. The pace of life was easy, the gentle climate suited him. He had brought up his daughter, tended his beloved garden and devoted himself to his life's work.

He had made it her cause as much as his. He had shared everything with her. From an early age he taught her to speak Russian. She looked like a child of his native Ukraine, with her Slavic bone structure and fair hair. He had bequeathed her everything but the piercing blue eyes. They were her Irish mother's legacy.

Lucy glanced anxiously at him. 'I've been so worried about you,' she said. 'But you are feeling better, aren't you?'

He thought, I've got to be brave. I've got to tell her. I've got to tell her everything. My time has run out. Hers has come. He reached for her hand and held it.

'No, Lucy,' he said gently. 'I'm afraid not. Listen to me, darling, and be calm. I have only a few weeks left. Maybe a few days. It could happen any time.' He heard her sob. 'Don't do that,' he said. 'You mustn't. I've had a very good life and much happiness. It's coming to an end, that's all.'

She stemmed her tears for his sake. With an effort she said, 'How long have you known?'

'Since the last test. I've been putting everything in order. I don't want you involved with lawyers. It's all clear cut now. There's only one thing left.'

'What is it?' she asked him.

'To tell you the secret I've been guarding since before you were born. And to show it to you. Help me in to the house.'

It wasn't the safe where he kept his papers and Eileen's jewellery. It was a trap door under his desk. When she moved the desk and took up the rug, it was almost impossible to see the join in the parquet floor.

'Put your foot on the fourth square to the left, Lucy.'

She did so and the flap rose up on a hidden spring. She knelt down to look inside. It was a cavity hollowed out and lined with lead.

'There's a box,' he said. 'Bring it to me.'

It was plain wood with a ring handle and a simple catch. 'What is it?' she asked him.

'A great treasure,' Yuri answered. 'But, before I show it to you, I want to tell you how it came to me. Put the box there, on my desk. When I've finished, we'll open it together.'

He waited for a moment. The past was dangerous for him. It made the failing heart beat faster. Keep calm, his doctor had insisted. Don't excite yourself. He had smiled and shrugged off the advice. For what purpose? To eke out a few more days?

'Some of it you know already,' he told Lucy. 'How I was taken for forced labour in Germany. How my parents were shot. How Major Hope got me to England after the war. You know all that. But I never told you about Boris.

'Boris was in the camp at Spittal. There were ten thousand Ukrainians from the division that fought with the German army. The war was over and they were waiting to surrender to the British. There were women and children mixed up with them, kids like me who'd been caught up in the retreat and taken along. It was very hot. I remember men swimming in the dirty river and the women washing clothes along the bank.

'I was hungry and lousy and lost. I'd been kicked and beaten till I was scared of my own shadow. Then Boris found me. I can still see him now.' He paused for breath. 'He was a big fellow, built like a bull. Ugly, with a shaved head. He had a loud voice and a laugh you could hear in the next camp. I don't know what he saw in me, although he said afterwards I looked like his little brother who'd died. But he adopted me, Lucy. He scrubbed me clean and fed me, and kept me by him. "Don't you worry, kid," he'd say. "You'll be all right. You stick with me and we'll get out of this shit." He was coarse and people were frightened of him. I saw him hit a man with one blow and he fell as if he'd been pole-axed. Nobody bullied me with Boris around. I followed him like a little dog. I slept curled up by his feet at night.

'He talked to me, telling me about what he'd done in the war. He'd been in the SS extermination squads, killing Jews, he said. He was proud of it. "I fought the bastard Bolsheviks," he said. "They threw my family off their land and my mother and my little brother starved to death. I fought them and the filthy Jews that were the cause of all the trouble." He had no shame about it. But I loved him, Lucy. Can you understand how I could feel like that for such a man?'

He didn't wait for her to answer. 'The German general and his officers had deserted the camp. The place was full of rumours. The Reds were killing any Russian who'd worn a German uniform, even the poor devils who had been conscripted in to labour battalions to dig earth works.

'The Ukrainians were waiting, not knowing what would happen

27

to them. Boris had changed his uniform for an ordinary infantry soldier's. He said anyone wearing the SS uniform was handed over to the Reds immediately. I was terrified he'd be taken away. I used to cry and he always promised me, "I'm not going anywhere without you, kid. Now stop your snivelling." And he'd give me a great bear hug that squeezed the breath out of me.'

Yuri was far away as he talked, reliving the trauma of those chaotic days. He could feel the heat of the sun on the trampled dusty earth and the smell of the camp was in his nostrils. 'The British came and took our surrender. I remember the officers had a big dinner after the terms were agreed. Our commander, General Shandruk, was dressed up like a real swell. Many of them were old Tsarist officers, and some of them had been living in exile since 1919.

'The British were friendly to us. They gave food and sweets to the children and there was quite a bit of fraternizing and drinking.

'Boris didn't mix. I could feel he was uneasy, in spite of the way he talked. He kept in the background. We didn't know where we would be sent; one day it looked good, the next people were panicking because they heard we were going to be put on trains for Lenz. The Red Army was at Lenz. They were taking people back and shooting them in thousands. One night hundreds of Ukrainians and their families just slipped away and the British let them go. Then there was an announcement. The Ukrainians were going to be moved to a camp at Bellaria, outside Rimini. Beyond the reach of the Soviets. I'll never forget the cheering. People were dancing with joy, hugging each other, weeping with relief. Boris got very drunk that night. He was still drunk when a British officer and four men came in to arrest him the next morning. There was a separate list of SS criminals who were being entrained at St Veit and handed over to the Reds. Boris's name was on it.'

Lucy saw his lip tremble and a tear rolled down her father's cheek.

'They took him by force. He fought and struggled and I was screaming at them to let him go, while the officer held me. I wanted to go with him. I wanted to die with him. He was all I had in the world.'

'Daddy,' she said in a whisper. 'Don't. Don't. You mustn't upset yourself.'

He didn't hear her. He said, 'I begged the officer to let me say goodbye to him. I was crying and pleading in Russian; he called someone to translate. He spoke a bit of German. He said to me, "All right. You can say goodbye. Come with me."

'They were loading men on to a truck. The soldiers had guns trained on them. I saw Boris, and the officer gave me a push and said, "Go on. But be quick."

'Boris was handcuffed. There was a big bruise on his face. He couldn't embrace me, so I just clung to him round the middle. "Look after yourself, kid." I can hear him now. His voice was thick as if he wanted to cry. "I've got a present for you. It's buried under my cot. It'll make you rich, Yuri. Hide it. Don't let anyone see it, or they'll take it from you. Promise me?"

I couldn't take it in properly. He seemed to realize that because he said it all again. "Under my cot. It's a treasure. Get it! Hide it!"

'They were separating us, pulling me away. They dragged him to the truck and he shouted back to me, "Think of me, kid. And do what I told you!" They were all loaded on to the truck and driven away.

'I went to Boris's tent. It was empty. There was his camp bed, which I'd slept beside, on the floor, to be near him. And I dug underneath and found what he'd given me. Now you can open the box, Lucy.'

She held it in both hands. The red stones and the delicate gold flashed in the bright Jersey sunshine. In the garden outside she heard the buzz of a lawnmower.

'The holiest Relic in Russia,' he said. 'It's been revered by Ukrainians for a thousand years. It's in our blood. We've been so close, Lucy. I've shared my dreams with you because one day I wanted to share this with you, too. I had it planned, and then I had this last attack. Russia is in turmoil. It's the time for us to strike. I won't live to do it, so you must take my place.'

'How can I?' she whispered.

'I want you to go to Volkov in Geneva. Tell him about the Relic. Bring him and our people together. Kiss the cross, Lucy, and swear that you'll do it!'

She hesitated. He was a bad colour and his breathing was uneven.

'You're the future,' he said. The young have shown us all the way. The students in China who died for freedom, the Germans, the Romanians, our Polish brothers. The day Volkov returns to Russia with the Relic, the Ukrainians will rise and declare independence. And Communism will collapse. It'll die from the heart, from Moscow. All the murdered millions will sleep easy in their graves.'

'I'll do what you would have done,' she said. 'I swear it.' For a moment she touched the big central stone of the cross with her lips.

'Thank you, my darling.' Her father's voice had sunk. 'Get me some water . . . my pills . . .'

She laid the cross back on its satin cushion in the box, made in her father's factory, like the flooring that concealed the safe. She pressed the hidden mechanism and the cover closed over it. She realized that she was trembling.

Her father had swallowed his tablet; his colour was less grey. 'I'm tired,' he said. 'But now I'll die a happy man. I'd like to rest now.'

She helped him to the downstairs room that had been turned into a bedroom once he couldn't walk upstairs. As he lay down, he raised his hand and stroked her face.

'I'm so glad I never had a son. There's an old saying, "A daughter gladdens her father's heart". How true it's been for me.'

Ten days later he died.

It was a private funeral. There'd be a requiem mass in the local Catholic church for his many friends in Jersey, but only a dozen came to the graveside. Like Lucy, the women were in mourning. It was their custom, and they cherished the old ways. One by one they came and kissed her, murmuring their sympathy. Then they came back to the house for the traditional funeral breakfast. Lucy

30

didn't weep; she had no tears left. Part of herself had been buried that morning – right beside the mother she hardly remembered. He often told her how much he had loved Eileen and how beautiful she was.

His old friend, Mischa, made a solemn speech. He called Yuri by his original name, Warienski, and spoke of his patriotism and his life-long devotion to Ukrainian freedom from the Communist yoke. He reminded them of his generosity in time and money, his involvement with the human rights activists inside the Soviet Union. His letters and articles denouncing the arrest of the bravest of the young intellectual dissidents, Professor Volkov. He had tears in his eyes and Yuri's Russian friends cried openly. Vodka was passed and drunk in Yuri's memory. And then Lucy called Mischa aside. He was the closest to her father and the president of their English association. She brought him in to her father's study and closed the door.

He said quietly, 'Yuri wrote to me before he died. He said you would take his place.'

'I'm going to try,' Lucy said. 'I promised him.'

He said, 'He asked a lot of you, even when you were a child. Perhaps this is too much. If you change your mind, nobody would blame you, Lucy. One of us could approach Volkov.'

She shook her head. 'You're known,' she said. 'You never made a secret of your activities. You'd be watched. Nobody will connect an English woman called Warren, on a holiday in Geneva, with anything subversive.'

Don't mention the Relic, her father had warned. All our organizations have been penetrated by the KGB ever since we helped to expose the Yalta Agreement. They learned we were more than a few exiles shaking puny fists at them from a safe distance . . . Only Volkov can be trusted. No one else must know.

Mischa said gravely, 'It won't be easy. Volkov has been silent for five years. He hasn't written a word or given an interview. There have been rumours that he was very ill. And his wife is an infamous woman. She worked in the Lenin Institute.'

'I know the risks,' Lucy said. 'But my father believed in Volkov. He said he was a patriot who would never spit on his own country as an exile.'

31

'Yuri was an idealist,' Mischa said gently. 'He wouldn't believe that Volkov might have changed.'

He came close and laid a hand on her shoulder. He had known her since she was a child. He had watched her grow in to a beautiful young woman. She should have married by now, producing grandchildren for her father. But Yuri had dedicated her on the altar of his own fanatical beliefs. And he was sending her out to fulfil his mission from the grave.

He tried once more. 'You know how much I loved your father,' he said. 'But I do urge you to consider very carefully. This could bring you in to considerable danger, Lucy. Take time to think about it.'

She shook her head. 'I'm booked to fly to Geneva tomorrow. Don't worry. I'll be careful. Wish me luck.'

He bent and kissed her on the forehead. 'I do,' he said. 'God go with you, Lucy. But promise me one thing. If Volkov is not the man you think he is, abandon it at once and come home.'

'I promise,' she said. 'But I know I won't have to keep it. I feel my father's near us. Do you feel it?'

'Yes,' he said. 'He's here. Open the windows in the house. It's what we do in the old country. It allows the spirit to leave in peace.'

When they had all gone, Lucy walked out to the garden. She sat on the empty seat and stared out at the sea below. Sailing boats glided into view, swaying and dipping like swallows in the breeze. It was so peaceful and secure. Sailing had been her father's hobby. As a child he had taken her out on a simple sailing boat, taught her the rudiments of handling a small craft, navigating the little inlets and outcrops of rock around the coast. She was an apt pupil; she loved the sea and had no fear of it.

The little boat had been replaced by a motor cruiser. Soon it was Lucy who sailed to St Malo and Yuri who crewed happily for her. They spent their holidays at sea; he had taught her to navigate and she took them down to the south of France the year before his last illness.

She thought of that time, watching the sea and the boats below. They had been so happy together, so deeply companionable. She'd had boyfriends, but no one had engaged her heart. That belonged to Yuri and to the man whose faded photograph was still pinned on her bedroom wall. The face haunted her; she kept it as others kept an icon, to remind them of their faith and to give them strength. Imprisoned, persecuted, defiant to the last, Dimitri Volkov was the dream that hadn't faded like his photograph. Mischa was wrong to doubt. Volkov hadn't changed.

She thought of the ancient cross, in its dark hiding place. A thousand years ago it had been given by the tyrant Vladimir when he converted to the Christian faith. Ever since, men had woven legends around it and invoked its mystical powers. Dark superstitions had invested the cross with a God-given power to bless or curse. No Tsar dared take the oath at his coronation without holding it in his right hand. Hands tainted by murder and sacrilege had reached out to seize and destroy it. But the shrine was empty. The priest who had been its guardian had died in torment rather than betray where it was hidden.

A life-span later, the old tyranny was crumbling. A people who had never known freedom were demanding it. All it needed was a man of vision and heroic courage to bring the cross back in triumph to Russia, to rally the millions of Ukrainians against the power of Moscow. Volkov was that man.

It was a smooth flight the next morning. Lucy landed at Geneva airport and took a taxi to Les Trois Fontaines, a modest family hotel in the Rue de la Tour Maitresse. The weather was glorious. It was a lovely city, built round the southern end of the spectacular lake. Her hotel room was pleasant and not too expensive. She explained to the proprietress that she was on a working holiday and would need to rent an apartment.

The first estate agent she visited suggested several properties, but none was suitable. Too smart and highly priced, or too geared to short-term family lets. There was one, the girl suggested, that might suit her at Petit Saconnex, but it was for a six-month tenure. Lucy didn't argue. The setting had to be right. Unobtrusive but congenial. The time didn't matter.

Volkov couldn't be won without careful preparation. He had to accept this strange emissary, to trust her. And she needed a place where they could meet without attracting attention.

She arranged to view the apartment the next day and went on

a brief tour of the city. That evening she sought out the proprietress. Unlike many Swiss, Madame liked to gossip. She
accepted Lucy's explanation that she was a journalist on a popular
English women's magazine.

A journalist with a special assignment. Her curiosity was
aroused. A film star? There were plenty living in the region. Pop
singer, perhaps? No, Lucy said, hesitating before she let Madame
in to her secret. Professor Volkov, the famous Soviet dissident
who had been exiled from Russia – her magazine wanted an
interview with him that would exploit the women's angle. Nothing
political, Lucy shrugged that aside. Just domestic details. How
he'd adjusted . . . what were his hobbies? That kind of thing.

Madame nodded her agreement. Just the sort of thing she would
like to read about someone so well known. 'But, he never gives
interviews. Never been seen on TV,' she said. 'I remember there
was an uproar in the Press when he came here first . . . must have
been several years ago. But he wouldn't see anyone or talk to
anyone. His wife said he was too ill. I don't think anyone bothers
him now. When people settle here they soon become private
citizens, never mind who they are. It's our way. His wife's a
doctor; she works in a very exclusive clinic up in Cologny. Only
very rich people can afford to go there.'

'I've got to try and talk to him,' Lucy confessed. 'It would make
all the difference in the world to my job if I could write something
about him.'

'You could try his wife,' Madame suggested. 'But she's never
encouraged the Press.'

'I wouldn't want to bother her,' Lucy answered. 'If I could just
bump into him. He must go out sometimes. They're not in the
telephone directory, I looked.'

Madame was sympathetic. She was such a pretty girl and so
friendly. It would be a pity if she went back with nothing.

'I can ask around if you like,' she offered. 'Hoteliers all know
each other; I've got relatives in the business. Everyone goes to
bistros and bars at some time. A lot of Swiss have regular places
where they eat every day. Let me see if I can find out anything
for you. After all, he's a well-known figure.'

Next day, Lucy took a taxi to Petit Saconnex and viewed the

apartment. It was in a pleasant block on the Chemin de la Tourelle. She rented it, but she didn't move in. And the next morning, when Lucy came down to take breakfast, Madame hurried over looking pleased with herself.

'I've got some good news for you,' she said. 'Apparently he's a regular at the Bistro St Honoré! It's a pleasant little place by the lake on the Place de Trainant. He goes there every morning for his coffee.'

'Oh, how kind of you, Madame!' Lucy exclaimed. 'I can't tell you how grateful I am! At least if I go along I can see him.'

'Smile nicely, my dear, and I expect he'll talk to you,' the older woman said. *What man wouldn't?* she thought privately.

Lucy didn't finish her breakfast. She took a bus to Quay Gustav Ador and walked along. The Bistro St Honoré was small, as Madame had said. Clean and bright like all Swiss cafés and restaurants, with tables where the customers could sit out, sipping their coffee and watching the passers-by.

She took a table set back a little and ordered coffee. The waiter lingered over the order. She was a foreigner and very pretty. He had picked up foreign girls before, by offering to show them the sights after work.

'You on holiday, Madame?' he asked.

'Working holiday,' she replied. 'I'm doing some articles for an English paper. It's my first visit to Switzerland. It's very beautiful.'

'Thank you,' he said. 'You staying long?'

'I'm not sure,' Lucy answered. 'Tell me,' she said, 'is that Professor Volkov?' She nodded towards an old man reading a newspaper. He was old enough to be Volkov's father.

'Oh no. That's Monsieur Fritche. He's one of our regulars, like the Professor. *He* hasn't been in since last Thursday. Maybe he's sick or something. He's here most days.'

'I've read so much about him,' Lucy prompted. 'What's he like?'

The young man shrugged. 'Quiet, doesn't talk to anyone. Just sits around. Wanders off after a couple of hours.' He hesitated, but she had a beguiling smile. He really hoped she might meet him one evening after work. He lowered his voice and said, 'He's

35

drunk most of the time. He starts on the cognac as soon as he gets here. Never causes trouble, though.'

'How awful,' she said. There was a sick feeling in her stomach. Drunk! It couldn't be. And the waiter said he hadn't been into the café since Thursday. Sick or something. *Starts on the cognac as soon as he gets here.*

'Talk of the devil,' the man said. 'Here he is!'

She recognized him at once from the faded photographs. The tall, slight figure. The face with the distinctive Slavic cheekbones and broad brow. He looked ill. There were bags puffed under his eyes; his dark hair straggled over his collar. He walked with his shoulders stooped under an invisible weight.

'He's pissed,' the waiter whispered. 'Same as usual. I better take his order. He still brings in the gawkers now and again.'

Lucy sat very still. She watched him take his place at a table under an umbrella. She saw the careful movements as he shifted the chair and lowered himself into it. As if he were in pain.

'*Oh God,*' she murmured quietly to herself. 'What am I going to do?' She was close enough to hear him speak. She started at the sound of the voice. It was deep and heavily accented. It reminded her of Yuri. She flinched at the memory.

'Some coffee – and a cognac. Lovely morning.'

And the sneering waiter, writing down the order, looked briefly across at her and winked.

She took a deep breath to calm herself. Her father's life-long dream, the hopes of so many helpless people, the saving power of the Relic that men had died in torment to protect . . . all to be abandoned, sacrificed in vain because a great man was drowning himself in drink.

She ignored the waiter. She pushed back her chair and walked up to his table. She stood in front of him and he looked up.

'Professor Volkov?'

'No,' he shook his head. 'I'm sorry, you're mistaken.'

'No, I'm not,' Lucy said firmly. 'I know who you are. Can I sit down?'

He frowned for a moment. She thought suddenly, he isn't drunk. That oaf was wrong. He's *been* drunk, but he isn't now.

'If you're a journalist, you're wasting your time. I don't give interviews. Please go away. I don't mean to be rude, but go away.'

She pulled out a chair and sat opposite him. She leaned towards him. 'I'm not a journalist,' she said in Russian. 'Please can I talk to you? Just for a few minutes?'

Immediately the shutters came down. Suspicion, fear, then blankness. 'I've nothing to say,' he said. 'If you don't leave me alone, I'll call the management.'

Lucy shook her head. She spoke gently. 'Professor, you needn't be afraid of me. I just want to talk to someone I've admired all my life. That's all. Please believe me.'

The waiter arrived, bringing the coffee and a large cognac. Lucy looked up at him. 'Coffee for me, too,' she said. Behind Volkov's back he pulled a face and winked again.

She said to Volkov, 'Thank you for not getting him to throw me out.'

'Who are you? What do you want?' He reached for the cognac; his hand was shaking. He said defensively, 'I'm not frightened of you. I need this because I've got a hangover.'

'I know,' she said. 'Why not take some coffee? It's better for you.'

'How do you know?' he demanded. 'You don't know anything about me!'

She answered quietly. 'I know everything about you, Professor. I've read every word you've written. I know your speeches by heart. I've had your photograph on my wall since I was twenty. The waiter told me you were drunk when you arrived. My name is Lucy Warren. Will you at least listen to me?'

'Why should I?' he asked. 'I don't know you. I don't want to talk to you. I don't talk to anyone from home.'

'I'm English,' she explained. 'I've never been to Russia. My father was Ukrainian; he taught me to speak Russian. His name was Varienski.'

'Means nothing to me,' Volkov said. 'I never knew anyone with that name.' He fumbled in his pocket and brought out a packet of *Disque Bleu*. He put one in his mouth and searched for matches. On the second attempt he lit it.

'There's no reason why you should know him,' Lucy answered.

'He wasn't famous, like you. He was an exile who loved his country and thought you were the bravest man in the world. He worshipped you, Professor, and he brought me up to feel the same. He's dead now, but just before he died, I promised him I'd come and see you. That's why I'm here.'

'Well,' he looked down, fiddling with the coffee cup. 'Well, you've kept your promise. You've seen the great Volkov at close quarters. At bit pissed from the last three days. Got the shakes. So you can go now and leave me alone.'

'I've come all the way from England,' she said. 'Just to meet you. Here, let me give you some sugar.'

'I don't take it,' Volkov muttered.

'It'll give you energy. Try one spoon.'

'You must be English,' he said. 'English women are so bossy.'

'If you really hate coffee with sugar, have mine instead.'

'No, no. It doesn't matter. Now will you please go away?'

'No,' Lucy said. 'I won't. You said to the waiter it's a lovely morning. Can't we just sit together and enjoy it. I won't talk if you'd rather not.'

He'd been trying not to look at her. He didn't want to see her, she realized that. With his eyes lowered, he felt safe. Now he gave in and met her eye to eye. His head ached and his nerves clamoured for more alcohol. But she was pretty, with piercing blue eyes like the lake water when the sun shone.

Why would they send her? Why would they try and trap him after all this time? They'd nothing to worry about from the wreck he'd become.

'Are you real?' he said. 'They use pretty girls to trick people into saying things. Are you sure you're not one of those?'

'No,' Lucy said firmly. 'I'm not. My name is Lucy Warren. I was born in England and, as you said yourself, I'm bossy. You really can trust me, Professor.'

Suddenly, he smiled. It was brief, but it lit the sad, dark eyes.

'I was locked up for a year,' he said. 'You learn not to trust anyone after that. I've been very rude. Most people would have gone away.'

'I'm not most people.'

'I can believe that,' he said. His cigarette had burned out in

38

the ashtray. He lit another, blew out the smoke, and stared at her. The coffee and the cognac were soothing; he felt better. He thought, *She has the most beautiful eyes. She keeps staring at me. I wish she wouldn't.*

Lucy let the silence continue. Under the table her hands gripped one another tightly with tension. So far so good. He hadn't got up and walked away. For a brief moment she had made him smile. He had drunk the sugared coffee. But one ill-judged word, one mistake and their flimsy contact would be broken.

The waiter was hovering. She avoided his enquiring glance.

'Anything else, Sir, Mademoiselle?'

'Have you had breakfast, Professor?'

Volkov shook his head.

'Would you mind if I had something? I'm starving.'

'I don't mind. It's bad to be hungry.'

She ordered croissants and more coffee. She didn't want them. Her throat was tight and her stomach knotted. Anything to keep him there, even food that she doubted she could swallow. She said gently, 'Why don't you eat anything in the morning? Isn't there anyone to get it for you?'

He drained his cognac.

'My wife leaves early. I'm asleep. It doesn't matter. I haven't felt hungry for a long time. When I was in prison I tried to eat the straw out of the mattresses. They stopped my bread ration for five days.' He put down the empty glass and looked at her.

Lucy couldn't help it. Her eyes filled with tears. One slipped on to her cheek and she tried to brush it away. But Volkov saw it. He leaned a little towards her.

'Don't cry,' he said. 'Nobody cries for me any more.'

'I was crying for all the people like you, Professor Volkov,' she said slowly. 'The ones who died and the ones who are still locked up.'

He made no reply.

'Are you forbidden to talk?' she asked him. 'Did they make you promise?'

'My wife promised for me. I wouldn't co-operate. Now.' He raised his hand for the waiter.

'Don't have any more to drink, Please!' Lucy said.

'That's what *she* says,' Volkov nodded. ' "Don't drink, Dimitri. Stop feeling sorry for yourself." Please don't sound like my wife.'

He let his hand fall. He had been a handsome man once; but the face was now drawn and hollow-cheeked, the fine eyes sunken and bloodshot. He looked so desolate that Lucy almost gave up.

'I'm being a nuisance,' she said. 'I'm sorry.'

'Why is it so important for you to sit and talk to a drunk who's opted out?'

After a moment Lucy answered him. 'My father said you couldn't be bribed or threatened into keeping quiet. When they were sending dissidents to mental hospitals, you drew the world's attention to what was being done. I had no right to speak to you that way. Please forgive me. If you want a drink so badly, Professor Volkov, I'll go to the bar and get you one myself.'

'If I'm not going to get drunk,' he said. 'I'd better go for a walk. We'll pay the bill and I'll say goodbye.'

'I'll pay the bill,' Lucy said. 'And if you don't mind, I'll walk with you.'

They walked slowly and in silence for most of the time. Once Volkov paused at the lakeside. Seagulls were swimming close to shore, looking for titbits. He felt in his pocket absentmindedly.

'I forgot,' he said. 'I normally take some stale bread from the café. I like to feed them.'

'We'll get some tomorrow,' Lucy suggested. 'I won't forget. At home we have a plague of seagulls; they come screaming in over the garden. If you're not careful they'll snatch the food out of your fingers.'

'You live by the sea?'

'I live on an island,' she said. 'Jersey, it's very beautiful.'

'I've never heard of it. You said you lived in England.'

'It's one of the Channel Islands; they're English. The Germans occupied them during the war. I was born in England. We only moved there because my father had a heart attack and had to retire. It was cheap and he had made a little money. You pay hardly any tax there.'

Lucy could sense him drifting away from her. She caught his arm, and felt him start nervously.

'There's a seat over there. Could we sit down for a while?'

'If you like.'

They sat and he lit another cigarette. He offered her the packet.

'Do you smoke?'

'I never really liked it.'

'My wife chainsmokes. Only Russian cigarettes. They get sent over specially.'

'You don't smoke them?'

'I hate the smell.'

'Why?'

His attention was focused again. *He can't relate to anything outside his own experience. I mustn't talk about myself or he'll drift away.*

'My interrogator used to smoke them. He'd say, "You'd like one, wouldn't you, Volkov? You'd like a cigarette and a hot meal and some coffee . . . and shoes? Your feet are cold, aren't they?" '

He gazed out over the placid water.

'Your wife should give them up,' Lucy said quietly. 'It's unkind when she knows it upsets you.'

'She loves me.' He turned his head and looked at Lucy. 'If it weren't for her, I wouldn't be here now. They took my shoes away when I was arrested. I got frostbite.'

'I don't know what to say,' she murmured. 'I've read what happens to prisoners, but hearing you say it makes it so much worse.'

'There's someone coming,' Volkov said. 'I hope he doesn't sit down here. What's the time? I forgot to put on my watch this morning.'

'Nearly twelve,' she said. 'I think he's going to sit here. Shall we go? I'm not tired any more.'

The man's shadow fell on them, directed by the bright sunlight. Lucy glanced up at him. He was elderly, grey haired, well dressed. He looked ill. He didn't speak. He sat at the far end of the seat and stared out over the lake.

'Ready?' Lucy whispered.

'Yes,' Volkov muttered.

41

They got up and as they did so, the man glanced at them without interest. In turn, their shadows fell on him.

Adolph Brückner had been walking. There was an hour to kill before his appointment. He believed in taking exercise, but his head was starting to ache and he was tired. He saw the seat in the distance with a man and woman sitting on it. He would have preferred to sit down alone, but there might not be another seat for some distance. His head was now throbbing. It wasn't the skull-splitting pain that immobilized him for days on end. Just the warning of the agony that was to come.

He had told his secretary that he was going on a short holiday. His wife knew the truth. She was so worried about him. Adolph was touched by her concern. She loved him in spite of their age difference. He had promised to phone and let her know what happened after the first consultation.

He came up to the seat and sat down, as far from the couple as possible. The last thing he wanted was a casual conversation with strangers. His doctor was a woman. He didn't like the idea of that; he had old-fashioned ideas about the female role, but she was said to be the best. His friend, Peter Müller, had recommended her. He trusted Müller's judgement in this, as he did his knowledge of antiques and works of art. He glanced up briefly as the couple got up. The girl was blonde and pretty. He liked beautiful women and beautiful things. Collecting was his passion. He watched them walk away together.

He stared out over the lake; he couldn't appreciate the splendour of the view. His mood was bitter because he was afraid. Afraid of the headaches, afraid of submitting to a science he had derided as the refuge of fools and weaklings – psychiatry.

He had tried everything else. Brain scans showed nothing. No tumours, no abnormalities. Business pressure was blamed and he went on a long cruise with his wife and his adopted children. It was useless. He lay in his cabin and groaned aloud with the intolerable pain. There was no rhythm in the attacks. They came without warning and as suddenly they stopped, leaving him shocked and exhausted. He had taken his head between his hands, crushing the temples as if he could drive out the excruciating agony. At times he had thought of suicide.

He had been forced to this as a last resort. Switzerland. He muttered the word to himself. Cuckoo clocks and numbered bank accounts. Watches and ski resorts . . . and clinics. Clinics as discreet as the banks.

A group of children passed by, laughing and shouting. He winced at the noise. He loved children, but he couldn't father any. His first marriage had broken up because he was sterile, and his wife wouldn't adopt. Eloise had been different. He had worn his second wife like a jewel. Thirty years younger, elegant, intelligent, she was a medal Adolph Brückner had awarded himself for his phenomenal success. But his wealth and his power couldn't help him now. Here he was, the famous West German industrialist with his millions, and his influence from the Bundesbank to the Bundestag, sitting on a seat, alone and vulnerable, while the headache tuned up for a terrible concert of relentless pain.

Clinics and cuckoo clocks. The words chased each other round his brain like some idiot jingle. He looked at his watch. He sighed. He had left his car and chauffeur while he walked. They were waiting on the road.

It was a short drive up the hillside. The clinic was built on a promontary, with spectacular views across the lake to the distant Jura mountains in their bridal wreath of clouds. He went up the steps and in to the reception.

It was a handsome modern building, with lots of glass. Cool colours, plenty of air. Pastel flower arrangements and smiling faces coming to greet him. Empty eyes and painted smiles. To soothe the mad, he thought savagely. Am I, Adolph Brückner, mad? What is it, inside my head, that all the skill of technological science cannot find?

A nurse guided him to a silent lift that stopped at the third floor without seeming to move. She came with him and he read the name plate. *Dr I. Volkov.* The nurse knocked, and then opened it for him. Her smile was painted, too. He stepped inside.

He had formed a mental picture of the famous Russian doctor. He was expecting a big, butch woman, with spectacles and shorn hair. The woman who came to meet him was slight, fair haired and in her thirties. She wore a well-cut blue dress and a gold necklace. She smiled at him and held out her hand, as if it were a social encounter.

'Monsieur Brückner. Good morning. Do come and sit down, please. Make yourself comfortable.'

A big leather armchair faced her across her desk.

'Do you smoke?'

He shook his head. 'Thank you, no.'

'Very sensible,' she said and smiled. 'But I'm afraid I do. If you don't mind.'

'I don't mind.'

She wasn't a health freak; that helped. He had no time for the anti-alcohol and tobacco lobby. People should make their own decisions about what was bad for them. And he had interests in the tobacco companies.

'I've been looking through your notes,' she said. 'You're a very healthy man. No illnesses apart from a remedial operation for a war wound.'

'I was shot in the leg on the Russian front,' he said. 'Army surgeons cocked it up. I walked with a limp till it was put right.'

She nodded. She wore her blonde hair in a short swinging bob. The colour of corn swaying in a light breeze. Fields and fields of corn as they rumbled through, cutting across them, scything down the crops.

'But you have this one problem,' he heard her say. 'Headaches. Acute attacks lasting for days, sometimes. Clinical investigations show no malignancy or physical cause. Migraine has been eliminated. Psychological stress is the diagnosis, but the attacks occur as frequently when you're on holiday or during leisure activities. You play golf, I see.'

'And I ski,' he added. 'I keep myself fit.'

'Well,' the doctor said; she put out her cigarette. 'I'll start by asking you some routine questions. Do you have any secret anxieties that you can't discuss with anyone? Any business problems? Personal relationships? Money?'

He said no, to each one.

'Sex?' she enquired and smiled at him, as if it were a foolish question.

'I'm seventy-one,' he said. 'I'm still able to perform, if that's what you mean.'

'I'm sure you are.'

He knew he was being aggressive; she didn't seem to mind. 'No aberrations, no perversions you're ashamed of? Don't think you can shock me. I've heard everything. I've great sympathy with problems of that kind.'

'I'm not a sado-masochist, paedophile or anything else,' he said. 'And I don't want to fuck men, or dress up in women's clothes.'

'Would you like a cup of coffee?'

It was a gentle put-down, and he knew it. She had a slight accent, not very thick, but with the lilt he recognized from all those years ago. He said, 'Doctor, I didn't come here to drink coffee. What can you do for me?'

'It's what you can do for yourself,' she said. 'Your headaches are self-induced, M'sieur Brückner. You are punishing yourself. *I* don't know why, but *you* do.'

He glared at her. 'That's nonsense. I'm not listening to a lot of psychiatric crap.'

'Then get up and walk out of here,' she suggested. 'I guarantee you'll have the worst headache of your life.'

He didn't move. He rubbed one hand against his forehead. There was sweat on his palm.

'What am I to do?' he said at last.

'You can trust me,' she said quietly. 'Try to think of me as a friend. Let me help you in the way I think best. I'd like to give you an injection, something to help you relax and make it easy to talk.'

He jerked suspiciously. 'Sodium Penthadol? I'm not having the truth drug!'

'No, you're not,' she assured him. 'You've been reading too many spy novels, M'seiur. That's a lot of nonsense. I'll give you something called Buscopan which simply relaxes the muscles and stops you feeling tense. It will hold that headache at bay for a little while. Now, why don't we start. Would you prefer to lie down?'

He grimaced. 'No couch for me, thank you.'

'If you're comfortable, you're just as well sitting up. Take off your jacket and roll up your right sleeve, please.'

She straightened up. He hadn't even felt the needle go in. 'You won't feel drowsy,' she assured him. 'Just loose, not uptight. So,' she went behind her desk and lit another cigarette. He remembered the smell. Strong, scented Balkan tobacco. 'Tell me about yourself. From the beginning.'

It was the third time Volkov had said goodbye. They'd been walking aimlessly, stopping to sit and gaze at the lake and the passers-by, mostly in silence. There was a bar up a side street. Lucy saw him glance towards it and then stop.

'Time for me to go home,' he said.

'And I must go back to my hotel,' Lucy said. 'It's lonely when you don't know anybody. There's a café over there. I wouldn't mind a glass of wine and a sandwich. Then I'll say goodbye. I promise.'

He didn't argue. They left the quayside and crossed over; Lucy asked if she could take his arm.

'I'm not used to the traffic yet.' She knew he didn't want the contact, but he was not going to refuse. He was a naturally gentle man, she realized that. A kind man. The courage, the self-respect might have been stripped from him, but his natural kindness remained. He guided her across the stream of traffic.

'This is a nice little place,' Lucy remarked. 'Do you come here every day?'

'If I walk this way. I have a routine, you see. I have a drink at the St Honoré, then I walk to the end here and sit down for a bit in the Jardin Anglais. I stop off here occasionally. There are bars and cafés everywhere. The Swiss like their food and drink.'

They sat down; the bar was already full of people eating snack lunches, drinking beer and coffee. The waitresses were busy. Volkov fidgeted.

Lucy said quickly, 'What do you do when it rains?'

'I go to the Bibliothèque in the Place aux Vivres and borrow a book. Or I go to the cinema.' He was looking around, trying to attract attention.

Lucy waved at a passing waitress. 'The menu please and a glass
of cognac. Bring the cognac right away, my friend's not feeling
very well.
'Why did you do that?' he said suddenly.
'I know you need a drink,' she said quietly. 'Tell me, what sort
of books do you like?'
'I'm reading about Buddhism at the moment. Ah, thank you.'
He took the brandy and sipped it.
Lucy waited. 'Do you believe in Buddhism?'
'I don't believe in anything. I live in a vacuum. Rather, I
exist . . . There was a Protestant pastor in prison with me. He
was a good man. He said I'd find it easier if I was a Christian. I
wonder what's happened to him . . . If he ended up in a labour
camp he's probably dead. He wasn't very strong.'
'But you survived,' she pointed out. 'That's what's important.'
Finishing the brandy, the sense of not being, not caring, spread
through him. She had such a delicate face, such an innocent
intensity . . .
'You're a nice person, Lucy Warren. But you're wasting your
time with me. I've nothing more to give. So, for the last time, go
away and leave me in peace. Please.'
'All right,' Lucy stood up. 'All right, I'll go. But I'll be back
tomorrow and the day after and the day after that. You're not
going to get rid of me, Professor. Because I'm damned if I'm
going to let them win!'
Then she was gone. He watched her walk away down the street.
It was peaceful now she had gone. And suddenly, lonely. The day
ahead of him seemed very long, but he knew the remedy for that.

Back at the rented apartment, Lucy felt tired and drained. Despair
was creeping up on her. The hero didn't exist; the fiery orator,
the fearless protester against injustice and oppression had become
a lost soul. Introverted, withdrawn, a drunk.
This man was no Andrei Sakharov, who, after years of exile,
could enter politics and rally the opposition. Volkov was dying
visibly, without even a martyr's crown. It was hopeless, and cruel
to harass him. As he had said himself, he had nothing left to give.

She sat down and closed her eyes. All for nothing. Her father's dream of a crusade, her hopes, the trust of Mischa and the friends who had lobbied and marched in protest all over the world when Volkov was arrested. A year in prison. That was all that was needed to break his spirit.

She opened her eyes and sat up slowly. A year wasn't very long. Others had survived much worse and come out stronger and more determined. Was Volkov fundamentally weak? He hadn't seemed so when the world was watching. Ringing statements of defiance had been smuggled out of his cell in the Lubianka prison and published, to the rage of the Soviet authorities.

Lucy got up and opened the window. She took deep breaths of the clear Swiss air. *I'll be back tomorrow and the day after and the day after that. For as long as it takes until I reach him. If his wife is part of what's happened to him, then she's not going to win, either.*

She slammed the window shut so hard that the glass rattled.

Adolph Brückner was relaxed. The chair was comfortable. He had no sense of drowsiness or lack of control. It was natural to talk about himself; the doctor was so unobtrusive. She just asked an occasional question to concentrate his mind.

He'd had an unremarkable childhood, devoid of traumas. His parents were affectionate, his home life stable. He was the only son; he got on well with a younger sister. Yes, he'd joined the Hitler Youth. It was compulsory, after all. And not a bad training either, he insisted. Discipline, physical exercise, pride in achievements. The present generation of young Germans could benefit from such a system. He wasn't a Nazi, no, he rejected that. He was a patriotic German.

The army, Irina Volkov prompted. Tell me about the army. What was it like being a soldier? She was sitting just out of his view, a disembodied mentor. She could see his reflection in a cleverly placed mirror in the wall.

He tensed. His jaw clenched. He shifted in the chair. He didn't want to talk about the army.

'There's nothing to tell,' he snapped back. 'War is filthy. I

48

survived with a bullet in my leg and that got me out of it and home.'

'You were lucky,' she remarked. 'Millions of Germans never got back at all.'

'Ten million,' Brückner said. 'Ten million dead. Don't talk to me about war.'

She had lit another cigarette. Her eyes narrowed against the smoke. 'Twenty million Russians,' she amended. 'If you went through that campaign, no wonder you get headaches.'

'It's got nothing to do with that! I was invalided out by the end of forty-two.' He was visibly disturbed; sweat was trickling down his face in the air-conditioned room.

Irina stood up. 'I think that's enough for today, Monsieur Brückner. You've made a good start.'

He was up, pulling on his jacket, running his tie in to place under his collar. He was anxious to get away.

'I don't see there's any point in going on with this. All I've done is waste time talking about myself.'

She said quietly, 'Do you have a headache?'

He paused. 'No.'

'One was beginning when you came here, wasn't it?'

'Perhaps; yes, it was throbbing slightly.' The fear came back, swamping him.

'Well, it's not hurting now, is it?' she said firmly.

'No. No, it isn't.' He was buttoning his jacket. He wiped his damp face with a handkerchief. 'I may not have another attack for weeks.'

'I wouldn't like to bet on that.' Her voice was very cool. 'I'd like you to come back tomorrow. Unless you want to wait till you get another headache.'

He raised his voice. He was used to shouting at employees and servants when they frustrated him in any way.

'What good can all this talking do me? I'm busy. I've a business to run, I haven't time to waste on a lot of clap-trap.'

She was quite unmoved. She shrugged slightly. 'It's up to you. I can't do anything for you except help you to help yourself. If you want to come back, there's a ten o'clock appointment reserved for you. Believe me, M'sieur, I have a waiting list of patients. I'm only seeing you because I know it's urgent.'

He went to the door. He turned the handle. Irinia Volkov didn't move. He opened the door; then he turned back and said, 'All right. Ten o'clock tomorrow then.'

She left her desk and came to him. She smiled and nodded in a friendly way. 'I'm glad,' she said. 'You've made the right decision.' She gave him her hand to shake and gently closed the door on him.

Then, she bent down to the recorder hidden under his chair and pressed the button to rewind the tape.

There were four more appointments that afternoon. It was already dusk when she closed up her office. Just before she left she checked with her secretary. Yes, Monsieur Brückner had confirmed the ten o'clock session.

Irina drove home, taking her time. She wasn't in a hurry to get to the apartment. She knew what she would find there. It was a lovely evening; Geneva was beautiful in the springtime. On impulse, she stopped outside the Hôtel Beau Rivage. She felt like relaxing with a drink before going home. And it was a good place to make her telephone call.

She knew she was attractive. Men glanced at her appreciatively. She gave no encouragement. She ordered a glass of Moselle, smoked a cigarette and watched people come and go without much interest. She was thinking about her patient, Adolph Brückner. She knew the type, A number had come to the clinic over the years. Arrogant, greedy products of the capitalist society that she hated. Their women were no better. Their children, spoilt and neurotic, were typical.

She loved her work; the mysterious mechanism of the human psyche fascinated her. She was euphoric when she dismissed a patient, cured and ready to resume a normal life; depressed when she failed and the solution eluded her. It was like winning or losing a chess game at championship level. She played chess as a hobby. She had been trained to regard human beings in her care as no more involving than amoeba under a microscope. Without a professional attitude, she couldn't have worked at the Lenin Institute.

50

Brückner was different. Brückner wasn't there to be cured of his agonizing affliction. Peter Müller had sent him, as he'd sent others over the past five years. Müller hadn't made one mistake in his selection so far. Brückner was going mad with guilt. He was driving himself to the point of suicide.

A ruthless opportunist who had fought his way to riches and power in post-war Germany must have something dreadful gnawing at his subsconscious to torture himself like that.

Irina stubbed out her cigarette and asked for the bill. And for a telephone. She dialled a number in Munich, closing the cubicle door. It rang for some time, and she exclaimed impatiently. Where was he? He was expecting the call. At last it was answered. She heard Peter Müller's voice.

'It's me,' she said. 'I've been ringing for ages. Are you having a party? There's a lot of noise . . . All right, so long as you can hear. Our friend came today. You're right, I'm sure we're on to something. I didn't rush him. He's coming again tomorrow . . . Yes, of course, I'll keep him in. Can you come up at the weekend? What an awful row. You must have hundreds of people!'

It irritated her trying to talk against a background of cocktail-party noise. It was unprofessional of Müller. She didn't like him from the beginning. He was too smug, too sure of himself. Now she had reason to hate him. But he was good.

'Oh, have you? That's nice for you. Make it Friday. I'll know a lot more by then.'

She rang off. He was celebrating, he said. A very big sale to some American collectors. She checked her watch. It was late. Time to go home.

Volkov was sober when the front door opened. He'd slept off the afternoon drinks, showered and made himself coffee. He didn't switch on the lights. He sat in the deepening gloom and thought of the girl who had come into his empty life that morning, and refused to go away.

When he was released he'd been plagued by waking nightmares; often reality and fantasy became indistinguishable. Irina's care had got him through the worst period. Her care and her medical skill. She'd healed his damaged lungs, insisting that he rest and avoid all mental and physical stress. No interviews with the clamouring

51

Western media, no Press conferences till he was stronger. He was so weak he didn't resist. His will seemed to ebb away; the fighting courage that had sustained him even when they forced him on the Aeroflot plane in handcuffs to fly him out of Russia, had deserted him.

He was in Irina's hands. Something in him had broken. Not in the cruel misery of cold and deprivation in his cell, but in the comfort of the Swiss environment. For many months he'd lived only to hear the door open and her step in the hall.

He had depended on her like a child. Irina loved him. Irina had fought for his release and finally persuaded the authorities to let him go. It was a long time since he had discovered the terms negotiated for that act of mercy. That was when he started to drink. He felt the helpless rage well up within him. And the despair.

She switched on the lights.

'Dimitri, what are you doing sitting in the dark?' She came towards him; he wasn't drunk and gratefully she bent and kissed him on the cheek.

She loves me, he said to himself. *She takes me in her arms in bed and I can't bear to touch her. . . .*

'What did you do today?' It wounded her when he flinched from her embrace. She bit her lips, as if one pain would drive out another.

'Went for a walk. Had a few drinks.' He heard her sigh. 'Came home again.' He didn't say, *I met this strange girl who told me how brave and wonderful I was and wouldn't go away. And she'll be there tomorrow.* He said, 'I won't ask what you were doing.'

'I'm going to change. You might pour me a drink instead of being nasty, darling. It doesn't do any good.'

She went in to the bedroom and stripped off the smart dress. *He has to hurt me*, she told herself. *He has to punish me. I must try not to mind. If only, if only that swine Müller had kept his mouth shut.*

He hadn't moved when she came back. She poured herself a glass of wine. 'I'll make some dinner in a few minutes,' she said. 'Unless you'd like to go out?'

'I've been out,' he said. 'And I'm not hungry.'

52

Irina looked at him. 'I wish you'd try,' she said suddenly. 'We could still be happy. We could have a good life here together.' She leaned close to him; he saw a film of tears in her eyes. 'It's all over now, darling. It's all in the past. You could stop drinking and start on your book. Don't you realize how things have changed at home? We could go back one day.'

'There's nothing to stop *you* going,' he remarked. 'You've given them enough victims by now, haven't you? Not to mention me. Why don't you go?'

'And leave you here to drink yourself to death alone?'

He shrugged.

She said desperately, 'I still love you, that's the reason. We go over and over it and nothing changes. You can't forgive me and you won't try. All you want is to destroy yourself and blame me.'

She got up, fighting back tears. At the door of her room she turned back to face him. But he wasn't even looking at her. She slammed the door.

He might have been able to forgive her. He still loved her in those days. He might have been moved by her distress. He might have accepted her explanation. If it hadn't been for Peter Müller.

'Peter, darling, the Baxters are going. Come and say goodbye to them. Who was on the telephone at this hour?'

Peter Müller followed his wife back to the party. The Baxters were rich American clients; they specialized in early German Gothic carvings and enamels. He had sold them a highly important ivory tryptich for an incredible sum of money. His wife, like all clever American women, had made a friend out of Mary Baxter and organized the party in their honour. She was a great help in the business. They had been married for twenty-two years and they were happy together.

'Who was it?' she whispered, the smile already in place on her lips as they emerged from his study.

'Only a runner,' he said. 'Thinks there's something to be looked at in Geneva. I chewed him up for calling so late. Ah, Joe, Mary – do you really have to go so soon?'

He had a wonderful warm manner. A typical Bavarian, cultivated, charming. Not at all like a German. Mary Baxter felt he was a friend. And that wonderful, wonderful tryptich! She couldn't wait to see it in their house in San Francisco. Thirteenth century, and the crispness of the carving! Joe loved their collection. It had made them famous, introduced them to interesting people in the art world. There'd been a whole profile on them in *American Connoisseur*.

They were escorted to the door, handed in to their car. Peter Müller kissed her hand.

'Enjoy your treasure, Mary,' he said. 'There's only one other like it and that's in the Getty Museum.'

'I wish we'd known you then,' Mary Baxter said. 'We'd have bought both!'

The party didn't break up for some hours. The Baxters were flying to London early the next morning en route for the States. The Müllers' friends settled down to enjoy themselves and talk about their clients and their businesses. He saw a slim, elegantly dressed woman getting a drink from one of the waiters and went towards her. She was thin and dark, and had been a photographic model in her youth.

'Eloise, my dear,' he said. 'Aren't you being looked after? You're always surrounded with admirers!'

'Not so many at my age,' she smiled at him. He made a gesture, dismissing the idea as absurd.

'My dear, a mature woman is more attractive than any girl. Have you heard from Adolph?'

'I spoke to him before I came this evening,' Eloise Brückner said.

'And how was he?' he asked. 'It must be so worrying for all of you.'

'He said he'd had one consultation. He was grumpy. You know what he's like. But no headache, thank God. I'm so grateful to you for persuading him to go and see this doctor. He'd never have listened to me!'

'I couldn't see an old friend suffer like that,' Peter Müller said. 'I've known a number of people who have seen this woman; they swore by her. It can't do any harm. Please God, may it help him.'

'I do hope so,' she said. 'Thank you, Peter. You've been wonderful.'

She didn't include his wife, Susan. The omission amused him. The two women didn't like each other. They were good at disguising it for the sake of their husbands.

It was past two o'clock when the last guest left. Susan Müller looked round the room. It was littered with empty glasses, plates of half-eaten canapés, full ashtrays. The staff were being slow about clearing up.

'Well,' she said. 'Let's hope it was worth all the expense. I've made a note of the spongers who come here and never buy a goddamned thing! Next time, they won't get an invitation!'

'From what we made out of that Baxter sale we could give a party every night for the next ten years,' Peter reminded her. She was always irritable after a party. She resented the expense. 'Come on, it was very successful. Let's go to bed.'

Before she went to sleep, she turned on her back and said, 'Peter? Is there something in Geneva?'

'There may be,' he said. 'I might fly up on Friday and take a look.'

'What is it? Why don't I come, too?'

'Because it's silver and most likely a fake. I'll only go for the day.'

'I don't know why you bother,' his wife said. 'There's no real market for silver at the moment.' She was far more dedicated to business than he was. Unfortunately, she had no natural feel or sympathy with beautiful things. She only saw the price tag.

He heard Susan's deep breathing. He lay beside her till he was sure she was asleep, then he got up and slipped out of the bedroom. He made some hot milk in the kitchen and sat down to drink it. The debris of the party was cleared away. The kitchen was its clean, clinical self.

He had known Adolph Brückner for nearly ten years. Brückner was a big prize for any antique dealer. He had a large fortune, and taste and knowledge acquired over years of collecting. He was an expert on early Russian art. Müller was as shrewd in his business as he was in his other profession. He set out to charm the wife. Eloise Brückner was a beautiful woman and he found he liked her very much. He didn't flirt; she wouldn't have welcomed that. He was astute enough to realize that she loved her husband. He wooed her in a different way, by praising Brückner's knowledge. She began inviting him to parties.

He thought back to that first party in the sumptuous Munich house. The big drawing room was set out like a museum, with rare Italian masters expertly lit and displayed, and, what caught his attention instantly, a large cabinet filled with Russian works of art. Fabergé boxes, photograph frames, copies of Japanese *netsukes* in various hardstones, with tiny jewelled eyes. And, in pride of place, glittering with frosty diamonds and translucent green enamel, a desk set from the Russian Imperial collection. A clock and an exquisite calendar. He noticed that the original Russian date card had not been changed. The set was priceless.

He cultivated Brückner carefully. He wasn't a man to be rushed into friendship. He didn't try to sell him anything. He flattered him by asking his advice and soon Brückner was consulting him. First one expensive rarity was found and purchased, then others followed. Brückner and his wife became close friends of the Müllers. Müller made a lot of money out of that friendship. And, one day, by chance, he caught Adolph Brückner out in a lie. They had discussed the collection of Fabergé at length. He had been allowed to handle the treasured clock, listen to the delightful silver chimes, adjust the calendar. And he had accepted Brückner's story without question. He had discovered the desk set in Paris after the war. He had named a famous French dealer, long since dead.

It was a lucky coincidence, a one-in-a-million chance that brought Müller on a buying trip to Sotheby's in New York, in pursuit of a Fabergé Easter egg made for a rich Russian merchant in 1912. He was acting for Adolph Brückner, who wanted this exquisite rarity for his collection. The estimate was over a million pounds sterling. Müller had his authority to go above the top estimate to buy it. He failed. The buyer was a New York dealer with a French name. The same name, he remembered, as the dealer in Paris who had sold Brückner his desk set. He had approached the man after the sale and introduced himself on behalf of his client. If the egg had not been bought on commission, might he be interested in an immediate profit from the under-bidder?

And Müller added the story of his client's purchase from the French namesake. No namesake, the American said, but his grandfather! The desk set rang no bells with him, he added. And he knew every important item of stock his grandfather had bought and sold. The old man had kept a meticulous record stretching over forty years. He'd check, but he would surely have remembered something so unique. Müller got a call from him that evening at the Sherry Netherland Hotel.

There was no desk set listed. He'd been through the ledgers. The name Brückner was not on his grandfather's list of clients, either, and he was equally meticulous about them. And he regretted that the egg was not for re-sale. His tone suggested that he regarded Müller and his offer as highly suspect. That was when, as Müller put it, he changed hats.

Adolph Brückner had lied about the Fabergé set, which meant that he had come by it dishonestly. And dishonesty was another commodity that excited Müller's interest. Theft, sexual delinquency, scandal – Müller traded in all of them. He had been working for Moscow Centre since 1957, using his contacts in the art world to supply them with agents. And for the last five years he had routed several highly important potential victims via the Geneva clinic – and Doctor Irinia Volkov. Müller alerted Moscow. Brückner would be a very useful tool.

He finished his hot milk, grimacing because he had sat there letting it get tepid. Eloise had told him about Brückner's headaches. No physical cause had been diagnosed. He wouldn't accept that it was psychological. She was in despair. Müller promised to talk to him.

He waited till he knew that Brückner was recovering from a terrible attack. Then, in glowing terms, he recommended the Russian psychiatrist to Brückner. Between them, he and Eloise persuaded him to consult her. It was possible his lies about the Fabergé treasure was part of something far more serious. Once in Doctor Irina's hands, he'd make a good confession. Thinking that, Müller grinned. He had been brought up a Catholic and it was the old injunction to children on the weekly visit to the priest: *make a good confession, Peter*. Brückner would confess, but there'd be no comforting absolution at the end of it.

He rinsed out his cup and went back to bed. Susan was lying on her back, snoring lightly. She had no idea of his other life. No idea of the bank account in Lichtenstein that was topped up so generously every time he pleased his Soviet masters. His controller over the last eight years was at the present moment leading a trade delegation in Berlin.

The Russian was an enigma to Peter Müller. Over the years he had surfaced in the West under a number of aliases and jobs. When Müller first came under his control, he was a military adviser to the East German army. He wore a moustache and cultivated a hard-nosed image, dour and stiff necked. A year later, he appeared as a naval commander attached to the Soviet Embassy in Paris. No moustache and a very different personality. A fun-loving, pro-Western Russian, with an eye for the ladies and the good life.

He had told Müller once that the French Intelligence, SEDECE, had tried to recruit him. He was much amused by the incident. He had, in fact, recruited one of *their* senior officers who'd been caught in bed with one of Rakovsky's young naval lieutenants.

He left Paris to re-emerge as a respected official in the Soviet Trade Ministry. And, this time he used his own name and assumed his real identity. The cloak-and-dagger days were over. He still ran a few selected agents like Müller, but in the new age of Gorbachev and glasnost, intelligence work was more specialized. A lot of the action men, as the assassins were called, and the sleepers waiting to be activated, would have to be retired.

As Müller would be one day, he realized. That made the nest egg in Lichtenstein so important. When Müller talked of retirement to his wife, he wasn't thinking of their pleasant Munich apartment and a holiday house on the Baltic coast. He had the golden shores and sunny skies of the Caribbean in his mind's eye.

He'd make the trip to Geneva on Friday. By that time Irina Volkov would have opened Brückner's skull to see if there were worms inside. He drifted off to sleep.

*

He was late. Lucy looked at her watch again. It was nearly midday. The same smirking waiter had given up trying to talk to her.

She had slept badly and woken with a sense of apprehension. He wouldn't come. Then, just as she was giving up, he came in to view.

He walked slowly, a traveller without a destination. If there was a ravine at the end of the road instead of a café, he'd step over the edge without looking down. She got up to meet him.

'I'm so pleased to see you,' she said. 'Where do you want to sit?'

'I didn't mean to come. I thought you'd have given up,' Volkov said.

'I never give up,' Lucy told him. 'And you wanted to see me again. What would you like? Coffee?'

'If you like. It's hotter today.'

'Then let's go into the shade,' she suggested. 'I've been thinking so much about you.'

'I wish you wouldn't,' he said.

'Do you always feel so sorry for yourself?'

It was a quietly spoken question and it took him by surprise.

'I enjoyed talking with you yesterday. Why are you being unkind?'

'I didn't mean to be,' Lucy answered. 'It's just that I'm not sorry for you any more. There's nothing wrong with you now, Professor. Nothing really wrong, or you wouldn't have come back here.'

'It's my favourite café,' he said. 'And I think I'd like a cognac.'

'I'll have one with you,' she said.

'There's no need. I'm used to drinking alone.'

Lucy opened her bag. 'I brought these,' she said. 'Copies of the speech you made about the Helsinki Agreement and the article published just before you were arrested. I was reading them last night.'

He took the photocopies from her almost absent-mindedly. He didn't want to read what he'd said and written when he was in Russia. But a phrase caught his eye.

'Liberty is the life of the human soul. The system that denies that

to its people must be resisted even at the cost of that life.' He put the page down.

'Why are you doing this? Why are you trying to revive a corpse?'

She said quietly, 'Because you owe a lot of people. Like my father, who spent his time and his money campaigning for you. And all his friends. And *your* friends, Professor!'

She reeled off half a dozen names. Members of the human rights movement. Imprisoned, dead, driven insane.

'You got out,' she declared, 'but they didn't. What would they say if they could see you now, if they were able to speak for themselves?'

He hadn't touched the cognac. He looked at her; there was a tinge of colour in his face.

'I don't have to listen to any of this.'

'No,' she agreed. 'No, you don't. You can turn your back on me, just like you've done with them! But you won't. You need me. If you're dead, Volkov, then I'm going to bring you back to life.'

'Where are we going?' he asked her.

She had hold of his arm. She'd been walking quickly, forcing the pace. Now she hailed a taxi cab.

'To my apartment. It's not far now. I've just moved in. I want to show it to you.'

When they got out at the entrance to the block he paused. 'Why am I doing this?'

'I told you,' Lucy said. 'Because you need me. We need each other.'

He followed her through the front door, into the apartment. It was a large sunny room, pleasing to the eye.

'You're very beautiful,' he said.

She put her arms around his neck and gently touched his lips. After a moment she parted them.

He said, 'I'd better warn you. I'm impotent.'

'You won't be with me.'

*

The blinds in the room were drawn; a single light shone on the ceiling above the bed. Adolph Brückner lay on his back and looked at it. He couldn't see Irina; he couldn't see his surroundings. He saw only the little circle of light over his head; it held his concentration.

He felt weightless; there was no pain, no sensation in his body. He had been talking, answering questions that unlocked doors he had kept closed for fifty years.

Irina's voice was cool and distant.

'You were sent ahead to scout the land,' she reminded him. 'What happened?' The tape recorder by the bed was taking it all in.

'We went too far. Boris wasn't looking for partisans. He was looking for some place to loot. I was scared. I thought we'd run into a Red Army patrol. He only laughed at me. He was like a bull. He didn't give a damn about anything.'

She had heard a lot about Boris, the big Ukrainian who'd volunteered to fight with the Germans when they entered his village. A powerful brute who couldn't wait to put on a uniform and rob his own people.

'We went through a wood,' the monotonous voice continued. 'We saw this house. Boris said, "We'll get some pickings in here! Come on, let's take a look!" We had our sub-machineguns out; Boris could move like a cat. He didn't bother being quiet. He'd seen through the window. We just shoved the door open and went in. There was a woman. With long blonde hair. She stared at us.'

As he talked he became a spectator. He saw it all happening again, as if it were a play. The blonde woman, terror contorting her face, backing away from him and Boris.

'She turned and ran in to a room, slamming the door. Boris laughed.' The laugh was ringing inside Brückner's head.

'Oh no, you don't. I'll get you, you bitch!' And Boris hurling himself at the door and bursting it open. He saw himself following; Boris had the woman by the hair. He was bending her backwards onto the bed, one hand ripping her skirt off. He felt the sexual excitement rise in him all over again as he watched Boris expose her naked thighs and the round belly. She had been silent until then. The scream echoed in his head as the man fell on top of her, his breeches dropped round his ankles. He was thrusting into her, grabbing at her breasts, shouting at Brückner to shut her up . . . to sit on her head.

Sweat was pouring down his face. He saw himself pinning the woman down, half-smothering her while Boris heaved and grunted, ripping her blouse away.

From far away he heard the doctor's voice.

'You held her down while he raped her. How many times was she raped?'

'Boris did it twice. Then turned her over and buggered her. He was like an animal. Then he said, "Here you are, kid. Now you get stuck in."

'She was still struggling, kicking out. He held her for me while I got on top. She managed to scream once. It was so loud . . . like a trapped animal.'

'Next thing there was a boy in the room. He was punching at me, trying to pull me off by the leg. He was yelling. Boris picked up his gun and smashed him over the head. I heard the skull crack. It made me finish too quickly.

'She was bleeding. She was bleeding all over the bed. I looked down and saw the boy was dead. I said to Boris, "Come on, let's get out of here."

' "Get your pants up," he said to me. "That little bastard spoiled a good fuck for you." He kicked the boy's body. Then he started pulling open drawers. Throwing stuff out, looking for money or jewellery.

'I ran out of the bedroom, I was watching out of the window. I was so scared someone might come and find us. The place was miles from our main force. I was scared of the partisans. I heard a shout from Boris and he came out holding a cross. Holding it up. It was big and flashing with red stones. I thought, "My Christ! He's got something there."

' "Well now, get a look at this," Boris was laughing. He was excited. "The Red bitch's been robbing a church! This might be worth a few roubles, eh? Gold and jewels, lad; gold and fucking jewels!"

'He told me to go back in and pick up some ornaments he'd found.'

In the shadows Irina sipped water. Her hand shook. She said, 'What did you steal, Adolph?'

On the monitor his pulse rate had steadied. He was past the worst trauma of the rape and the murder of the child.

'My desk set,' he answered.

'Volkov,' Lucy whispered. 'Wake up.'

He was lying across her, his head pillowed on her breast. She stroked the dark hair, trying to rouse him gently. He stirred and lifted himself, gazing at her. She reached up and kissed him on the lips.

'I want you to make love to me again,' she said softly.

He said in Russian. 'You're a witch. A white witch.'

It had been an extraordinary love-making. Compulsive, mindless and without words. Words might have given him time to doubt . . . to remember the empty shell his body had become. She didn't let him speak; she kissed him till his mouth burned and suddenly his tongue thrust fiercely back against hers. They undressed each other, still in silence.

There was no sophistication in their love-making. She opened herself and grasped him to her and he reached a swift and violent climax. He fell into an exhausted semi-sleep, while Lucy lay passive under his weight and held him in her arms. He was spent, but he was a whole man. She had made him whole. No failure, no impotence with her.

The second time was leisurely and there were many words, even laughter, between them. They were intimates now, finding out about each other, exploring their bodies with sensitive touching.

'You're wonderful,' Volkov told her. 'You smell like flowers.'

And he made love with subtlety and tenderness, stifling her sharp cry of pleasure with a gentle hand over her mouth.

Then they both slept in one another's arms. It was dark when they awoke. They lay and watched the lights blink and flicker from the window and Lucy said, 'I'm going to make you love me, Volkov. I'm going to make you want me and love yourself because I love you. That's a promise!'

He smiled at her. 'And you keep your promises, don't you, Lucy?'

'I keep them,' she said. 'Are you hungry?'

'No. Are you?'

'Ravenous. Stay there and I'll make something for us.'

'You're always hungry! You wanted breakfast the first time we met.'

'I didn't. I only ordered it to keep you talking to me. Do you want a drink? I've got some wine.'

He lay back against the pillows, watching her. She put on a dressing gown. She switched the light on and drew the curtains.

'I might get drunk,' he said. 'I'm always drunk by now.'

She paused by the door. She said, 'You'll never get drunk again. You're not alone any more. We'll have a glass of wine together!' She sat on the bed and they touched their glasses in a silent toast.

She made sandwiches and they ate them crosslegged on the bed, finishing the wine together.

'Why aren't you married?' he asked her.

'I never met anyone I wanted to marry,' she said.

'But you've had lovers?'

'Only two. There was a student at the college in London where I was studying interior design. It lasted about a year. It wasn't serious; we were both very young. Then there was a man in Jersey. I decorated his house and we became involved, but that didn't work out either.'

He said slowly, 'I don't want to hurt you, Lucy. I don't want to disappoint you. But I must go home before my wife gets back.' He sat forward, not touching her.

'Tell me about your wife,' Lucy said. 'Talk to me about her. You said she loved you.'

'She calls it love,' he answered. 'She's tried in bed with me for a long time. I can't bear to touch her. She says we could start again. The other night she said we could be happy. There have been nights when I lie there, listening to her breathing beside me and I think of killing her.'

'Why? Whatever did she do to you?'

He lay back and she moved close to him, taking his hand in hers.

'When I came here first I had TB. I caught it in prison. I was ill, I couldn't concentrate, I couldn't see people or face interviews. I didn't know what was the matter with me. Then I had an accident. I hadn't left the flat for so long. I remember it was sunny outside. I wanted to go out, to walk on the street alone. The flat was like a prison. I didn't get far. I fell and knocked myself out. Someone called an ambulance and I woke up in hospital. They found the pills I was taking twice a day. I believed they were for my lungs. My wife, Irina, prescribed them. They were drugs, mind-numbing sedatives. The dosage was so strong the doctor at the hospital said it was no wonder I fell down.

'They kept me in overnight. I wouldn't let them send for Irina. I wouldn't see her. By the time I went home I'd thought it out. My wife had been controlling me, just like they do with the poor devils in the special wards. Keeping me quiet, doping me so I didn't talk to journalists, give interviews . . . turning me into a sleepwalker who'd never cause Moscow any trouble. I threw the bottle of pills at her.

'She tried to lie. But the hospital had X-rayed my lungs and they were clear. She's not the sort of woman who cries, but she did. She begged me to forgive her, to understand that she'd had to promise to do it before they'd let me out of prison.'

'She kept saying, "You'd have been dead of TB if I hadn't agreed to what they wanted." '

'You couldn't forgive her,' Lucy said at last.

'I could have forgiven her for what she did to me,' he said. 'I'd escaped total addiction; that was lucky. I wouldn't let her even give me an aspirin for a headache, so I had a drink when I got withdrawal symptoms. I could have let her persuade me, I suppose. She'd given up so much to follow me. She had a brilliant career; she was dedicated. Her father was a powerful Party man with friends in the Politburo. She'd worked hard to get me released. In the end, I could have come to terms with the way she'd betrayed me.

'I would have forgiven her. Until I found out why she was really in Geneva.

'I thought of killing myself many times. But I didn't. I gave up on life and went on living. Drinking! Making Irina suffer.'

'What exactly is she doing?' Lucy asked him. 'Can you tell me?'

'She works for the KGB,' he said. 'She has special patients at the clinic. She tortures them with drugs; she breaks them into little pieces so they can be blackmailed into doing whatever Moscow wants. It was part of the deal she made when they let me go.

'I said I'd denounce her. She just looked at me and said, "I got you out of prison. I'm doing it for you. Go on, have me arrested. I'll get twenty years under Swiss law."

'I couldn't betray her, Lucy, and I couldn't speak out on the old issues unless I did. So I opted for the Russian alternative. I got drunk.'

After a time he said, 'You despise me, don't you? *You* wouldn't have compromised.'

'I would have done the same as you,' Lucy said. 'She saved your life; you couldn't have denounced her. You're not that kind of man.'

She put her arms around him. He saw how pale she was. The blue eyes blazed.

'I hate her for what she's done to you. But you're free of her now, Volkov. You won't feel guilty and you won't drink. And very soon the world will hear your voice again. Don't go back tonight. Stay with me.'

'I want to,' he said slowly. 'But it wouldn't be wise. She mustn't know about you. She'd find some way to hurt you.'

'Where do you live?' she asked him.

He told her. 'You mustn't try to contact me,' he said. 'You must be careful.'

'I'll wait for you outside, tomorrow,' she said quietly. 'If you don't show up I'll know there's something wrong. I'll come up and get you.'

He held her tightly, kissed her hard and hungrily. 'She leaves for the clinic before nine,' he said. 'There's a flower shop on the corner. I'll be there at ten o'clock.'

He let himself out of the apartment. Lucy watched him from the window. He turned, looked up and waved. Then he disappeared from view.

*

66

'I won't take any calls this afternoon. I'm having a long session with Monsieur Brückner.'

'Yes, Doctor,' the nurse said.

At the door of Brückner's room, Irina Volkov paused.

He'd been given a light sedative after the morning; she'd watched him drift off to sleep. He'd laid his bloody ghost to rest. Or so he thought.

While she wrote up her notes and locked the first of the tapes in her desk, she thought of the woman, violated and degraded and the child who had tried to save her. She opened the door and went in. He was still drowsy. She prepared another injection, pinched up a vein and shot the drug in to him. Then, after checking her watch to let it take effect, she slapped him hard across the face.

'Wake up! Wake up!'

She had hit him so hard there was a red mark on his cheek. Her own hand stung. She lit a cigarette and took her seat. He was awake and muttering in confusion. She reached over and switched on the powerful light above his head.

'Look at the light! Look at it, or I'll have to slap you again. Good. Now, Boris had killed the woman. The boy was dead and you'd stolen the desk set. Tell me, Adolph. Tell me what you did then.'

'Boris was gloating over the cross,' the voice was low and slurred. 'He kept rubbing the red stones and holding it up to the light. "Gold and jewels," he said over and over. "It's worth a fortune. Boris, you're in luck, you clever fucker! You'll be rich when this war's over."

'I was wrapping the clock and the calendar in a skirt I'd found in the bedroom. He'd thrown everything on the floor, emptied the drawers. I wanted to get out, take the stuff and get the hell away from the place. I remember I was so scared I was peeing myself, thinking what would happen if a Red Army patrol caught us coming out of that house. Then I heard a moaning noise.

'I shouted at Boris. He heard the moaning, too, and he shoved the cross in to his jacket. He picked up his gun. "Watch outside," he told me and he went back in to the bedroom. I thought we'd killed her, but she was still alive. I stood by the window looking out again. The sun was shining in. Then I heard a noise. It was coming from a big cupboard by the door. I got ready to open fire and then I opened it.'

Irinia noticed that the monitor attached to his wrist showed a violent rise in his pulse rate.

'Tell me,' she said. 'What was in the cupboard?'

'Two kids. A boy, holding a baby. He had his hand over its mouth to stop it crying. He just stared up at me.'

'Did you kill them, too?'

'No. I heard shots in the bedroom. I knew Boris had finished off the woman. I made a sign to the boy to stay quiet and I shut the door. I didn't say anything about them to Boris. I knew what he'd do. I used to dream of that kid's face and the eyes, staring up at me. I had nightmares about it for a long time.'

'Didn't you have nightmares about the woman and the boy being murdered? Didn't that worry you?'

'Not so much. I'd seen a lot of corpses by then. We always looked for women when we took a village. Everybody did it. She wasn't the first one I'd had. But the boy in the cupboard, holding the baby. I couldn't get it out of my mind. The way he looked at me.'

'That must have been his mother then, and his brother,' Irina remarked. 'She tried to save them by hiding them in the cupboard. She didn't have time to save herself.'

Brückner's mouth trembled, and tears spilled out and ran down his cheeks.

'It was the war! It was the same everywhere. I wasn't the only one! I could have shot them. Boris would have done it! I just couldn't. That boy staring up at me. I couldn't. Oh Jesus, my head hurts.' He began to sob.

Irina stood up. She looked down on him. Remember, remember your training. You are not involved. You are objective, unemotional. It means no more to you than a test-tube experiment. You struck him because you had to wake him up. You had to demonstrate your power over him. You are a scientist, a rationalist. You are superior to feelings of hatred and rage.

She switched off the tape recorder, put the tape in her pocket, shut down the harsh overhead light and rang for the nurse. Brückner was moaning, holding his head and tossing to and fro.

The nurse came in and Irina said, 'We've had a very good session. Very productive. But he's experiencing some distress.'

'Yes, I can see. What medication shall I give him, Doctor?'

Irina paused on her way out. She said coolly, 'None. He'll just have to suffer through it. It's part of his therapy. If necessary, restrain him. I'll be in early tomorrow morning.'

She closed the door.

Volkov saw her car draw up and turn into the garage space reserved for residents in the apartment block. She was late; another special patient. He hurried in ahead of her. *I must be careful*, he kept saying to himself. *She's clever, she's trained to observe people. She mustn't notice any difference in me.* He wondered if it showed – wasn't a man who's found his sexual powers after five years of flaccid impotence, visibly changed? Isn't it obvious when a dead man comes to life? Won't she see at a single glance that something has happened? Part of him wanted to flaunt it. Part of him wanted to taunt her.

What did you do with yourself today? She always asked that question, never expecting an answer, only the same sullen negative. *Nothing. I walked, I had a few drinks.* But not this time.

How much he hated her, he realized, waiting for Irina to let herself in. *Perhaps it's because I loved her so much in the beginning. I wanted to change her, to open her heart and mind to the goodness and the truth in human beings. I failed. I couldn't change her.* The only thing that touched her soul was love for him. And that's why he tried to kill it. That's why, if it weren't for Lucy Warren, he'd cut her heart out tonight. *So long as she loves me, I'm not free of her*, he thought. *I'm tainted with her cruelty, her heartless commitment to the Soviet ideal.*

'Hello,' she said. 'Sorry I'm late, darling. How was your day?' She wasn't really listening. She was making herself a drink, frowning, absorbed in something far from her surroundings.

He shrugged. He didn't answer. She didn't notice.

'Oh!' she exclaimed impatiently. 'I forgot. I said we'd have dinner with the Schmidts tonight. I'd better hurry up or we'll be late.'

The Schmidts were her friends. He was a lawyer, his wife a research chemist. They tolerated Dimitri, ignoring his drinking. They were sorry for Irina, with such a burden to carry.

She had a circle of acquaintances. They all treated him as if he were some kind of mental defective who had to be humoured. Poor Volkov. Just a shell. Put him in a corner with a bottle and forget about him.

'I don't feel like going,' he said. 'You go. They won't mind.'

Irina didn't mean to lose her temper. She didn't realize how the sessions with Brückner had frayed her nerves. She wanted to relax, regain her professional composure. She liked the Schmidts. Dimitri didn't like anyone. He had no friends. He lived in a limbo of his own making.

She swung round on him.

'They're expecting you. Frieda's cooking dinner. What am I supposed to say at the last minute?'

'I'm drunk,' he suggested.

Irina glared at him. She was trembling.

'You're not,' she countered. 'You're just being swinish. I've had a long day and I'm not going to play games with you. We're going out to dinner and that's the end of it. Get drunk if you like. They won't be surprised! Now I'm going to change.'

He said, 'I don't like them. He's a bore and she talks about animal experiments. She makes me sick. I'm not going, Irina. I'm not going out with your friends any more.'

She paused then. She made a great effort not to lose control. He was challenging her in a way he never had before. Not with the petulance of the weak; not striking a feeble blow that she could ward off easily. She was used to his gestures of defiance, tokens of independence that meant nothing.

'What's the matter with you? Why are you suddenly saying all this?'

'Because I'm sick of being put on display. Here's Irina with that poor dummy of a husband . . . Wasn't he something to do with the human rights movement in Russia? Never sober. Must have had a hard time in prison. Only it wasn't prison, Irina. It was you! I wouldn't make me go if I were you.'

And then he said, from the comfort of his armchair, 'What kind of a hard day *did* you have? Found some poor devil to set up for those bastards back home?'

She snapped. She stood facing him and shouted. She was shaking with anger.

'I'll tell you. I'll tell you about the poor devil! I spent my day listening to how he helped to rape and murder a Russian woman and her child in the war. How he held her down while she was sodomized by another brute. A Ukrainian, one of the scum who joined the Germans. Ukrainians like you! He robbed her and he's got the loot out on display in his nice big mansion! He's going to pay for it. And I'm going to see that he does!'

She rushed into the bedroom and slammed the door. She stripped off her clothes, changed into a silk dress, put on earrings and a necklace. She took deep breaths, urging herself to be calm. She dialled the Schmidt's number and said she'd be a little late. And Dimitri wasn't too well, so she was afraid he might not make it.

She lit a cigarette and walked out to face him. He was reading. There was a glass full of cognac beside him.

'I'm going,' she said. 'I made up some excuse for you. I'm sorry I shouted. Forget what I said. It's nothing to do with you anyway. It's my problem. Try not to drink too much.'

'Have a lovely evening,' he said, putting the book down.

She turned her back on him and left the apartment.

Volkov waited. He went and watched from the window till he saw her car edge out from the garage, its headlights raking the road, then turn and speed away. He took the glass of brandy in to the kitchen and poured it down the sink.

2

'Good morning, Sister Duval.' Irina had changed into her white coat. She never wore it with ordinary patients. It intimidated them. She liked to project herself more as a friend than a doctor.

'Good morning,' the sister said. Her tone was hostile. 'Here are the night staff's notes on Monsieur Brückner. As you instructed, we gave no sedatives. He became seriously agitated. We had to call in male nurses to restrain him. I couldn't take the responsibility for what was happening. At six a.m. I called in Doctor Minden and he sedated the patient.'

She was a very experienced psychiatric nurse and Doctor Volkov's callousness verged on deliberate cruelty. The unfortunate man had suffered such violent panic attacks that he tried to throw himself out of the window. She saw the Russian flush angrily.

'Doctor Minden had no right to interfere with my treatment programme,' she snapped. 'I shall take this up with him. You should have called me, Sister!'

The sister said, 'I'm sorry', in a chilly voice.

'I'll see my patient now,' Irina said. 'We're not to be disturbed.'

He was unconscious; his pallor was frightening and he'd bitten through his lower lip. He was strapped down to his bed and as Irina stood watching him he stirred, the eyelids fluttered open for a second and then closed tight. There was nothing she could do till the sedative wore off. She had cancelled all other appointments. The morning was free.

She'd slept very badly. She felt tired and low spirited. And frustrated because Brückner was out of her reach for some hours.

Volkov had been asleep when she came home. The dinner with the Schmidts hadn't been a success. It was her fault; she had been tense and ill at ease. Volkov worried her. She sensed he was pretending to be asleep when she got in to bed. How many times had she reached out to him, trying to rouse the passion they used to share? And been rejected. In the end she had subdued her body as she disciplined her emotions.

Sex had brought them together, bound them through the difficult and dangerous years when he was actively opposing the authorities. Sex and a strong maternal instinct made her love him. There was no child at her breast, but a vulnerable, misguided husband who was doomed unless she took control. They might still have come together in spite of what she had done. If it hadn't been for Müller.

She sat in her bright office and thought of Müller coming to the apartment that day. He often visited her in the early months, talking as if the passive figure in the background wasn't there. It hadn't mattered what he said. Dimitri Volkov was in a fog of mental apathy and confusion. Müller had said to her once, 'How can you live with him like that? Why don't you just keep him in the clinic?' and shrugged her angry retort aside. And then, that fatal day when he came early. She hadn't time to get Volkov out of the room. He had been off drugs for three months. Müller in high spirits, boasting, 'I've got a client for you Irina. French diplomat. Likes little boys. Doesn't fancy anything over six years old. He's got a big job in the French Foreign Ministry. Centre will love this one!' And he'd laughed out loud, talking through her, ignoring her frantic attempts to stop him.

It had been too late. He had seen the signals too late. He had stared at Dimitri Volkov and grimaced. 'What's the matter? He wouldn't know if it was Christmas or Easter.'

That was how Volkov had discovered the real implications of his release. His wife had been put in place as a Soviet agent.

Evelyn Anthony

Centre was Moscow Centre, the heart of Soviet Intelligence. They had financed the clinic and prepared the set-up in Geneva especially to make use of her talent. A unique talent, honed and polished in the Lenin Institute, where brainwashing was a fine art.

Müller had brazened it out. He'd tried to bluff and bully his way out of his terrible mistake, but Volkov wouldn't be intimidated. He was physically frail, but mentally clear. He had got up and faced them both. He'd said to Müller, 'You do it for money. You'd have sold Christ for dollars,' and turned his back on the German.

'You fool,' Irina remembered shouting in desperation at him. 'You big mouth! Get out! Get out of here!'

She sat for a while, the inevitable cigarette burning out in the ashtray.

She had tried to explain, to make excuses, but he wouldn't listen. His contempt shrivelled them on her tongue. She had burst into tears. He was so soft-hearted, he hated anyone to cry. But he recoiled in disgust when she came near him. He had actually held up his hands as if to ward off something evil.

'If I'd know what you were, I'd have killed myself in the Lubianka.'

He'd locked himself in their room and drunk himself insensible. He hadn't denounced her. Irina had waited, gambling that he wouldn't turn her in.

For the next four years he had lived in his private hell, and his silence had condemned her to live in it with him.

But last night he had been different. It wasn't brandy bravado that spoke. She knew that too well. She was reminded of the man she had seen fight the invincible power of the KGB and refuse to back away. For only a moment, hardly discernable, except to a trained eye, the old Dimitri Volkov had shown himself.

Her telephone rang. She was startled back in to the present. It was the ward sister.

'Your patient, Monsieur Brückner, is awake.'

'Thank you,' Irinia said. 'I'll come right away.'

Brückner was sitting up in a chair. He was gaunt and hollow-eyed; his voice trembled. Irina sat behind him, a disembodied

74

voice asking questions through the drugged haze that was his mind.

'Why did you spare the two children, Adolph?'

'I didn't want Boris to kill them.'

'That was a good thing you did. A kind thing. I'm proud of you for doing that. Did Boris like killing people?'

'He didn't care. If it suited him, he'd kill them.'

'Were you together for long?'

'About a year. We were a team. We fought at Kiev together. He was decorated. He only laughed. "They can stuff the Iron Cross," he said. "The one I've got is going to make me rich!" '

'The cross he stole from the woman?'

'Yes. He was always talking about it. He was going to sell it to some Jew. That's why he joined the Einsatz Commando.'

'The SS extermination squad?'

'They were wiping out all the Jews they could find. He thought he'd find a rich one and sell him the cross for a good price. Then shoot him. He thought it was a great joke.'

'Did you join with him?' the quiet voice asked him.

'No. I was a soldier. They were murderers. The Ukrainians hated the Jews as much as we did. A lot of them joined the SS. We got drunk together the night before Boris left. He got the cross out and showed it to me. He kissed it. "There's my beauty," he said."With what I'll get for it, I'll live like a prince! All the girls I want, all the drink. You'll make a few roubles out of that clock, old lad. But I'm going to be rich!" '

'When did you see him again?'

'I never saw him. I was wounded and sent back home. I was put on light duties. My leg was very bad.'

'So you never found out what happened to him?' She went on probing.

'No. I didn't even think about him. I wanted to forget. I never told anyone about what it was like. I kept the clock and the calendar. I didn't want to sell them. They were beautiful. I wanted to make money, so I could have more things like them.'

'And you did,' she encouraged him. 'You worked hard after the war. You made a lot of money and became a powerful man, didn't you, Adolph? You're well respected. You have a lovely wife and three nice children. And a fine art collection. So long as nobody knows how it started.'

She had inserted the point of the knife. He didn't seem to notice.

'That's the irony,' he muttered. 'If it wasn't for the desk set I wouldn't have got interested in Russian art. I'll never forget the day I saw it. I couldn't believe it. There it was. Boris's cross! The medieval treasure lost during the Revolution.'

She said sharply, 'What was lost? What are you talking about?'

'The holy Cross of St Vladimir. Priceless. Thirteenth-century gold and jewels. It was the same. It was the cross Boris stole. And he'd taken it. Without knowing what he'd got. I could have wept thinking what I'd missed. I made enquiries. I tried to find it. I'd have paid anything.'

'What did you find out?'

'Someone had taken it to a French jeweller after the war and tried to sell it. The jeweller said the jewels weren't rubies. They were spinels. He offered very little, so the man didn't sell.'

'Was the man Boris?'

'No way of knowing. The jeweller was vague. He said the man was a foreigner. He wouldn't part with the cross. If that fool had known what it was, he'd have given him the money!' Brückner wiped the saliva from his mouth. 'To think of it – what a treasure I missed! With such a history! I found out all about it. It's in all the reference books. The Bolsheviks never found it. It disappeared from the cathedral at Kiev. The White armies would have beaten the Reds if they'd got that cross.'

Irina didn't move, she didn't interrupt. He was ranting now, venting his frustration.

'When I think of that marvellous treasure being hawked around for sale . . . I went back to that idiot, the jeweller who turned it down. I kept asking him questions. What did the man look like? Couldn't he try and describe him? He couldn't. I told him what Boris looked like. He didn't think it was the same man. I could have strangled him. He was my only link with the cross. I put detectives on it; they found nothing. I even advertised in the art magazines. I was careful, very careful.' He looked sly. 'I didn't want the Russians on my track if they knew what I was looking for – just think what it would mean if it turned up now? Just think – that'd put Gorbachev in trouble! There'd be a blood bath.' He cackled wildly. He was becoming very agitated.

Irina interrupted him. 'You were mistaken,' she said firmly. 'It wasn't a treasure. The jeweller would have known. You've imagined it, Adolph. It's not what you think.'

He croaked at her, trying to raise his voice. 'I held it. I counted the stones. It's unique! There's not another cross like it in the world. Don't you know I'm an expert on that period? Just because of that cross. I've spent all these years thinking about it, wondering how it got in to that house. Like the Fabergé.' Sweat was running down his face. 'If Boris had known they weren't rubies, he'd have taken that instead.'

He leaned back exhausted. 'He couldn't have sold it to a Jew. All the Jews were killed. Perhaps he was killed. Perhaps it was stolen from him. I'll never know. I'll never find it now.'

'No,' Irina said quietly. 'You never will. But you couldn't have shown it to anyone, could you? You couldn't have risked people finding out you'd stolen it from a woman you'd raped during the Russian campaign. Fabergé pieces were on sale. You could lie about them. But not a holy Russian cross. The only one in the world. People would have found out you were a thief and a rapist who'd let a woman and child be butchered in cold blood. No wonder you got headaches, living with a crime like that for all these years. No wonder you were driving yourself mad. You wanted to kill yourself last night, didn't you?'

He had sunk again, and his eyes were full of tears.

'Yes.' It was a mumble.

'And you will kill yourself if I don't help you. You know you can trust me, don't you?'

'Yes.'

'You're safe, so long as nobody else finds out. And you won't have headaches any more because you saved the other child and the baby. That was a good thing to do, Adolph. Boris did the killing. But other people wouldn't care about that. They'd think you were as bad.'

He was crying. 'I was punished. I am sterile. I was punished.'

'That's enough for today,' Irina got up. 'You'll have a sleep

77

now. We'll talk again tomorrow. You'll feel better. Much better. Get up.'

She wouldn't help him; he was weak and unsteady, but she wouldn't take his arm or guide him to the bed. She let him stumble and fall to his knees. For a moment he looked at her with lucidity.

'You hate me,' he said.

Irina pressed the bell for the nurse. 'I'm helping you,' she said. 'You hate yourself.'

Müller arrived at Geneva Airport just after eleven in the morning. He wandered down the Rue du Rhône, admiring the window displays. It was a rich city, comfortable and self-confident. He stopped to inspect the latest Piaget watches and was tempted to buy one for Susan. She loved jewellery. She had done a lot towards making that sale to the Americans. She deserved a present.

They had two boys, both at college in America. He didn't want his sons to grow up in Germany. They were not going to be involved in what he did. Their lives lay with the capitalist world he had hated so bitterly in his own youth.

He didn't hate it now. He accepted it, enjoyed what it had to offer and lived his secret life because he loved it. He loved the game for its own sake. If it had ever been necessary he could just as happily have switched sides.

He decided to be generous and went in to the shop. He bought a gold Piaget with a diamond-set face, had it gift-wrapped and went out to find a cab and go to meet Irina.

He was on the pavement, waiting, when he saw Volkov on the opposite side of the road. The same familiar figure, untidily dressed, with too-long hair and a hang-dog look about him. Then he saw the girl. She was beside him and she had taken his arm as they waited on the pavement across the road. Müller stared hard. She was young, in her late twenties, very blonde and pretty.

'I'll be damned,' he said to himself 'I wonder what Irina would think of that!' He turned away, not wanting Dimitri Volkov to see him. He was in luck because a cab drew up alongside him and a man got out. He jumped in and set off for his rendezvous with Volkov's wife.

Müller grimaced at the thought of her. He had grown out of fanaticism. He despised the single-mindedness of people like Irina Volkova. They were blinkered by their own convictions. Often they did their cause more harm than good. Even more important to Müller, they harmed others more flexible than themselves. He didn't like her. She was a type he found threatening.

But he had despised her husband from the beginning. A fiery orator, and self-styled leader of the persecuted and oppressed, consumed with a reckless urge to sacrifice himself for his ideals. Müller hadn't admired him for it, even when he was a thorn in the Soviet government's side. He thought Volkov was a fool. There was no place in Müller's scale of values for a loser. He had long since abandoned heroics. They were all losers; the Jewish refusniks, the intellectual dissidents, the scattered Christians asking to be eaten by the KGB lions. All the men and women of conscience who had confronted the invincible system. The jails, the labour camps and the asylums were full of them. They were building railways and digging roads in the frozen wastes of Siberia. They had changed nothing. Change had come in spite of them, that was the irony. Change was a mass movement; it owed nothing to the puny efforts of the individual. Gorbachev and the new era in Russia was the result of the great pendulum swing of economics.

Inequity and deprivation had brought Marxism to birth. The same forces were calling for freedom and democracy. What people wanted was food in the shops and a slice of the materialist cake they saw being gobbled in the West.

Few things surprised Müller; he had lived through the trauma of Germany's defeat and the painful reconstruction of a shattered and divided people. He had come out of it successful, respected and secretly wealthy. But the sight of Dimitri Volkov with a woman gave him pause. It was no chance acquaintance. They were isolated from the crowd, their arms linked, the woman gazing up in to his face. Volkov had been written off for the last five years. He was drowning himself in booze and self-pity. He posed no threat to anyone. He was the last man in the world with the guts to deceive his wife. But even in that brief glimpse, Müller was certain that he *was* deceiving her.

She should be told, of course. He should mention it, alert her in their mutual interest. But he disliked her enough to postpone it. What harm would come if she were being fooled for a change? He had never forgiven her for reporting his indiscretion in front of her husband. Even though the husband had made no use of it. She had rounded on him without mercy. If his controller had taken her seriously, he might have been in real trouble. No, he decided. Let Volkov cheat on her. A little adultery now and then was harmless. As harmless as the man himself. And Müller could play that particular ace if and when Irina Volkov needed a slap in the face.

'Tell me about yourself, Lucy. I want to know about you.'

She smiled at him. They were together, sitting in the sunshine on the balcony of her apartment. They had made love that morning and it was better than the day before.

'I've told you all there is,' she said. 'The only interesting thing about me is finding you.'

He had a strand of her hair in his fingers; he played with it, twisting it round until it curled.

'You have lovely hair,' he said. 'Tell me about your father then. How did he get to England? And your mother?'

He was happy; he had lost the familiar feeling of dread and despair. The elation, the excitement and the wonderful afterglow of making love to her had left him in a mood of carefree tenderness. The sun was shining and they were warm on the pretty little balcony with its boxes of flowers. He was in the mood for confidences. He wanted to extend their intimacy, to hear about her childhood, her family. He wanted to imagine her growing up.

'My father was in a camp at the end of the war,' Lucy said. 'He'd been taken back to Germany for slave labour. His parents were shot. The camp was run by the British and one of the officers had taken an interest in him.' The same officer who had let him say goodbye to his friend Boris, but she didn't tell him that.

'He got my father to England after the war, gave him a job

and helped him to get settled. My father became naturalized, but he was always a Ukrainian. My mother was Irish; she died when I was seven, but I remember her very well. She was so pretty. My father brought me up. Major Hope left him the business when he died; he'd lost his only son through drugs, I think, and he more or less adopted my father. They were very close.'

He held her hand. 'I'll take care of you now,' he said gently. 'Your father taught you to speak Russian?'

'He taught me everything,' she said. 'He'd had so little education, but he loved books and believed learning was the key to living. And to being free. That's why you meant so much to him. He'd lost his freedom, his parents . . . He was beaten and half-starved . . . But he never gave in. Like you, Dimitri.

'He wrote letters to politicians, to Church leaders. He got up petitions and raised money when you were arrested. And he gave me a picture of you to put in my room. Every Sunday we went to Mass and prayed you'd be released. I wish he'd lived long enough to meet you.'

'I didn't deserve anyone's prayers.' Volkov said slowly. 'I don't deserve you. What are we going to do, Lucy? This can't go on forever.'

'No,' she said. 'It can't. But we have a little time left. We've got today and we're going to be happy together. The sun's gone in, and you look cold. Come inside and I'll warm you.'

In the evening they went walking, hand in hand, as if it were the first love for each of them.

'How long must I wait,' he said suddenly, 'till you tell me why we are here together?'

'Not very long, I think,' Lucy answered. 'I never thought I'd love you, you know that? I imagined meeting you, talking to you, but nothing like this. I'd built up a picture of you, like the one my father cut out and gave me, but it's nothing like you, Dimitri. You can't fall in love with heroes. You trust me, don't you?'

'I trust you,' he answered.

'My life is in your hands, Lucy. And your life in mine. It frightens me.'

She stopped and they faced each other. 'Your wife won't find out about us,' she said. 'But if she does, it won't matter because we will be out of her reach. I'm going to say goodbye, Dimitri, my love. It's getting late and you should go home. I don't worry about that any more. I know you won't drink. I know she can't hurt you. I won't come to the flower shop tomorrow. I'll wait at the apartment.'

He bent and kissed her. She gasped as he opened her lips. He held her tightly.

'I'll come to you tomorrow,' he said.

Irina was early. They met in the cocktail bar of the Richemond. There was an old Intelligence adage which held that if you want to hide something, put it on public view. If two subversives want to meet and pass unnoticed, then do it in the smartest, most exclusive hotel in Geneva. She waited irritably, smoking, checking her watch.

He came into the bar without any sign of being flustered. He walked up to the table, smiled, pulled out a chair and sat down.

'Irina,' Müller said. 'What can I get for you?'

'You're late,' she said icily. 'I have afternoon appointments.'

'So have I,' he retorted. 'I'm going to waste my time visiting two dealers, both of whom will try to sell me items I don't want – and one of which I know is a nineteenth-century fake. But I had to have an excuse to see you, so I'm not complaining. I shall have a Kïr. The same for you?'

'I hate liqueur in wine,' she said. 'A glass of Moselle will do. Now, can we be serious?'

'You're always serious,' Müller remarked. 'How is our friend Adolph? Have you discovered why he has his headaches?'

She was a very cool, self-composed woman, who seldom showed her feelings. Except on that one occasion when she lost her temper and shouted at him like a fishwife in front of her husband. He would never forget that. Now he saw anger in her eyes and a faint flush of colour in her cheeks.

'Rape and murder,' she said. 'It's taken a long time for the guilt to surface.'

Müller raised his brows and pursed his lips in a tiny whistle. 'Adolph? My God! Tell me about it.'

'He and a Ukrainian Nazi attacked and killed a woman during the Russian campaign. He stole the Fabergé desk set from her. That's why he lied about it. That's not the important point. The Ukrainian stole a cross. Does St Vladimir's Cross mean anything to you?'

He set his glass down on the table. 'It does indeed. What are you saying?'

'In a minute,' she leaned towards him. 'What do you know about it?'

'It was an early thirteenth-century gold cross which vanished from Kiev during the Revolution. Most likely the Bolsheviks destroyed it. With all due respect, my dear Irina, they were a lot of barbarians in those early days.' Then he frowned. 'You're not suggesting there's a connection with it and this cross Adolph told you about. That would be impossible!'

She said quietly. 'It was a humble farmhouse. They were country people. But they had a Tsarist treasure hidden there – that desk set. He told me about the cross. He ranted and raved because he found out years afterwards what it was the other swine had taken. He's a world expert on Russian art, isn't he?'

Müller said, 'He likes to think he is. I've told him so anyway. So?'

'He swore it was the genuine cross. He tried to find it after the war. He thinks the Ukrainian probably was killed and someone stole it from him and got it to Europe.' She paused. He didn't interrupt her. 'He used his resources to try and trace it and he came up with a French jeweller who'd been offered it about twenty-five years ago. He wouldn't pay good money because it was set with spinels instead of rubies, so the man took it back.'

Müller said slowly, 'It would be spinels. There weren't any rubies of large size in that period. And that was all? He got no further?'

'No,' Irinia said. 'He knew its significance. He said he didn't want the Russians getting on to him, so he had to be very discreet. But he came to a dead end with that jeweller.'

'What exactly is its significance?' Müller asked. 'I assume you mean political?'

'Political disaster, if the wrong people got hold of it,' she retorted. 'Brückner knew how dangerous it was. He said it this afternoon.'

'And you want me to make enquiries?'

'I want you to tell our friends at home. This is too big a responsibility for us to take on our own. It must go to the top. At once.'

'You don't think you're being alarmist,' he suggested. 'It's very unlikely that it survived the Civil War in 1919, and even less likely that it was looted during the war and brought out of Russia in one piece. Personally, I don't believe the story.' He shrugged. 'No doubt there was some cross or ornament they found when they robbed that poor creature, and Adolph had made a fantasy out of it. He's half-mad anyway, from what you tell me. I'll pass it on, but I must add my own disclaimer. I don't want to look a fool.'

Irina got up. 'I have to see my evening patients,' she said. 'As for looking a fool, I wouldn't play this down if I were you. I have an instinct that he's right.'

Müller summoned the waiter for the bill. He got up, bent briefly over her hand. It was a charming display of good manners by a suave middle-aged man to an attractive woman.

'I have a great respect for female intuition,' he said. 'But I never suspected you relied on it. My contact is in Berlin at the moment,' he added. 'It wouldn't be wise to communicate with him in the usual way while he's there.'

Irina looked at him. 'You can fly there yourself. If you don't, I'll make contact.' She turned and walked away.

Müller sat down again and ordered another Kïr. He had time to spare before his appointments. She meant what she said. If he didn't go to Berlin, she'd pre-empt him. She believed in Adolph's fairy story. But then she would, he thought, sipping the delicate drink. Superstition was embedded in the Russian psyche. Not even the dehumanizing process of Soviet medical training could eradicate the myths and legends of a thousand years of Russian Christianity. A brand of religion peculiar to the country and its people, where saints and miracles were part of everyday life and idiots were revered as the children of God.

Part of Irina Volkova would believe in a cross that might cause people to rise up and start a counter-revolution. Being Russian she knew it was possible . . . After seventy years of atheism, religion was re-emerging in the Soviet Union. When official attitudes relaxed, the Easter services had been packed with worshippers. And not just the babushkas, mumbling their prayers, but with young men and women. Perhaps Irina was right to be alarmed.

He finished the glass of Kïr and decided that he had better see his controller in person. He travelled all over Europe on buying trips. He wouldn't be suspected. He paid and left for his first call at a dealer's house in the Place du Bourg-de-Four. He planned to catch the 6 pm flight back to Munich. And then go on to Berlin the next day.

Irina had cooked dinner; she noticed that Volkov refused wine. 'What's the matter?' she asked him. 'Aren't you feeling well?'

He said, 'I've decided to give up drink.'

On an impulse she reached over and touched his hand. 'I'm so glad, darling. I'll help you. It won't be easy.'

He pulled his hand away. 'No, thank you,' he said. 'I'm never taking medicine from you again. I'll manage.'

She said, 'Why? After all this time, when I begged and begged you to cut down, why suddenly say you're going to stop?'

'I'm taking your advice,' he answered. 'I'm pulling myself together. That's what you keep telling me to do, isn't it?'

'Yes, yes, of course. But why do you have to be so hostile?'

'How's your patient?'

She saw the contempt in his eyes. She bit her lip; he knew the mannerism well. It signified that he had hurt her.

'He's recovering,' she said. 'I don't want to talk about it. There's a play on television. I want to watch it.'

They didn't sit together. He avoided contact with her even more these days, she noticed. She tried to concentrate on the screen, but she kept looking at him. Watching him. He made her uneasy.

'What have you got there?' she asked. He was eating something out of a box.

'Chocolate,' Volkov answered.

'You would need sweet things,' Irina said. 'It'll help if you feel a craving.'

He stared at the screen. She knew he hadn't been paying any attention to the play.

'I don't feel a craving,' he said. 'And I don't want advice from you. I thought you wanted to watch this nonsense?'

She got up. She switched the set off. 'I'm going to bed,' she said. 'I've been miserable with you for five years, Dimitri. I don't know why I don't throw you out on to the street!'

'Because you love me,' he said coolly. 'You said so not long ago. "I love you, Dimitri. I betrayed your trust and I betray sick, helpless people who come to me for help, because I love you." '

'Don't count on it,' she said slowly. 'I'm only human. There's a limit to what I can endure.'

'Unlike your patients.'

He didn't turn round when he heard the door bang. He switched the set back on, changing the channel to a news programme. It was so long since he had taken an interest in anything. Years of self-induced coma. An abdication from life and from reality. Sexless, motiveless, enmeshed in guilt for the crimes of someone else. He knew she would cry when she was alone. He had seen her weep when he turned away, chilled into impotence at her touch. He had made her suffer and further imprisoned himself by doing so.

Courage was what he needed. The courage to leave her and beg public forgiveness for his desertion of his cause and his friends. Love, his terrible wife called her obsession with him. But love was what he felt for the stranger who'd thrust herself upon him. Not just the love for her body, for the softness and the scent of her, but for the person inside that body. The spirit that believed in him and would dare anything in its innocence. She had made him come alive in heart and mind.

He sat forward and concentrated on the interview being screened.

A first-floor office had been made available to Müller's controller in the new Soviet Embassy in Berlin. From the windows he had a clear view of the Brandenburg Gate. So much had changed in the city. The wall was long gone, the divided city was united like the country. Germany was one.

Viktor Rakovsky had made a sketch of the scene; he would finish it later. His speciality was water colours. He had exhibited in Moscow under a pseudonym and been pleased with the critical reaction. The painting of St Basil's Cathedral was highly praised. He preferred not to think that everyone knew the artist had painted his best-known work from the window overlooking Dzerjhinsky Square.

He had chosen his stepfather Lepkin's old office when he made his permanent headquarters in Moscow. He had a photograph of him enlarged and framed in silver gilt on his desk. There was another photograph, the same size and framed identically. It showed the famous partisan leader, Ivan Zakob, wearing the medals bestowed on him by Stalin. The two men that Viktor loved. There was no picture of his mother or his murdered brother Stefan. His childish drawings of them were in his bedroom, the only visible momento of their lives.

Rakovsky was thinking of them as he sat there in the borrowed office in Berlin. It was late afternoon and the sky was turning red outside. He remembered the vivid sunsets of his boyhood and the way the sun would hang like a crimson ball above the edge of the trees surrounding their house and then plunge out of sight as if it had been dropped in a moment of carelessness. He had been frightened until Ivan explained to him that the sun went to bed like everyone else and would be up and shining for them in the morning. Ivan was a fanciful fellow, and he loved to tell the boys stories. Who would have thought he could turn into a hero – leading his partisans against the Germans.

Ivan had become a legend, a symbol of all the other Ivans who died on the battlefields and fought village by village and street by street to drive the invader out of Russia. He had stood for them all, when he was made a hero of the Soviet Union by Stalin himself.

Ivan was old and dying, but he lived in Rakovsky's handsome *dacha* and his days were comfortable. Rakovsky called him Little Father and Ivan called him son.

There was a report on the desk in front of Rakovsky. His agent, Peter Müller, had prepared it and left it in one of the embassy 'letter boxes' for collection. It was in the sleeve of a classical album which Rakovsky's junior secretary had picked up from one of Berlin's best-known music shop on the Tiergarten.

The words leapt at Rakovsky off the page. The words of a man confessing under duress, from drugs and a long festering guilt. Rakovsky could see it all. The house in the woods. His mother screaming as she was raped; his brother bursting from their hiding place to run in and try to save her. Sweat broke out over his body. He couldn't go on reading. He had a bottle of Scotch whisky in his office; he poured a half tumblerfull and drank it down. Now he saw the missing details in his nightmare. His brother lying on the floor with his skull crushed. His mother stretched mute and bleeding on the bed. The sound of shots as her ravager murdered her. And then the moment when the cupboard door opened and he looked up in terror at the German soldier staring down at him. He was still stifling his baby sister's cries. Then the door closed.

He heard the roar of the motorcycle being started up and then fading until it was silent. A long silence afterwards. He hadn't dared to move. He was trembling with shock. He was in the dark. At last he let the baby cry. He was afraid she might suffocate. He didn't open the cupboard door till he heard Ivan's voice calling when he came in. Then Ivan's terrible cry of anguish from the bedroom.

Ivan had gathered Viktor and the baby Valeria in his arms; tears were streaming down his face.

He heard his own voice saying over and over, 'Germans. Germans did it.' Ivan had held him back from the bedroom by force. They had dug the grave together. He remembered how deep it was and how hard it was to break the earth. He hadn't seen their bodies. Ivan had wrapped them together in the curtains his mother had made for the sitting room, and laid them in the bottom of the grave. Even so, Viktor had seen the red stain spreading amongst the bright colours of the makeshift shroud.

They didn't get the train to Moscow. The terminal at Kharkov had been bombed. There were no trains and the roads were under constant air attack.

The days afterwards were blurred in his memory. He was in shock. He screamed if Ivan left him alone, even for a few minutes. They journeyed into the countryside, sleeping under the trees, eating what Ivan could trap or shoot. When the partisans found them, they gave Valeria to one of the women to look after, but he stayed with Ivan. The camp in the forest was their home. It moved as the Germans advanced. They lived like nomads, ambushing, killing the enemy, moving on.

Some of them were captured. Viktor had seen their bodies swinging from a gallows in a little hamlet after the Red Army had retaken it. He had been given a rifle and Ivan taught him how to shoot. He'd said, 'You're a man now. You're old enough to kill Germans.'

They never took prisoners. They lined them up and shot them. The first time Viktor saw an execution, he vomited. Then he remembered his mother and Stefan and made himself go back and look up at the bodies till he didn't mind any more. Ivan had understood. Ivan was beside him when he shot his first German. He was ten years old.

'Now you'll sleep better, he had told him. 'Your mother is smiling on you from heaven.'

Viktor drank more whisky. He had lived through the war with the partisans. He had learned to accept death. His little sister had sickened and died before her second birthday. There were no drugs in the camp. A lot of the children died. He had seen horrors committed by the enemy, and horrors that were the doing of his comrades-in-arms.

Lepkin had been captured during the Battle for Smolensk. He had been denounced as NKVD by one of his own men and executed.

Viktor was twelve when the war ended and by that time he had forgotten how to cry. Now he sat and stared out at the Brandenburg Gate, lit by the bloody glow of a German sunset and saw it through a mist of tears. After thirty years, he could come face to face with the soldier who had spared his life. And raped and robbed his mother.

Lepkin's gift to her was on display in the German's Munich mansion. Viktor had sketched the green enamel and the twinkling diamonds in the tattered book he'd taken with him from the charnel house that had been his home. Ivan had given it to him, with the wooden doll he'd made for Valeria. They'd buried the doll with her in the forest.

And he'd drawn and coloured the cross that he'd seen on his mother's bed. The cross she spoke of with hatred, as if she feared it. Her ravisher and murderer had stolen it.

Müller had ended his report: 'If the cross Brückner describes could possibly be the genuine Relic from Kiev Cathedral it could present a serious threat to Soviet stability in the Ukraine.'

Rape and murder, wartime looting – a dark stain on the past of a very important German industrialist. Such incidents were not unique. It was the cross that had prompted Müller's journey to Berlin, and the rarely used 'urgent' signal he'd sent to the embassy.

And he was right. The threat was incalculable. Rakovsky forced himself to be calm, to consider the wider implications. The great Soviet Empire was only just holding together; if a group of Ukrainian nationalists were to raise St Vladimir's Cross as a rallying point, the most important state within the Union would erupt into rebellion against Moscow.

Müller was not only a very good agent, but an old partner. He had asked for an urgent meeting with Rakovsky to discuss the report and get instructions.

They hadn't seen each other for a long time. Both had been comparatively junior when their association started. Rakovsky was embarking on his career as a diplomatic spy, moving under different names and jobs from one Western embassy to the next. He had personally recruited the antique dealer. Over the years they had worked well and closely together until the political situation in Russia underwent the first dramatic changes. It was time for Rakovsky to leave the field and work in Moscow. Another reason was his beloved Ivan. Terminal cancer was diagnosed. But Rakovsky kept one or two special agents under his control. He wouldn't relinquish Peter Müller to anyone else.

The light was fading; lamps were aglow in the streets and the shop windows were lit invitingly, tempting the late shoppers. There was a reception at the Italian Embassy; he was expected as a special guest. A dinner and the theatre afterwards, arranged by his own ambassador to entertain the trade delegation he was leading.

Trade interested him now, as other intelligence spheres had done in harder days. Industrial espionage was high on the list of Soviet priorities. They were starved of the technical skills of Western manufacturing industries. The best brains and resources had gone into military research and development until Gorbachev came to power.

Rakovsky drank another whisky. He would go to the Italians. He would attend the dinner and the theatre. He would smile and talk engagingly and hide his feelings. And then, when he was alone, he would get drunk enough to sleep without dreaming of his mother screaming.

Müller was a little early for the rendezvous. Rakovsky was visiting a Russian arts and crafts shop selling embroidery, pottery and lacquer work. Müller arrived ahead of him by twenty minutes and waited in the private room at the back. He thought the goods on display were crude and tasteless; but sometimes it was possible to find a little gem amongst the mass-produced dross. One small lacquer box had caught his eye. It was the work of an original craftsman. He asked to buy it. His wife liked little trinkets for her dressing table.

He was surprised at how much Rakovsky had aged when he came in. They hadn't seen each other for so long. They shook hands and then embraced like old friends. He *had* aged, Müller decided, noticing the puffy skin under his eyes. He looked as if he had hardly slept.

They drank tea together and Müller went over the report with him. Rakovsky was quiet, which was unlike him. He let Müller talk while he listened. He was not only older, but subdued.

Müller said suddenly, 'You don't seem well, Viktor. Is anything wrong?'

'It's been a heavy schedule,' Rakovsky said. 'Too many parties every evening. Peter, I've decided to go to Geneva. I'm going to see this man, Brückner, and check his story for myself. I'll make the travel arrangements. What you must do is tell Irina to keep him in the clinic till I can come. And not to lean on him too

heavily. I know her methods. They don't leave much at the end.
I want to talk to him myself.'

Müller hid his surprise. Rakovsky had never visited the clinic.
He knew Irina very well from her Moscow days. He had been
instrumental in getting Volkov released so she could take up her
appointment in Geneva. But he had left the running of the operation to Müller.

'Of course I'll tell her.'

'And Volkov? Still drinking?'

Müller shrugged. 'Still drinking. She leads a hell of a life with
him. And he's cheating, which is interesting.'

Rakovsky glanced up at him. 'You mean with a woman? How
do you know?'

'I saw them together, by chance. Young, very pretty. They
looked like lovers to me. Irina doesn't know. I saw no reason to
tell her. She might do something stupid. She's still obsessed with
him.'

'It was her one weakness,' Rakovsky remarked. 'Everyone
warned her; her father, all his friends, but she would marry him.
Her own career was at risk. Even her loyalty came under suspicion
because of his activities. I remember her coming to see me and
begging me to help when he was arrested. She was crying. She
was an attractive woman, but I never thought she had a human
feeling in her. To me she was just a brain, a scientific machine in
a bedworthy body. She'd have agreed to anything to save his life
and get him out. And this is how he's showing gratitude. Well!'
He paused, then he offered Müller another glass of tea. Müller
declined. He didn't like Russian tea.

'Perhaps we'd better find out about the woman. Just routine,
Peter, but we don't want that drunken fool getting into mischief.
And we don't want Irina upset. She's much too valuable.' He
finished his tea and stood up. He shook hands with Müller.

'You were right to bring this to me direct,' he said. 'I'm going
home at the end of the week and I'll make arrangements to go
to Geneva as soon as possible. And I'll authorize another payment
for you. Look after yourself, my friend.'

'And you, Viktor. I'll go out the back way.'

'My love,' Lucy said. 'He wants to speak to you.' Volkov hesitated.

'Go on,' she urged. 'He's waiting.'

He took the receiver from her. She had dialled the number in London.

'Mischa is my father's oldest friend,' she said. 'He worked so hard for you, getting signatures, writing to the newspapers.'

She had described Mischa to him, and his wife and his children. How they worked for the dissidents, raised money, edited a Ukrainian language broadsheet. Now he was going to talk to the man himself.

Lucy watched him; she came and stroked his hair with tenderness to give encouragement.

'I love you,' she whispered, and then left him to speak.

He had changed so much in the time they'd spent together. He was still hesitant, still uncertain. His hands shook and he was suffering, but he didn't drink. Mother, mistress, friend, Lucy filled whatever role he needed, when he needed it. Her little apartment had become their home, where she cooked for him and they shared all the daylight hours together. He went back to prison at night. They were his words and as soon as he said them, she knew she had won him to freedom. Mischa was the next step. Mischa knew what to say. Lucy had primed him carefully.

She went out of the room while he spoke on the telephone. There was a fine line to walk between protecting him and urging him to self-reliance. If she crossed it, he regressed.

When she came back he had finished speaking. There was a little colour in his face and a brightness in his eye. He drew her close and kissed her gently.

'You were talking for a long time,' she said.

'He reminded me of so many things I'd half-forgotten. The way we used to fight at home; our little victories. I never realized how the world was watching us. That was the worst thing they did to you in prison. They said it every day. "Nobody even knows you're here. Nobody cares whether you're alive or dead. You're just a number. You'll be a number till the day you die." It used to frighten me. I kept saying my own name so I wouldn't forget it. Your friend told me they held vigils outside the Soviet embassies all over the world when I was arrested and when Sakharov went on hunger strike. Lucy, how could I have abandoned people like that?'

'You mustn't say that,' she said quickly. 'All that is in the past; you're not to think about it. You've come back to lead them.'

He looked at her solemnly. 'How can I lead them, Lucy? History's overtaken me. I've been left behind.'

She stood up and looked down at him. 'When my father was at the camp at Spittal, another Ukrainian looked after him. He'd joined the SS. He'd done some dreadful things, but my father was only a boy and this man took care of him. He was sent back to be shot by the Red Army.' She paused for a moment. 'Do you want me to go on?'

He nodded.

'Before he was taken away, this man gave my father something he'd stolen during the war. He thought it was valuable and my father could sell it. He knew he was going to die. But my father kept it. Then, when my mother was so ill, he did try and sell it to get money for treatment for her. He told me that. He said, "The hand of God saved me, Lucy." The jeweller didn't know what it was my father showed him. He saw an old paste cross and he wouldn't offer any money for it.' She slipped to the floor and knelt beside him. 'My father came back with the cross; his friend, Major Hope, paid for my mother's treatment.

'Before he died, he showed it to me. He'd kept it hidden for fifty years. He'd tried to sell the Holy Relic, St Vladimir's Cross. And what's why I came to Geneva. To find you and give it to you.'

She couldn't help herself; she burst into tears. He raised her up and held her.

'No, my darling,' he said very gently. 'That was destroyed. Everyone knows the Reds destroyed it.'

'I have it,' she said. 'In my house. It's the Relic. I can prove it to you.'

He left her early. He took one of the water buses that ferried across the lake. He needed to be alone. She understood and accepted it. When he left her she was very pale and quiet.

'I'll be back,' he promised. 'Just give me a little time to take it in.'

She had shown him the book where it was illustrated. And he had the article written a few years ago about the missing Tsarist treasures. It featured another illustration, large and faithfully depicted. The delicate gold filigree, the massive red gems.

Paste, the jeweller had said, refusing to buy the cross. Missing from the cathedral at Kiev since 1919. It was a learned article; it went into details about the workmanship, the size and influence of Byzantine art on the beautiful object specially commissioned by Vladimir to mark his conversion from paganism. And the writer hadn't spared the legends, because it explained the Bolshevik obsession with the Relic. If the White armies could claim it, the Civil War might go in their favour. The Reds spread the rumours of its destruction, but there was no evidence to support this. There was evidence that despite torture and execution, the clergy at the cathedral had managed to conceal it. *There was no evidence of its destruction.*

Volkov had the article in his pocket, the pages scissored out of a famous art magazine. They were creased and folded, a little frayed at the edges. He looked at the cross. Besides the colour reproduction, there was an old scale drawing, and an enlarged section of a painting of the last Tsar's coronation, with the Relic in his right hand.

Lucy had said simply to him, 'It's the real cross. This is the photograph my father took. Compare them. The scale is right, the goldwork is identical. No one ever copied that cross; it would have been blasphemous.'

He put the pages back in his pocket. There was a restaurant on board the ferry. All he had to do was get up and walk a few steps and he could escape it all.

He could be what his gaolers had told him he was. A number. No identity, no name, just a set of numerals. Numbers didn't have responsibilities. They weren't presented with ancient symbols of faith with powers to topple a tyranny. They weren't challenged to do anything. They hardly existed. Prisoner 36672. That's who he was. Five digits. One brandy would make him in to a number. His hands trembled. Sweat broke out all over his body, chilling him. One brandy. Then two and afterwards he'd lose count. He wouldn't remember his number even. He got up and went to the restaurant. He put money down.

The waitress said, 'What can I get you?' She had very pale blue eyes. Not the same limpid colour as Lucy's eyes, but pale and blue.

He said, 'A glass of mineral water, please. I'm thirsty.'

He had been gone for a long time. The little clock in the sitting room struck the hour. It could have been the span of her whole life. She paced up and down; she went backwards and forwards to the windows, stepping on to the little balcony where they sat together in the afternoon sun, peering down the street.

There was no sign of him. Other men walked along, passed underneath. But not Volkov. Volkov had gone away to think. Or to escape! To step backwards into the limbo of the last five years. If he drank, he would be lost for ever. . . .

She almost cried out in desperation and self-blame. She'd acted too soon, burdened him before he was ready. She went into the bedroom and gave way to a burst of weeping.

She heard the clock strike again. She washed her face and went wearily back to look out for him, but she was losing hope. She was leaning by the window, watching the first clouds creeping up from the horizon to challenge the sun, when the door opened. She heard her name.

'Lucy?'

She turned and saw him. He walked towards her. He was steady, sober. She ran into his arms.

'I took the water bus,' he said. 'That's why I was so long. Were you worried? Did you think I wouldn't come back?'

Lucy held tight to him, 'No,' she lied. 'I knew you would.'

He didn't contradict her. In her place, he would have doubted, too. Then she managed to smile up at him.

'That's not true,' she said. 'But thank God you did.'

Later, he said. 'I'm not going home tonight.'

'You must. What will your wife think? Darling, you mustn't be reckless. You said she was dangerous.'

'Dangerous to you,' he corrected. 'But she doesn't know about you. I've stayed out before. I went to sleep at an all-night cinema once. I don't want to leave you tonight. We've got so much to think about. Will you let me stay?'

Lucy drew him down to her. 'Kiss me,' she said.

Irina hung up in exasperation. She had been trying the apartment since seven o'clock. She had an emergency patient to attend to. A rich Italian suffering severe post-natal depression had been brought in by ambulance, having tried to kill her six-week-old son, and then taken an overdose. The family were following on in a state of high Latin hysteria.

Irina didn't know when or if, she would get home that night. There was no answer to her calls. He was either out and hadn't switched on the answering machine or he was tormenting her by ignoring the telephone. He sometimes did that.

She wondered whether he'd started drinking again. She hadn't taken him seriously when he said he was giving up. Even though he'd never said it before. Miracle cures for alcoholism didn't happen. He'd slip. It was inevitable. And he'd been more unkind than usual in this odd period of sobriety. That was a common symptom, but she didn't welcome it. Mute, drunken dislike was easier than the cold hatred of the last few weeks.

She put her unhappiness aside. She had a seriously ill patient to contend with and she'd just had a telephone message to say that Brückner's wife wanted to come up and visit him. She'd deal with that in the morning. Müller's instructions were clear. Keep him quiet, but don't disorientate him. Viktor Rakovsky wanted to talk to him. A most significant departure for someone so senior to involve himself personally. She had been right about the importance of Brückner's story. Right to overrule Müller's judgement. No doubt he had claimed the credit for himself. She would let Rakovsky know the truth. *I hate Müller*, she thought. *He ruined my happiness. If it wasn't for him, I'd have talked Dimitri round. We'd be living together like in the old days.*

Her internal phone rang. The patient was recovering consciousness. Her mother was being treated for shock by one of the junior physicians and the husband was creating hell. Could she *please* come down and deal with the situation? Irina hurried out. She forgot to call the apartment again, and decided by two in the morning that she might as well stay at the clinic for what was left of the night.

Volkov had woken early. He was restless and excited. Lucy watched him in wonder.

'I nearly had a drink yesterday on that boat,' he told her. 'I went to the restaurant and put the money down for a large brandy. Then I thought of you. It was easy then, my darling. I can't believe how easy it was. It's over. I know I'll never drink again!'

'You've got to get away from here,' she insisted. 'We can go to England. Mischa will organize meetings. He has contacts inside the Ukraine. We can't plan anything till you're safe and out of their reach.'

Volkov said, 'I disappear and then I reappear very publicly. I do all the things I didn't do the first time. I give interviews. I hold a Press conference. I've thought it out already. I draw so much attention to myself that they won't dare touch me.'

'We shouldn't waste time,' Lucy said. 'We should get away from Switzerland.'

He was bold and confident, almost euphoric. Suddenly she was afraid. Afraid for him and for herself. And the fear was growing as he made his plans. She came up and put her arms round him.

'We could leave here tomorrow. Why don't we? Why don't we just go to the airport and get on a plane?'

He shook his head. 'We can't travel together,' he said. 'And there is a practical problem – I have to find my passport.' He frowned. 'It may be out of date. It may have been renewed. I wouldn't remember. Irina took care of everything. I was just a piece of luggage to be labelled and sent wherever they wanted. You speak to Mischa. Ask him if he could help with papers. Say I'm sure it won't be necessary, but just as a precaution. Meet me at seven at the St Honoré. We'll hide ourselves in a corner and celebrate!'

He hugged her tight. 'I feel like Lazarus,' he said. 'Out of the tomb and into the sunshine! How much I love you, Lucy! Seven o'clock – at our café.'

Then he was gone and she watched him striding away down the street. Now he was a traveller with a destination. *This* was the Dimitri Volkov the world had watched in admiration.

But the fear stayed with her, its cold hand on her heart.

The big Illuyshin jet made a smooth landing at Sheremetov airport. Viktor watched the descent over the city he loved. He was glad to be home. He had always felt the same elation at the end of his long tours abroad. When he came back to Russia he shed his aliases. He was himself.

The official Zil, with his driver, was there to meet him. There were no airport formalities for him and the rest of his delegation.

It was a warm evening and the air was sweet. He opened the window after they turned in to the country. His *dacha* was in the woods on the banks of the Moscova river. He loved Moscow, but he didn't like living there. His *dacha* was home to him. The forest and the lapping water of the great river were a balm to the spirit.

His housekeeper came out to greet him. He kept his mistress in an apartment in Moscow. He never brought women to the *dacha*. He made his way to the upper floor. He opened the door of a big airy room with views down to the great river itself. The old man sitting in his chair by the window turned round and smiled at him. Ivan! Cancer had eaten in to him, but he was still alive. A wraith with bright eyes in his gaunt face. He was too feeble to leave his room now, but Viktor had the window specially made so he could sit and watch the river.

Viktor embraced him. The body was a skeleton wrapped in a winding sheet of clothes, but the eyes were bright and the smile was glad.

'How have you been, Little Father?'

'Well, son, well. And you?'

Viktor offered him a drink. A very small drink, since he had only half a stomach. In the old days Ivan could swallow a bottle of vodka and keep his legs.

'I want to show you this,' Viktor said.

He put an exercise book on the old man's lap. The cover was faded from bright red to pink. It was creased and frayed. He turned the pages. The childish drawing of rabbits sitting under the trees among the spring daffodils; his sketch of Ivan on the sled, of Lepkin dozing in his chair by the stove. The cat with yellow eyes crouched in the long grass in pursuit of a bird.

The old man nodded. 'Your drawings,' he said. 'You could have been an artist.'

'A bad one,' Viktor answered. 'Anyway it wasn't a time for painting pictures, Little Father.'

The sketch was from memory, but he had an eye for detail. He had drawn the cross he'd seen so briefly, and coloured the stones red and the setting yellow. Ivan looked at it and didn't speak.

'I can't remember why I drew that,' Viktor prompted.

'It belonged to your father,' the old man said at last.

'To Lepkin?'

'No, your real father. The minister Rakovsky. I think he gave it to Lepkin as a bribe.'

'How do you know?' Viktor asked gently.

'I saw him look at it in the car when we were driving to the Lubiyanka. It was tied up in a parcel. I saw him in the driving mirror. I thought, he's got something valuable there. He's in trouble; he's going to buy someone with that cross. It was full of red jewels. He didn't know I could see him. I saw a lot of things, but I never let on. It was safer to look stupid.'

'You're a fox, Little Father,' Viktor said.

The light was fading. Clouds were creeping up over the edges of the trees and the river's surface was turning black. His father had given the cross to Lepkin. A bribe, Ivan had said. Viktor watched the darkness spreading. Lepkin had saved Rakovsky's family. He'd married the widow and been a father to Rakovsky's children. Rakovsky had bought their lives with that cross.

He took the drawing book and said, 'I have work to do. I'll come up later and say goodnight. Is there anything you want, Little Father?'

'Some tea,' the old man murmured. 'And that stuff that stops the pain.'

'I'll send the nurse,' Viktor promised.

Viktor had dinner alone. He went up to see Ivan and found him asleep.

'He was uncomfortable, comrade Rakovsky,' the nurse explained. 'I increased the dose as you instructed. He drank some tea and then he slept.' *No pain, no sorrow, no cloud to blur the sunset of his life.*

That was his decree for the man he loved best in the world.

'Watch him tonight,' he instructed. 'Call me if he wakes or he asks for me.'

The next morning he was assured by the nurse that Ivan had slept peacefully and eaten a little breakfast. He was in good spirits. There was no immediate danger.

Viktor went in to his Kremlin office. The necessary papers were provided for him, the travelling arranged, and by noon he was on an Aeroflot plane to Geneva.

He was met at the airport. He travelled on a Polish passport. His occupation was given as manufacturer of industrial components. He went unnoticed through Swiss immigration. Poles were travelling freely these days, seeking business, and Western commercial and technical expertise. He spoke perfect Polish. Also excellent German and fluent English.

He had learned his languages at the highly sophisticated KGB school in Leningrad. He had been recruited on the strength of his life with the partisans. He was the kind of material Stalin's Intelligence services needed in the Cold War.

The taxi took him through the city and up into the countryside beyond the lake, where the Amner clinic commanded its famous views. He was shown up to Irina's office immediately.

He hadn't seen her for five years. She had changed. She was slimmer, more sophisticated. He noticed the artful make-up, the elegant hair style. A very good-looking woman.

He was fond of women; he enjoyed their company and he liked making love. He wondered whether she had taken a lover during the last five years. Then he remembered that it was Volkov who was being unfaithful.

101

They shook hands. They were on first-name terms. He and her father were friends.

'It's good to see you, Irina. You're looking very well. Swiss air suits you.'

'Thank you. You look well too, Viktor. Please sit down. Can I get you a drink? It's not too early?'

He smiled. 'It's never too early. But I won't have anything. How is your husband?'

She shrugged slightly. 'The same. He's never recovered from Müller's visit.'

She still held that grudge, he noted. *Müller, beware*, he thought.

He said, 'That was a long time ago. Müller wasn't to know he'd come off your medication. And I haven't come all this way to listen to the same complaint, Irina. You've made it officially and it's been noted. I want to see Adolph Brückner. How is he?'

'I've kept his sedation to a minimum. And I haven't advanced his re-education since I got your message. His family are agitating to get him home. I'm glad you've come; it was getting difficult to stall them.'

'So far he's responded well?' he asked.

'Well enough. The trouble is, he hates himself. There's a strong suicidal tendency. That's why I've decided to let his wife and children come and see him. He needs motivation. I can advance the programme; that's no problem. He's already highly suggestible.'

Rakovsky listened to the cool voice describing the intensive hypnosis and subliminal suggestion that would distort Brückner's mentality. Visual images flashed on and off at fractions of a second to imprint themselves on the subconscious mind. Images of guilt, of fear, of the excruciating headaches he had inflicted on himself which only the doctor could hold in check. Obedience and trust. The treatment hammered them into the defenceless mind. Trust in the doctor. Obedience to the doctor.

'I'm glad you've come,' Irina said again. 'I insisted that Müller contact you at once. He thought it was a fantasy. I had such difficulty persuading him to take Brückner's story seriously. I had to practically draft the report myself!'

Oh yes, Rakovsky noted, *Müller had better beware.* He said, 'I'd like to see him now.'

'Of course. He's had some medication. He'll be pliable.'

They went down in the lift. Irina spoke to the nurse on duty in the corridor.

'I have a visitor for Monsieur Brückner.'

He stood back while she approached the bed. Fifty years had passed. The man lying there was in his seventies. He was white haired, with dull eyes and a slack mouth; saliva dribbled from one corner.

'Wake him up!' Rakovsky commanded.

Irina bent over and shook him. She shook him hard. 'Adolph! Adolph, pay attention!'

He focused on her, he mumbled something. Viktor came to the edge of the bed.

'He can see you,' she whispered. 'He's sedated, but he might recognize you.'

'It won't matter,' was the answer. 'I'm going to question him. Tell him he's got to answer me. Go on, tell him!'

Irina glanced quickly at Rakovsky. There was a terrible rage in him; she could feel it like an electric charge in the room. She raised her voice to the tone of command that meant, obey me or you will suffer for it.

'My friend is going to ask some questions. You'll answer them, Adolph. You tell him everything he wants to know. You understand me?'

'I understand.' The voice was tremulous.

Viktor Rakovsky came very close to him. He loomed over the prostrate man in the bed. 'Tell me about the cross that was stolen,' he said. 'Describe it to me.'

'It was gold. Very old workmanship. With big red stones. It was so beautiful.'

'How many stones?'

'Seven. Boris counted them. Three in the traverse and four in the body. He kept saying he'd be rich.'

Rakovsky's hands were clenched in to fists. Irinia thought he was near to striking the old man. She had begun to feel uneasy. This was no ordinary interrogation.

'How big was the cross?'

'Bigger than my hand. He let me hold it once. It felt so light.'

The description fitted exactly. Filigree goldwork, seven red spinels. The right measurement. He leaned closer, nearer to Brückner. Brückner was watching him with wide, frightened eyes.

'What happened to the man you call Boris? Tell me!'

'I don't know. He was SS. I heard they'd all been killed. The Reds never took SS prisoners.'

'No,' Viktor said. 'They didn't. You raped the woman in the house, didn't you?'

Irina protested. 'Please, you mustn't talk about that. You don't know what harm it could do now.'

She came and caught Rakovsky's arm. He thrust her away. He seized Brückner by the jacket of his pyjamas. He heaved him upright.

'You raped her, didn't you? You held her down for the other one. Didn't you?'

'Yes.' It was a quavering cry. 'Yes.'

'You raped my mother and you're going to die for it. You understand me? You hear me? You're going to die for what you did to her.'

Behind him, Irina gasped. He didn't hear her.

'You should have shot me. I was the boy hiding in the cupboard, gagging my little sister so she wouldn't cry out. You made a mistake. You didn't kill me. Now you're going to be punished. You're going to die!'

Brückner screamed. It was a thin sound of rising terror.

Viktor turned to Irina. She was filling a syringe. She paused for a moment, staring at him.

'Is it true? *You were there?*'

'It's true,' Rakovsky said. 'What are you giving him?'

Brückner was moaning, tossing to and fro.

'I'm going to knock him out,' she said. 'I don't want that busybody nurse coming in if she hears him.'

Viktor stepped away from the bed. He laid a hand upon her arm. It gripped so tightly it hurt.

'I meant what I said. Give him a lethal injection. That is an order. I'll wait in your office.'

He didn't look back. He walked out of the room and closed the door. He went up in the lift and sat down in Irina's pleasant office. He wiped sweat from his forehead. Now he would sleep as peacefully as his mother and brother in their unmarked grave in the woods. The time passed. He was calm. He waited. At last the door opened and Irina came in. She was very pale. He stood up.

'Is he dead?'

'Yes. Why did you make me do that? I've never killed a patient.'

He dismissed the protest. 'Don't be a hypocrite. You destroy their minds. This is cleaner.'

She sat down. She gripped her hands together.

'I feel very shocked,' she said. 'I've killed in cold blood. You must excuse me.'

'You'll get over it,' Viktor said. 'You did your duty, Irina. I gave the order. You obeyed it. That's all. How did you explain it?'

'Cardiac failure. I overdosed him and then rang for emergency resuscitation. I knew it couldn't work. They went on and on trying. I'll have to call his wife,' she said. 'I have to make a full report. There'll be an inquest.'

'But they won't find anything?'

'Nothing. Not a trace. He had a heart attack. I gave him digitalis. His heart couldn't stand the shock.'

He could see she was recovering her composure.

He said, 'You were serving your country. Times are dangerous for us all. One life is nothing compared to the survival of our system. He'd lived fifty years too long. Remember that. I'm staying at the Hôtel d'Angleterre. Get through to Müller and tell him to contact me there. I'll be in Geneva for only two days. There's a lot of work to be done. If the cross still exists, we have to find it.'

'It was so kind of you to come with me, Peter.' Eloise Brückner's eyes filled with tears. Müller shook his head.

'My dear,' he said. 'It's the least I could do. It's been so sudden, such a terrible shock!'

The children were with her. They were white-faced and dumb.

'I couldn't have managed without you,' she insisted. 'All those dreadful arrangements to make and that inquest. Oh, I'll be so glad to get home!'

Müller knew that her grief was quite genuine. It had been a happy marriage, in spite of the difference in their ages. It had shocked him, too, when he heard of Adolph Brückner's sudden death. Irina had been brisk when she called with the news and told him to telephone Rakovsky at his hotel.

She hadn't wanted to discuss what had happened. A heart attack, she said, and rang off before he could ask questions. It was unlike her to miss a heart condition in a special patient. They weren't any use to Moscow dead.

He was sorry for Eloise, but a rich and attractive widow of forty wouldn't grieve alone for long. She wiped her eyes with a lace handkerchief and he caught the drift of her exotic scent. He had toyed with the fantasy of sleeping with her; the rich smell aroused him. He had never dared do more than imagine it while Brückner was alive. Now – why not? A shoulder to cry on. He put his arm around her. She didn't resist.

'Some of Adolph's cousins are coming for the funeral,' she said. 'I don't know them. I think they're only coming in case there's any money for them.'

Müller said gently, 'Adolph left everything to you and the children. He told me. Don't worry about them. Susan and I will be there to support you.'

'I know,' she murmured. 'I'm so grateful to you. We're not going to be late, are we? I couldn't bear it if we missed the flight.'

She had begun to panic about things like tickets and timetables. For twenty years all these details had been arranged for her. It was a symptom of widowhood.

'Plenty of time,' he reassured her. 'Just relax, my dear. Let me take care of you and the children.'

Her luggage was packed. They waited in her suite at the Richemond for the hire car to take them to the airport. When reception rang through Müller answered it. It was not the car. There was a lady asking to see Madame Brückner. He looked over to Eloise.

'Someone's downstairs. You're not expecting anyone?'

'No, no. I don't want to see anyone.'

The receptionist sounded apologetic. The lady was very insistent. Could she speak to Madame Brückner? Just for a few minutes? It was very important.

Müller said, 'I'm afraid not, just get rid of her. Oh it has. Very well. We'll come down.' He hung up. 'The car's here. They're coming up for the luggage.'

They went down in the lift and crossed the big reception hall. A woman moved quickly and caught up with Eloise. Eloise stopped.

The woman said, 'Madame Brückner? Please excuse me. I saw you at the clinic. I've got to talk to you. It's about your husband. I was the sister on his corridor.'

They didn't catch the flight.

She was in her mid-forties, neatly dressed with a quiet air of authority. She spoke calmly enough. She had insisted on seeing Eloise Brückner alone. Müller had smelled trouble the moment she said who she was. He'd tried to hurry Eloise away, to sidetrack the woman standing in their path. But he was overruled. Eloise Brückner wasn't going without hearing what the sister who had nursed her husband had to say. They all turned back and went up to the suite.

'My name is Beatrice Duval. Your husband was admitted to my corridor. Let me say first, I've been nursing psychiatric patients for more than twenty years and I know what I'm talking about. I've never experienced a case like this.'

'Why? What do you mean?' Eloise stared at her.

'The way Doctor Volkov treated him was nothing less than sadistic. I'm sorry, this isn't going to be easy for you, but I've got to say it. It was deliberate cruelty. And it's been on my conscience ever since.'

'Cruelty? How? I don't believe you!'

'I've nothing to gain,' Beatrice Duval said. 'I expect I'll lose my job for telling you. But it's preyed on my mind. The doctor wouldn't allow sedatives, or painkillers when he had those dreadful headaches. She put him through the most intensive analysis with nothing to help him afterwards. 'It's a wonder he didn't go mad.

107

He suffered such terrible symptoms he tried to kill himself. He had to be tied down. In the end I got another doctor to sedate the poor man. She was off duty and I didn't call her. She had me moved to another patient after that.'

'My God,' Eloise said. 'My God, it's like a nightmare.'

'It was a nightmare for *him*,' the sister said. 'I don't know why she did it, Madame Brückner. If he hadn't died of that heart attack, he'd have been a mental wreck.'

'You're sure? You're sure this is true?' Eloise was standing now. The scented handkerchief that had roused Müller's lust was tearing in her hands.

'As God's my witness. I asked the nurse on duty about the day he died. She said the doctor and another man, a visitor, were in his room. She told me she heard him scream. A few minutes later *she* came rushing out saying he'd collapsed. I say she brought on that heart attack!'

Eloise said at last, 'I'm going back home and I'll contact my lawyers. They'll want to see you and take a statement. All expenses will be paid, you won't be out of pocket. You will come, won't you? You won't change your mind?'

'I won't. I wouldn't have come if I wasn't prepared to tell the truth. What will you do?'

'If we prove mistreatment, they'll bring criminal charges. I've got the best lawyers in Germany. I'm very, very grateful to you. You're still working there?'

'Yes. I've been there since it opened. It's a very good place. It was just that one case. I hadn't worked with her before.'

'Give me your private address and telephone number,' Eloise said. 'Don't talk about it to anyone else. Wait till you hear from me. It'll be very soon.' She went to the door of the suite. Her eyes filled up. 'Thank God you told me.' she said. 'I won't let her get away with this, I promise you. My poor darling Adolph.'

She turned away. When the door closed after her visitor she broke down in tears.

'I wouldn't believe a word of it!' Müller insisted. 'The woman's got a grudge. She's probably trying to get money out of you.'

'No,' Eloise countered. 'She said herself she could lose her job. I believe her, Peter. I don't want to, but I do. Something dreadful happened to Adolph and I'm going to find out what it was!'

'It's nonsense,' he said. 'Doctor Volkova is a famous psychiatrist. That nurse didn't understand what she was doing. He was getting better. You were going to take him home very soon! For God's sake, Eloise be careful. If you defame the clinic or the doctor you could be sued for a fortune!'

She looked up at him. 'You needn't worry because you recommended her, Peter,' she said. 'I'm not blaming you. I know you were trying to help.'

He hadn't expected that. He backtracked. 'My dear! I'm not thinking of myself. I'm thinking of you.'

'I'm thinking of my husband,' she said slowly. 'I'm going to follow it up. I can't forget what she said. He tried to kill himself. He was tied down. If that's medical treatment, it ought to be stopped! I'm not frightened of anything that doctor or her clinic can do to me. If she hurt Adolph she'll face criminal charges. And who was the visitor she took in there the day he died? She told me *no one* was allowed to see him. I want answers. I want to know why my husband was heard screaming.'

My Christ, Müller said to himself. If I go on defending Irina, I'm going to lose out. He moved closer to Eloise Brückner.

He said seriously, 'You're right. I was only trying to spare you. Of course, this must be investigated. I'll come to the lawyers with you, if you like. Adolph was my friend, and I do feel responsible. I did recommend the clinic. I'm with you every step of the way.'

'Thank you,' she said. 'Thank you, Peter. Now for God's sake let's go to the airport and get on the next flight home.' She looked round her at the luxurious suite and shuddered. 'I can't wait to get away from this awful place.'

The flight to Munich took just two hours. They ran into bad weather and the turbulence upset the youngest Brückner child. She was frightened and she was sick. Müller made soothing noises while Eloise moved seats to comfort her and then he settled back to plan what he must do. By the time they had risen above the storm, there was a slight smile on his lips, as if he were thinking pleasant thoughts. And they were pleasant. Now it was his turn.

109

Irina had put a black mark against him with Rakovsky. Fortunately, Viktor valued him and they had a long association before he ever worked with Irina. Otherwise he might have been in serious trouble.

He wasn't going to warn Irina. He was going to report direct to Rakovsky in Moscow. She was about to be investigated and charged with malpractice towards a patient. Under Swiss law she would get a long prison sentence. She'd exceeded her brief with Adolph Brückner and the operation through the clinic would have to be closed down. That, he decided, would put an end to Irina's career, if not to Irina.

He was very solicitous to the Brückner family when they landed, paying particular attention to the sickly daughter clinging to her mother's arm. He would end up in bed with Eloise; he was hot with excitement at the thought of it. And he would somehow persuade her to part with the Fabergé desk set.

Rakovsky wanted that. *Steal it if necessary. But get it. It belongs in Russia.* No Irina Volkova to goad him with her arrogance and her interference. An affair with this lovely woman who was so rich and inviting, and Viktor's brief to him, track down the cross. Use any means, spend whatever is necessary. Find it if it exists, or prove it if it doesn't. I'll make sure your reward will be in proportion to the value of your information. It was a glittering prospect and gave him the courage to brush his hand against Eloise's breast as he kissed her goodbye.

'We'll go to the lawyers,' he said. 'We'll see it through together. Now sleep well, my dear. I'll call you in the morning.'

Eloise's daughter frowned. When he'd gone she said, 'Mummy, I don't like that man.'

'Now, darling, you mustn't say that. He's been so kind.'

Viktor Rakovsky was in conference when the message came. He couldn't leave, duty came first. His self-discipline had been forged and tempered by years of training. He glanced briefly at the written note, put it aside and went on with the meeting. His concentration was equal to his self-control. The last item on the agenda was the renewed activities of anti-Soviet groups in Europe and the North American continent.

Not just the normal fundraising and propaganda through the media. After the uproar created by Nicholas Tolstoy over the Cossack repatriations, the fringe groups had been taken very seriously. Their leaders covered a wide spectrum. Free Ukrainians, Catholics, Orthodox Christians, Liberal Socialists, even the anomaly of a tiny White Russian remnant hoping for the restoration of the monarchy. They were moving, these disparate community leaders; visas and travel arrangements were reported and the rendezvous was in Europe. The KGB had penetrated all these organizations over the years, but the purpose and the location of this summit was kept secret.

In the days of Andropov, the solution would have been easy. Selected targets would have been eliminated. The rest would have understood the warning, and the plot, whatever its form, would have fizzled out, as so many had done over the years. But not now. Now the KGB itself was subject to scrutiny, to accountability.

The murder of anti-Soviet activists abroad would stir up fierce controversy at home. The old powers and the impenetrable secrecy that protected them had been breeched by the new liberties. It was ironic to Victor and the colleagues sitting round the table that morning that Gorbachev had been the KGB choice as leader.

Other, more subtle methods had to be employed. Rakovsky suggested that one of his protégés, an able and dedicated counterespionage officer, should take over the activist case files and plan the Soviet response. At thirty-five, Leon Gusev had reached colonel's rank on account of his excellent work with agitators in the Baltic Republics. He had scored notable successes in Estonia and Latvia. It was agreed and at last the meeting ended. Viktor made the announcement.

Ivan Zakob, the father of the partisans in the great patriotic war, was dying. His name and his exploits were part of every Russian child's curriculum. He was a hero who had become a legend. Every man there expressed his sympathy. They were genuinely moved by the news.

Viktor reached his *dacha* before noon. The nurse was waiting.

111

Victor raced up the stairs and the doctor opened the door to Ivan's bedroom.

'He's still conscious,' he said. 'He's been asking for you.'

Viktor sat by the bedside. He held the frail hand.

'I waited for you, my son,' the weak voice whispered. 'I wouldn't go till you came.'

'I'm with you, Little Father,' Victor said. 'I won't leave you.'

'You've been a good son to me,' the old man said. 'We fought together and we suffered together. I want to tell you something.'

'Tell me,' Victor bent close to him.

'I loved your mother. There was no harm meant, but I loved her.'

'I know you did,' Victor answered. 'I found one of the men who killed her, Little Father. He was punished.'

Ivan's eyes opened; he gazed up at Rakovsky.

'Too many dead,' he said. 'Too much pain. It's time to forgive, my son. I want to die in peace. I want you to live in peace. Remember that. I'd like a priest to bless me.'

'I'll send for one,' Viktor promised.

'Then I'll wait,' the old man murmured and closed his eyes.

The priest was young and flustered; a number of churches in the district were open for services. Viktor stood while he blessed the dying man and anointed him. The priest intoned the prayers in a nervous voice, pulling at his beard. It was a privilege to send such a hero on his way to heaven. He summoned his courage and said so to the grim-faced man before he left the sick room. He knew he was a very important Party official.

'Thank you, Father,' Viktor said. 'It's been a comfort to him.'

He came to the bedside. The priest had gone, but he had left the smell of scented oils behind him. Viktor knelt beside the bed and bowed his head.

'Don't cry, my son. I'm happy now. I'm not afraid to go. Maybe I'll see your mother . . . and Stefan.'

He died so quickly that Viktor didn't know he'd gone. The silence told him. When he laid his hand against the old man's waxen cheek it was already cold. He got up and did what Ivan would have wished him to do. He opened all the windows to give the spirit easy exit.

*

Volkov looked round the apartment. There was no smell of Balkan tobacco. It was Irina's signature. Whenever she was at home, he smelled her cigarettes.

He went in to their bedroom. The bed hadn't been slept in. He knew because his pyjamas were exactly where he'd left them, dropped on the end of the coverlet. Untidy! She hated untidiness. Making a mess was one of his little rebellions against her. How trivial and demeaning it seemed to him now. How low he'd sunk through his own choosing. There were no messages on the machine. He'd forgotten to switch it on. She hadn't been home and she hadn't been able to call in. That would have infuriated her. When that happened it meant he was drunk, sprawled out on the sofa if he hadn't been able to reach the bed.

He went to the window, made sure her car wasn't coming, or turning into the communal garage. Then he started looking. He opened the drawers in her dressing table. They were full of make-up, boxes of this and pots of that; a case with her expensive jewellery, all the pieces meticulously fitted in to their places. He opened everything, searched, put everything back. He'd learned to be very tidy when he was in prison. If the straw mattress was an inch out of line with the plank bed base, his food was reduced by one meal. A few drops of urine on the floor by his slop pail merited a scientifically aimed punch at his kidneys from the guard. He had thrown his clothes on the floor, spilled his food, deliberately kicked over the stinking pail in the first weeks and suffered terribly for his defiance.

Searching for his passport, he paused, remembering it all. The battles he won at such a cost to his health that he couldn't help but lose the war in the end. The pain of coughing and the blood that frothed up in his sputum. The cold, that cruelest of all tortures. And the smell of those cigarettes in his tormentor's office, where he stood barefoot and shivering for hours on end.

He paused and suddenly tears welled up. He felt weak and overwhelmed. No passport in her private drawers. He forced himself to search the wardrobe, the chests full of her clothes. He went to the kitchen and found nothing but food and neatly arranged cooking knives and spoons, hanging like guardsmen from their hooks in perfect rows.

There was a desk in the sitting room. She never locked it. He'd gone through the drawers once, looking for something – he couldn't remember what, but there was nothing personal in that desk. Writing paper, envelopes, address book, a list of numbers where Irina could be contacted, paper clips, stamps, an India rubber, a packet of rubber bands, a stick of unused red sealing wax. He opened and shut the drawers and the flap and found what he expected. Nothing! She must keep her documentation at the clinic.

He sat down and wiped his brow. It was wet with sweat. The sweat of old memories, buried horrors, miserable lonely fears. No alcohol to dull the nerves; no soothing glow to warm the chill of despair into a muddled kind of peace.

Anger instead. Anger was making him sweat. Not anger for what he had suffered, but a deep and terrible rage for what had been inflicted upon others. Friends, colleagues in the movement who'd never left their bitter cells, or spent their lives in labour camps till they died of exhaustion.

He had no passport, but that wasn't going to stop him. He'd been offered a second chance of salvation. The girl who found him that day by the lake was sent by destiny, by fate, the atheists' substitute for God. The Holy Relic passed down by who-knows-what route out of Russia, given to an orphan in an Austrian prison camp. Into Lucy's keeping, so she could give it to him and with it, he could challenge the system that had tormented him and millions of the innocent. And win.

The front door opened. He saw his wife come in to the room. It was strange, but his hatred was purged. He looked at her and saw a stranger, who had never been anything else.

'You're up early? I tried to ring last night to say I wouldn't be home, but the machine wasn't on.'

She looked very tired, he noticed; pinched and pale. He felt nothing. He wasn't glad.

'I do wish you'd remember,' she said irritably. 'It's not such a lot to ask! God, I'm exhausted. I think I'll go to bed and get some sleep.'

'Did you have a crisis?' he asked her.

The passport must be in the clinic. But it wasn't going to stop him.

'Yes. Attempted suicide. God save me from Italians! They had the place in an uproar.'

'It wasn't your special patient then?'

She stiffened, anticipating an attack. 'No.'

'Is he still there?' Volkov said it casually.

She was caught off guard. 'No, he isn't. He had a heart attack. He died.' She was on her way to the bedroom, slipping out of her jacket.

Volkov said quietly. 'He was lucky. Are you off duty for the day now?'

She stopped at the door. 'Why? What do you care? You're never at home these days anyway.'

'I don't care,' he answered. 'I don't stay around here because I get bored. That might make me drink. I go out and about and keep busy. You ought to be pleased.'

She sighed. She was tired and her spirits were low.

'I'm not pleased,' she said. 'I don't care either! I'm going to bed.'

She went in and closed the door. He waited. She had left her handbag on the chair. He waited for a full half an hour by his watch before he opened it.

'What are we going to do? You can't go near that place!' Lucy leaned towards him. 'Dimitri, you mustn't!'

He said, 'It's the only way. My darling, you're not to worry, I'll be careful, I promise you. Now, drink your wine. This is our celebration, remember?' He smiled and reached out for her hand. 'It's no good complaining now. You were the one who made me brave.' He turned her hand upward and kissed the inside of the soft palm. 'When we're ready to leave I'll go to the clinic, get my passport out of the desk and meet you at the airport. Simple!'

Irinia's passion for neatness had labelled the key in her handbag. 'Office, drawer. Doc.'

'If she misses the key out of her bag,' Lucy protested.

Nothing could shake his calm or give him pause. He only laughed at her fears.

'She won't,' he countered. 'Because I've got this.'

He put an envelope on the table and slid a rough white square out of it. 'I'll have another key made with this,' he said. 'Candle wax, Lucy. You melt it and take an impression.'

'Oh, darling, why don't we just try Mischa? Please? I can't bear it if you take any risks now!'

'Life is a risk,' he said. 'Every time you cross the road, get in a car, climb a ladder! The risks are all ahead and I don't give a damn! We're going to succeed, you and I. How strange it all is! If I believed in anything, I'd say it was part of a divine plan.'

'My father was convinced of it,' she said. They had chosen a table out of view in the café he called 'their café'. The waiter who'd tried to pick her up that first morning wasn't on duty. It was warm and there were flowers in a little silver vase with candles lit for them. He'd ordered champagne for her. He was flushed and happy and he hadn't let go of her hand since they'd sat down.

'You look so beautiful,' he whispered. 'When we're back home I want to marry you.'

'Home?' she questioned.

'In Russia,' he said. 'I can't wait to show it to you. I want to drink tea with you at the Samoyovska Hotel in Kiev, and vodka with you in the evening in a place where they used to play gypsy music when I was a student. If it's still there.'

'It'll be there,' Lucy said.

He leaned close to her. 'Nobody's looking. Kiss me. Ah, that's better. Again, sweetheart. I love the taste of you. Why don't we get under the table and make love?'

'You're crazy.' Lucy protested.

'In that café where the gypsies were, we used to do that. When we were very drunk. I was wild in those days.'

'You're wild now,' she said.

By the end of their dinner she was imbued with his optimism. He talked of the future; he made light of the present and its difficulties until Lucy lost sight of them too. They went home, walking the streets with their arms around each other. They walked slowly and clumsily, her head resting on his shoulder. The private detective following them cursed when they stopped and kissed in the middle of the street. By the next morning he had a full report on Dimitri Volkov and his lover, ready for despatch to Peter Müller in Munich.

3

Leon Gusev was a Muscovite by birth. He had been born in one
of the hideous concrete blocks of flats erected after the Great
Patriotic War. His father was an engineer and his mother worked
for a minor official in the Ministry of Post and Communications.
He was an only son; his mother's old father and his aunt lived
with them. The flat had three rooms. He shared his parents'
bedroom and the old man and his widowed daughter slept in the
other room with a blanket on a line dividing them.

Leon was clever as a boy; he was a dull-looking child, hampered
by short sight. He had a squat body of surprising strength and
quick fists which deterred bullies. Once the glasses came off, they
ran away. He had a mind that delighted in problems. Mathematics
fascinated him. He seemed destined for a career as an engineer
like his father, but with much brighter prospects. But human
puzzles intrigued him more. He graduated from Moscow
University with degrees in psychology and political science and
joined the internal security.

As compensation for his lack of height and pebble glasses, he
was gifted with a charming smile and a friendly manner. He
wooed and married one of the prettiest secretaries in the office on
Dzerjhinsky Square.

Promotion came rapidly once he caught Viktor Rakovsky's attention. He joined Rakovsky's select team of young Intelligence operatives. He saw service in the Baltic Republics and earned a special commendation for his analysis of the situation among the ethnic groups.

He had a pleasant apartment on the outskirts of Moscow with his young wife and baby daughter, and hoped to achieve a small *dacha*. He was a dedicated follower of the new political initiative begun by Gorbachev. He believed in reform and modernization. He also shared Rakovsky's dread of the Soviet Union becoming fragmented by the Republics' achieving independence. A loose federation meant weakness. They couldn't contemplate such a situation with a united Germany and their allies in the Eastern bloc in chaotic pursuit of democracy. His colonel's insignia was still bright and new; he was very proud of it. Now he had been given an assignment that demanded intuitive analysis to a sensitive degree. The anti-Soviet activists abroad were planning to strike a blow. Discovery and prevention were the methods available. The old strong-arm KGB response was not an option.

Gusev sensed that his *dacha* and further promotion was in the balance. He immersed himself in his work. Every file, every data sheet on the exiles and *emigrés* who'd caused trouble over the past thirty years was computerized and collated for him.

He noted the dead as well as the living. The dead had children who might carry on their work.

In the very recent past, an English-based organization of so-called 'Free Ukrainians' had led a worldwide campaign on behalf of the gaoled dissident, Dimitri Volkov. The organizer and prime motivator was of Ukrainian birth, though a naturalized British citizen, Yuri Varienski. He had died early that year. He had one child, a daughter, who had a Jersey-based interior-decorating business. Independent income from her father's estate.

The name Lucy Warren went in to the computer at Moscow Centre, along with hundreds of other names on the periphery of the various movements. Even a seventeen-year-old schoolboy in a French *lycée* was documented because his father and grandfather were involved in exposing the executions of the Cossacks after Yalta.

Gusev likened himself to an industrious spider, sitting at the heart of a complicated web, pulling a thread here, tightening one there, until finally he began to see a pattern. There was no pattern as yet. KGB agents among the various groups had no information beyond rumours of some kind of summit meeting between the leaders. Their destination was being kept so secret it emphasized its importance. Activities in Canada and America were even more alarming. There were powerful and vociferous organizations of anti-Communist Russians in both countries, backed by considerable funds.

The venue of this gathering must be Europe. But its location and its purpose was Gusev's first priority. There must, he rationalized, there *must* be a unifying factor to bring so many divergents together. Something that bonded them closer than a shared hatred for Communism and the Soviet Union. If he could identify that . . .

There were many rumours. He didn't dismiss the wildest of them. Not even the fantasy that one of the Tsar's descendents was preparing to come out and offer himself as a leader within Russia itself, defying the authorities to arrest him and prove that they hadn't changed after all.

The theme of a leader kept recurring. Check and triple check the likely candidates. More lists, long computer analyses of each individual – background, ethnic origins, age, record, previous political activities. The web spread and became more entangled. Gusev recommended night and day surveillance by expert watchers on the heads of the organization and their families. Moscow Centre had facilities in all the countries concerned. Manpower was a problem, but he felt this deserved top priority.

An agent was despatched from London to Jersey to check on the dead activist Varienski's daughter. His report that she had left the island, and had not been seen or heard of since, went into the computer bank with hundreds of similar reports and remained on file. Gusev knew from experience that sooner or later something would emerge and give the vital clue. It always did. Either by accident, or carelessness, or simply luck. And he believed that luck was the reward of diligence.

'It's late, honey,' Susan Müller said. 'Aren't you coming to bed?'

Peter Müller yawned and stretched. He smiled at his wife. 'I'll just finish these accounts,' he said. 'I won't be long. Don't go to sleep.'

'I won't,' she promised.

He kept the smile on his lips till she had closed the door. The accounts were his coded report for Rakovsky. With a new and important addition from the Swiss detective agency. Eloise had conferred with Brückner's lawyers that morning. Müller had gone with her. The lawyers were cautious in their attitude to the nursing sister's story. He could see they regarded Eloise as overreacting. 'Naturally', they said to her, 'she was shocked'. The senior partner explained patiently that the nurse herself might have suspect motives in accusing the doctor of malpractice. Her reputation and experience would have to be investigated very carefully. Their case would stand or fall on her reliability.

Müller was surprised by Eloise's resistance. He'd always thought of her as pliable, sexy, more of an ornament than a partner for a man like Adolf Brückner. Now he saw another side of her. She was determined. She possessed power and she knew how to exercise it. She had silenced them all.

'I believe this woman. I believe my husband was badly treated. I don't want arguments, gentlemen. I want this matter investigated. I want you to bring the nurse down here and let her tell you what she told me. Then, I want the best legal advice you can get for me. Good morning.'

It made her more fascinating to Müller. If he wanted the elegant clotheshorse, even more did he desire to strip and possess the woman of character. He had spent so much time with Eloise that he felt he must make love to his wife that night, however tired he felt.

That tiredness disappeared when he got his detective's report on Volkov and his girlfriend. He rewrote his original report for Viktor Rakovsky, incorporating the results of investigating the affair. Brückner's widow was determined to pursue Irina through the courts. And Irina's husband, Dimitri Volkov, was involved in a passionate relationship with a woman of Russian descent, the daughter of a well-known anti-Soviet activist who'd recently died, Yuri Warren, alias Yuri Varienski.

His admirable Swiss detectives had checked up on her with the central police register of foreigners, and then elicited the information from the police in Jersey. Her reputation was confirmed as impeccable. In the course of establishing this, the agency had extracted the other information about her background.

Müller urgently advised the recall of both Volkovs to the safe confines of the Soviet Union.

Lucy took the call. Volkov had gone out. He liked to buy their food; he even enjoyed cooking it sometimes, and was putting on a little weight. He seemed to take pleasure in the simplest things, like touring the delicatessens in search of a special cheese, or taking the water bus across the lake and just mingling with the tourists.

She was waiting for him to come back when the telephone rang. It could only be Mischa. No one else knew where she was.

He spoke in Russian. 'Are you alone?'

'Yes. Is anything wrong?'

'No. No, everything is good. The meeting is in two weeks. The twenty-seventh. In London at the Makoff Galleries. There's an exhibition of pre-Revolutionary photographs and memorabilia. It's a perfect cover. But is he ready? Is he strong enough?'

Lucy turned round as the door opened. Volkov was surprised by the brilliance of her smile and the heightened colour in her cheeks.

'Ask him yourself,' she said. She gave the telephone to Volkov. 'It's Mischa,' she said. 'They've set the date!'

She watched him, listening to the one-sided conversation. There was no hesitation. He spoke calmly and with authority.

'I shall be there,' he said. 'I'll be happy to address them. No. That won't be necessary. I'll be with Lucy.' He turned and looked at her. 'As soon as possible,' he went on. He hung up and he held out his arms. 'I told you it would happen,' he said. 'Now we're ready to go. In two weeks I shall be speaking to the people who worked for me and campaigned and raised money when I thought I was as good as dead and buried. I'm going to make the speech of my life. A new Russia will be born in the Ukraine!'

They held each other close. Then he said, 'I must get that key cut today. If it goes well, we'll be on your island by the end of next week. And you can show me the cross. I dreamt of it last night.'

Lucy didn't look at him. She was pale now instead of flushed. The key. He had to get into his wife's office, open the desk and trust that his passport was inside. That was when the idea came to her.

'Darling,' she said. 'Why don't I take that wax and get it done for you? Please let me. I know a little place not too far from here. Please.'

Lucy drove in to the centre of the city before she found a locksmith near the Chemin de la Tourelle. The man looked at her suspiciously, the piece of hard white wax in his fingers.

'You want a key cut from this, Madame?'

'Two keys,' Lucy said. She forced herself to smile at him. 'It's a bet,' she said. 'My friends said I couldn't get it done from a wax impression. I said I could. I do hope you can do it for me?'

'I could,' he said, 'but I won't. No responsible locksmith would make a key from a wax impression, I'm sorry.' He turned his back.

At the rear of the shop his young assistant looked up from his work and grimaced at Lucy.

'It's an impression of my own key.' Lucy insisted. 'I told you – it's a bet – nothing illegal.'

'I'm sorry, Madame.' The locksmith cut her short. 'Jean if anyone wants me, I'll be back in a minute.' He went out through a door in the back.

The assistant grinned at Lucy. 'Gone to make pee-pee,' he said. 'Quick. Let's have a look.' He took the wax from her and examined carefully. 'This is good. Very clear, I can make two keys for you. Come back tomorrow, after five. He's gone then. 50 francs?'

'That sounds fair enough.' Said Lucy. 'And I win my bet.'

Two keys. She drove home slowly. One key for Dimitri. And one for herself.

Müller's decoded report was given a yellow sticker. It arrived via the diplomatic bag on Saturday morning. Viktor Rakovsky had left for his *dacha*. A courier was despatched on the strength of that yellow signal. Blue was urgent, yellow was most urgent.

He was fond of fishing. When he wasn't sketching or painting as a relaxation, Viktor took a rod and line down to the banks of the Moscova and fished for the grey roach that lurked in the sluggish water. Mostly he threw them back. They weren't edible and the two cats at the *dacha* couldn't eat too many of them. Viktor kept cats. The cat with the yellow eyes had disappeared into the forest the day the Germans came. He remembered pleading with his mother to take the little creature on the train to Moscow and safety. He loved cats.

He laid his tackle aside and opened Müller's report. He didn't fish that day. He went back to his office and summoned Gusev. Gusev's family didn't see him for the rest of the weekend. The banks of computers were busy, and together Viktor and Gusev read the long print-outs and the cross-references and the counter-checks on the information. At the end, Rakovsky opened a bottle of his favourite Scotch whisky and offered a drink to the young colonel. It was a great mark of favour.

Rakovsky listened to Gusev's summary.

'The daughter of Yuri Varienski disappeared after her father's death. She reappeared, according to this, in Geneva, where she has made contact with Dimitri Volkov and became his mistress. For the last five years Volkov has been drinking himself to death. He had ceased to be a problem to us. This is the first woman he's been connected with in all that time. He's taken no part in politics since his release. Suddenly he becomes involved with someone whose father was an active anti-Soviet right up till his death. I think, comrade, that we must conclude that she has seduced Volkov in order to use him politically. The surveillance team,' he glanced down checking something. 'The Swiss surveillance team employed by our agent doesn't mention seeing him drunk at any time. His behaviour is sober and normal. That is remarkable, given his alcoholic addiction.'

'Very remarkable,' Viktor said slowly. He was thinking while he listened to the logical thought processes of Leon Gusev. Irina had killed Brückner on his orders. Only Irina knew that he was responsible for the collapse of Moscow Centre's operation at the clinic. If Brückner had lived, there wouldn't have been a complaint made to the widow. If he'd let his mother's violator escape punishment . . . Müller said she and Volkov must be recalled. Ironic, he thought, that Müller had plunged the knife in to her back instead of the other way round. She must be brought home, before any further investigations were made by Eloise Brückner's lawyers. She couldn't be charged with anything once she was out of reach.

But Volkov's infidelity was more important than Irina's blunder. Volkov was not drinking. Gusev deduced that Volkov was in love with a woman who'd been sent to entrap him for political purposes, so Gusev deduced. He paid full attention again.

'Varienski was the originator of the London-based "Free Ukrainians". The "Free Ukrainians" are in close contact with Catholic *emigrés* in Europe and the United States. They are a significant part of the dissident organizations we have been monitoring. As we know, they are suddenly very active.'

He cleared his throat. 'Excuse me, comrade,' and took a sip of whisky. He didn't like it. 'It seems to me that we are missing the key factor. The common denominator between them all. Is it possible that Volkov is this factor?'

He waited for Viktor's response. There wasn't one. He just nodded and said, 'Go on. Take it further.'

'Why should Dimitri Volkov, after five years of obscurity, become valuable to any anti-Soviet organization? That question has to be asked. The answer lies in his birthplace in the Ukraine and the reputation he enjoyed among dissidents and refusniks before his arrest and during his imprisonment.'

Viktor interrupted. 'I know all that. I know how dangerous he was. Go on,' he said again.

'He could be used as a figurehead. But a figurehead for what?' Gusev enquired and answered his own question. 'For a full-scale political movement outside the Soviet Union. What purpose would that serve? I can't see the exiles and *emigrés* banding together and achieving anything of importance but limited media coverage.' Gusev paused; he frowned.

Viktor thought, *The keys are clicking in to place in that computer brain of his. I can almost hear them.*

'His real use would be inside the Soviet Union. Here, he could be exploited by elements already working against the central government. Which brings us back to the Ukraine, where Volkov was born. If there is a link and I believe there is, then that's where we must look. That's where we'll find the heart of this conspiracy. In our present circumstances, we couldn't do anything to stop him returning here and openly declaring himself. And he'd have huge popular support. I'm not suggesting he'd last long,' Gusev continued. 'Once the Ukraine demanded independence he could drop out of sight. There are plenty of others who'd come forward. I don't have to name them!'

'No,' Viktor muttered. 'You don't. You may have found your missing factor. We can't take any chances. We bring Volkov home. Once here, we can make sure he gets inside the brandy bottle and stays there.'

Leon Gusev said, 'I'd like to investigate a little deeper. I'd like to run some cross-checks on Varienski. Before you take any action. Will you give me forty-eight hours?'

Viktor looked up at him. 'I know you, Leon. There's a bee buzzing between your ears, isn't there? What is it?'

'There's more to this than Volkov and the girl.'

'We both agree he has a limited potential, but he *could* be used to detonate a big political explosion. Isn't that enough?'

'It should be,' Gusev said thoughtfully. 'It should be, Comrade, but I still feel there's something we've missed. Let me research Yuri Varienski. Right down to the time he was born.' He smiled at Rakovsky in his friendly way. 'If there's nothing to find, I won't find it. If there is, we'll still have Volkov back in Russia.'

Viktor stood up. 'I'll make sure of that,' he said.

Müller flew to London. He was popular in the trade. He was amusing and knowledgeable, and he'd made no enemies. He started with the top dealer who specialized in Fabergé and Russian works of art. He called on Wartski in Conduit Street. Collectors from all over the world went to the firm for advice and to buy the exquisite objects fashioned for the Imperial family and the old nobility. If a collector had acquired the ancient cross, Wartski's experts might have heard of it through the dealers' grapevine.

An hour later, after admiring some of the rare and beautiful pieces in the shop, Müller left, having learned nothing. He was advised to consult Eckstein, who also specialized in Russian and Eastern European art. He had perfected a glib story. He had a client who thought he had missed a fabulous bargain when he refused to buy a paste cross from an impoverished Russian aristocrat.

This client was not only obsessional, but extremely rich. Müller had offered to help in the hope of persuading him to invest in something less fantastic. Heads were nodded in sympathy. Clients like that were not uncommon among the super rich. It irked them unbearably to let something slip through their fingers. But they had to be humoured before they could be diverted from the unobtainable to the treasure that was actually for sale.

From the best in the business he worked his way down. He went from the reputable experts to the shadier middlemen, who traded in dubious goods, and from them to those who traded in anything without asking where it came from. Shops and dealers who specialized in old paste, in decorative objects, phoney icons and faked religious relics. He made two calls to contacts who sold to a private collector in New York. The collector was a woman. She hoarded like a magpie. The house in Long Island was referred to as Xanadu in the specialized trade that supplied her. It was crammed from the cellars to the roof space with furniture, pictures, sculptures, jewellery and *objets d'art*.

They were never displayed. Her criterion for any purchase was that it was the only example of its kind. Then she bought whatever it was and paid their price without worrying too much about the provenance. She was the kind of acquisitive neurotic who would hoard a medieval cross or a Papuan shrunken head.

Nobody could help him. One even suggested he try a firm of theatrical costumiers. They had a mass of worthless artefacts from crowns to Papal tiaras that they hired out. Müller realized he was being ridiculed and hung up.

He decided to stop over in Paris and spend a couple of days

following a similar route. He paid calls to Le Vielle Cité, famed for its antiquities, where he was politely entertained and actually bought a little Renaissance bronze relief, but no one had heard of a cross coming on the market in recent years. He knew the fakers and the fences in Paris as well as London, and he skimmed through them, without any hope of success.

He was tired and frustrated by the end of his stay. The charming little bronze was a compensation. He decided to sell it to the Americans who had bought the tryptich.

He always stayed at a high-class hotel on trips abroad. He liked comfort and it was part of his image. He was packing in his room at the Georges V when his telephone rang. He supposed it was his wife, Susan. Or maybe Eloise. He'd kept in touch with her since he left home. She'd told him the nurse was coming to see her lawyers and make a statement at the end of that week. Things were moving, she'd said, and the steely note in her voice had excited him.

'I'll be with you,' he'd assured her. 'I'll hurry back.'

It wasn't his wife and it wasn't Eloise Brückner. It was a woman; she had a vulgar Parisian accent. She had heard, she explained, that he was enquiring about an old Russian cross.

Müller kept his voice cool. Yes, he agreed. He was asking around. Did she have one? No, she answered. But she had some information. She could come to his hotel if he liked.

Müller didn't like the sound of her. He suggested they meet at a bar he knew round the corner from the Place de Grève. Six o'clock, she suggested. He paused; he'd have to catch a later flight.

'My name's Levison,' she told him. 'I'm wearing a red dress.'

'Six o'clock,' he said and hung up.

He was five minutes early, but she was already there, conspicuous in the red dress which was too tight for her. She wasn't what Müller expected. She was middle-aged, overweight and ill at ease in the chic little bar. He came up and introduced himself. She got up and they shook hands. Her bag and shoes were cheap. He had expected some kind of tart from Les Halles and found a respectable Jewish matron in an unbecoming colour.

'Would you like something to drink?' he asked.

'No thank you. I don't drink.' She brought out a man's handkerchief and loudly blew her nose. People at nearby tables looked round.

Müller said, 'I do have to catch my plane, Madame Levison, so if you don't mind, I'd like to get down to business. How did you hear about me?'

She had gentle brown eyes; they were her best feature.

'I've got friends in the business,' she said. 'My father was well known in the old days. He had a fine shop in the Avenue de l'Opèra. Everybody respected him.' She put the handkerchief away. 'Excuse me,' she said. 'I've got a nasty cold. Summer colds are always the worst. My friend called me and said you'd been to see him and were asking about a Russian cross. He knew my father very well. He thought I might know something and he wanted to do me a good turn.'

'That was kind,' Müller said. 'Who was this friend?'

To his surprise she named a reputable dealer in fine art that he had been to see that afternoon.

'Times have been hard since my father died,' she explained.

'He took in a partner and we got married.' She shrugged. 'He was not like my father. He ruined the business. When he died I had to sell up. There wasn't much left. I do a little dealing from home. Small things. People offer me stuff they don't want.'

Müller had wasted enough time. He interrupted. 'You said you had information about the cross.'

She nodded. 'My father used to talk about it. He was nearly eighty when he died, but he had such a memory! Someone came to the shop and tried to sell him an old cross with paste stones in it. A long time ago – twenty years or more. He didn't offer for it. When he was telling the story, he used to bang his fist on his forehead like this. "I wouldn't offer for it! I ask you!" '

Müller was on the edge of his seat. Brückner's investigators had found a jeweller who'd refused to buy a cross that fitted the description of the Holy Relic. Twenty-five years after the war ended a man had gone in to the shop and been told that his treasure was studded with spinels instead of rubies. Paste wasn't accurate, but it served well enough. There the search had ended. Until now.

129

'He never got over it,' Madame Levison said. 'He only found out what he'd missed a few years ago when some German came in asking questions. By chance, he said. The Germans were asking everywhere, advertising, making enquiries all over the trade.

'My father remembered the man with the cross; he remembered him because he was young and so nervous. He didn't want to sell the cross unless there was a lot of money. The German wanted to know about the man. My father got suspicious. He just said he was a foreigner, he couldn't remember anything else. He didn't want to help a German. Forgive me, but you can understand why. He'd lost a lot of relatives in the war.'

'I understand,' Müller said. 'I'm sorry.'

'It's not your fault,' she said simply. 'You weren't even born. I don't think you can hate forever.'

'No,' Müller agreed. For a moment he felt the old shame rise in him. 'Tell me about the man. Tell me what your father said about him. You're being very helpful, Madame.'

'He was a Russian,' she said. 'My father talked Russian. He'd learned it from his grandparents. They left Russia after one of the pogroms. He told the man it was very old, but the gold work was too fragile to be reworked and the stones weren't worth anything. He said the Russian said to him, "Then it's God's will I keep it." And he walked out. My father didn't think of it again till this German visited the shop and showed him an illustration. He recognized it. Then he looked it up and found it was some priceless Tsarist cross he'd turned down.

'He loved telling the story. My friend must have heard it from him, and after you left remembered and telephoned me. He said you were a gentleman who'd pay a fair price for anything I could tell you.'

'What do you consider a fair price, Madame?' He could think of some people who'd say she'd told him nothing he didn't already know and offer a few hundred francs. But Müller had never done business that way, and it was evident that she was her father's daughter. She was a trader.

'Five thousand francs was what my friend suggested.'

Müller smiled. 'And how much are you giving him out of that?'

She blushed. 'He made the introduction,' she said. 'Fair is fair.'

'I don't have that much in cash. Do you mind a cheque?'

'No. A cheque is fine. Thank you.' She opened the bag, took out the handkerchief and made a louder noise than before. 'I hate colds,' she said morosely. 'Especially summer colds. Goodbye, Monsieur Müller. If you're looking for this cross, I hope you find it. It must be worth a fortune!'

'Money couldn't buy it,' Müller said. 'Goodbye, Madame.'

Müller got to the airport and caught the seven o'clock flight home. He had gone as far as he could go. He had no more resources to call upon. The cross had never surfaced since that one appearance in the shop owned by Madame Levison's father. Who ever had it then still had it, or had passed it on. A German would have thrown away worthless loot. A Russian who talked of God's will would have kept it. It was up to Moscow to start checking among the *emigrés* and escapees who'd gone to Paris after the war ended.

That evening he showed his wife the little bronze relief. Afterwards, when she was preparing dinner, he slipped into his study to telephone Eloise.

'I'm home,' he said in his warm voice. 'I just wanted to you know I've been thinking of you.'

He was thinking of her. And thinking that if he pleased her as much as he hoped, she might be persuaded to part with the Fabergé desk set.

The letter reached Irina by special courier. She was at the clinic when it was delivered, working on some case notes. The Italian lady suffering post-natal depression was proving difficult to treat. Her husband and relatives were virtually camped in the clinic, driving Irina mad with their interference. She had been tempted to banish them and forbid all visits, but they wouldn't be intimidated. The director of the clinic was a reputable Swiss psychiatrist. He had no idea of the real identity of one of the major shareholders in the enterprise and he regarded Irina as a dedicated and skilful doctor. He insisted that the Italians should be humoured. They were related to the Agnelli family and he was impressed by the connection with such wealth and power. Irina suspected that his own Italian origins made him sympathetic to the fuss they created.

She slit the envelope open. It was written in Cyrillic. There was no heading on the paper, but she knew the signature. The *chargé d'affairs* in Geneva was Moscow Centre's top man.

The message was brief. 'A civil action is pending against you brought by Adolph Brückner's widow, alleging mistreatment of her husband. You are recalled to Russia as a matter of urgency. Your husband is to accompany you. You are responsible for his return.'

She felt her pulse rate double; she flushed hot and then went cold. She was recalled to account for what had happened. Why had her methods been exposed? Why had Brückner died, putting the clandestine operation at the Amtel clinic at risk? Serious charges could be brought against her when she got home. Unless Viktor Rakovsky took responsibility. She snapped at her lighter; her hands trembled. At last the little flame flared and she set it to the paper, watching the end blacken, smoulder and curl as it burned. It lay in a charred heap in her ashtray among the cigarette butts.

Who had betrayed her? Who had given information to Brückner's wife? A civil action alleging misconduct leading to her patient's death. It was Rakovsky's fault. She pushed her chair back and threw the debris from the ashtray into her wastepaper basket. Rakovsky had pursued his private vengeance. Then she paused, realizing that he had a faultless motive. The Holy Relic was his alibi. Brückner couldn't be left alive with that knowledge. His defence would stand. Hers wouldn't.

She'd aroused suspicion in some member of the staff and they'd reported her to Brückner's widow. And she realized at once who it was. The sister who'd protested and overruled her by bringing in another doctor to relieve Brückner's suffering. She'd seen the hostility in the woman's face and had her moved to another ward. That must be who had accused her.

Irina swore in fury. She should have taken precautions against such a mishap. She'd become careless, complaisant. Five years ago she'd have got the woman sacked on some pretext, rendering her harmless if she alleged anything against a reputable doctor in a famous clinic. The grieving widow was rich and powerful enough to hound anyone through the courts.

Irina forced herself to calm down. She lit a cigarette . . . composed herself. The pulse steadied, the cold sweats stopped. She would go home. She had given years of valuable service. Rakovsky would support her. She hadn't missed the sting in the tail in that curt directive. It was her responsibility to being Dimitri back to Russia with her.

Easy for them to say, she thought bitterly. If it hadn't been for Müller's exposure, he might have been amenable. He might still have loved her and been capable of persuasion. But not now. Now Dimitri hated her. He hated her more in his sobriety than when he was drunk. And he was still sober, much to her surprise. The distance between them widened every day. They saw little or nothing of each other. He lived his separate life and she waited for him to falter and slip back into alcohol. But he didn't.

Irina stubbed out her cigarette. She went to the window and opened it, gazing out at the magnificent view over the vast lake. Five years of exile among strangers would soon be over. Suddenly her heart ached for the sight of her native country, for the sounds and scents and the voices of her own people. Once a Russian, always a Russian. She remembered reading a biography of a Tsarist *emigré* after the Revolution and the phrase came back to her. It was the only thing in the whole book that she related to, '*We cherished our language and our culture. We never wanted to lose our Russianness, no matter what country we lived in.*'

She thought. 'I'll come out of it unscathed. And when I'm home maybe I'll be happy again. No Russian is truly happy outside Russia. And I'll bring Dimitri with me, however I have to do it. Switzerland destroyed us. Russia may give him back to me.'

She took the key out of her bag and opened the locked drawer in her desk. Her passport was in order. His was out of date. She picked up the telephone and asked for a courier service. That afternoon the passport was delivered to the Soviet Embassy for renewal on an emergency application.

When Irina got home that evening Dimitri was not there. She realized suddenly how empty and unlived in the apartment had become. There were no signs of him about the place. No books left lying about, no newspapers scattered or folded untidily on a table, no dirty cups or glasses. He came home to sleep and as soon as he woke after she'd left for the Clinic, he went out.

There were no weekends for them. No days spent together. He left the apartment in the morning. If she enquired, he merely said he was going walking and he didn't know when he'd be back. She wasn't to wait for him if she had anything else to do. It was so cold and self-contained, his eyes were empty when he looked at her. He hated her so much that he refused even to see her as a person.

She had tried to follow him once. She wasn't skilled enough and a tram ride lost him to her. She came home in despair and went back to the clinic to work rather than spend the Sunday alone, or try to pass the time with friends. She went in to their bedroom. He'd made his bed when he left; that was unlike him, but then the sober man was neat and organized.

Irina sat on the bed. He'll never come back of his own free choice, she admitted. There's only one way to get him home and I'll just have to take it. As soon as I have his passport.

Lucy dialled the number. A bright voice answered on the third ring. 'Good morning, Amtel clinic. Can I help you?'

Lucy's mouth was dry. She said. 'Doctor Volkova's secretary, please,' and swallowed hard.

'One moment,' the switchboard said.

She waited; it seemed she waited for an eternity. Less than a few seconds, but it seemed longer than time.

'Doctor Volkov's office.'

The same honeyed tone, she thought; they must be trained to speak like that, oozing reassurance. She realized that she had betrayed her knowledge of Russian by using the feminine version of the doctor's surname.

'Good morning,' Lucy forced herself to sound calm. 'I would like to make an appointment with the doctor.'

'And have you a letter from your doctor? Normally it's your doctor who makes the appointment.' The voice was a little less friendly now.

'I'm visiting,' Lucy said. 'I came specially in the hope of seeing Doctor Volkov.' She was careful not to make the same mistake. 'I have no letter. My doctor's in England, but he promised to write to her before I arrived. Could you just check for me, please?'

'May I have the doctor's name, Madame?'

'Harrison,' Lucy invented. 'Doctor Philip Harrison, 27 Sloane Square, London. I've been getting attacks of giddiness and I'm not sleeping well. He wanted me to see a specialist in Harley Street, but I'd heard so much about your clinic and Doctor Volkov, I said I wanted to consult her. Are you sure you haven't had a letter?'

'One moment. Doctor Volkov is off duty today, but I'll see if I can check through the files in case.'

'Thank you,' Lucy said. She hung up. Today. Her heart gave a frightened leap. She'd planned it differently. She had to do it today. No doubt the secretary would dismiss the call as the work of some crank hoping to bluff her way in without a doctor's recommendation.

She took a deep breath. They'd made their plans for escape. She argued in favour of a direct flight to London and then on to Jersey. Dimitri would be safe there. Nobody would think of looking for him in the Channel Islands. He would meet Mischa and the others in London at the exhibition in the art gallery.

The next step would be to come out in public and call a Press conference. That would guarantee his safety. So long as he was in the limelight, he couldn't be attacked or abducted. The media would be the best bodyguard of all. He was fired with enthusiasm. His spirits were so high he didn't detect the chill of fear in Lucy. She was proud of him. It didn't seem possible for her love to deepen and grow, but it did. If she loved the sad victim of despair and betrayal, even more did she love the brave idealist. Loved him enough to steel herself to lie and excuse herself that afternoon, while she made her way to the Amtel clinic.

'Don't be long, my darling,' he said. 'I'll miss you.'

She forced herself to smile, to be lighthearted. 'No, you won't; you'll be busy.'

He was working on his speech and his Press statements. He said, 'I could come with you. Why don't I?'

She put him off with a kiss. 'I can't see you sitting in dress shops all afternoon,' she said. 'I won't be long. If I buy something nice, I'll wear it home for you.'

She waved at him from the door and went down to the street. She'd hired a car a few days before, with the trip to the clinic in view. No taxis, no chance of being delayed. In and out, and drive like the wind.

She got in, checked that the newly cut key was in her purse and switched on the engine. Clouds were gathering overhead and the windscreen was spotted with rain. At mid-morning the traffic was heavy, slowed down by the showery outbreak. Lucy kept looking at her watch. She had decided to reach the clinic by lunchtime. There was a good chance that the secretary would take time off for lunch while the doctor was absent. It was Lucy's hope of getting into the outer office unchallenged. Once there, she had to gamble on the consulting room being unlocked. Her hands were sticking to the wheel. She sat behind a stream of cars stopped at the traffic intersections till they surged onwards and then stopped again. The rain grew heavier and thunder rumbled over the mountains. At this rate, she thought desperately, the lunch hour will be over before I even get there. Then she remembered how things were here, and calmed down.

The Swiss enjoyed their food. They started early and worked late, but they took an hour and a half for lunch. If the woman she'd spoken to was having a break, she wouldn't be back to her desk before two o'clock.

It was just after one, when Lucy crossed the Pont du Mont Blanc, and the traffic was lighter. She drove as fast as she dared past the Jardin Anglais and at last swung out on to the Quai Gustav Ador. The sky was bright, the distant grumble of thunder died away and the sun shone, striking light off the puddles that had gathered from the downpour.

Driving along the Quay, Lucy thought about that morning when she had gone to the little bistro on the Place de Trainant to find Volkov. She remembered the sinking despair when the smirking waiter had shrugged and said, 'He's always drunk.' She'd needed all her courage then, to stand over him and introduce herself; to refuse to be sent away, to admit that she had come to Geneva in vain. Perhaps I fell in love with him then, she thought; when I discovered that he was a man and not a shining hero. The first time I looked into his eyes and saw how much he'd suffered.

And I'm taut with fear, she reproached herself, when all that can happen to me is to be thrown out of this damned clinic. If they call the police that would be different. I'd be arrested, Volkov wouldn't know what had happened to me. Panic rose for a moment. She crushed it ruthlessly. I can't afford fear. I've got to succeed. I've got to get his passport and take him away from here. Before our luck runs out. It's been too easy for us; we've led charmed lives till now. There was a Russian saying her father liked to quote: *'God doesn't always frown upon the wicked.'*

She put her foot down on the pedal and the car leaped forward. In her agitation she had taken the longer route on to the Quay de Cologny. She slowed and turned right crossing the Chemin de BelleFontaine and down the Route de la Capite, upwards off the main highway and into the Chemin Faguillon. There was a discreet sign pointing higher still to the Amtel clinic.

She turned into the big car park. Expensive cars parked in neat rows that the staff had reserved for them. She spotted the name Dr Volkov on a smart little board above an empty space and her heart jumped. She found a parking space close to the main entrance. She put the key in her pocket and left her purse in the car.

She saw the building that Adolph Brückner had looked at on his arrival that day, the pain in his head threatening like the thunder clouds that were drifting back over the mountain tops. Clean architectural lines, gleaming glass, flower beds so neat and regimented that no weed would dare to seed itself.

Two nurses in crisp white came down the main steps, laughing and talking, hurrying away. Lucy walked up the fight of steps; the plate glass doors slid open electronically as she crossed the beam.

More flowers inside. A small fountain pattered gently in the big reception hall. A desk with 'Reception' in French, German and Arabic loomed on her left. She absorbed every detail, her senses sharpened by a flood of adrenalin. She went to the reception and a smiling woman in a white blouse and neat grey skirt rose up and asked if she could help her. Lucy smiled back.

'Doctor Volkov's secretary,' she said.

The receptionist made a quick assessment. Nicely dressed, but not expensively enough to be a client.

'She may still be at lunch,' she said. 'I'll ring for you.'

'Oh, don't bother,' Lucy said quickly. 'I'm a friend of hers. I've only popped by for five minutes. Second floor, isn't she?'

'Third,' the receptionist corrected. 'You can take the lift over there.'

'Thanks,' Lucy said. Lifts could be on the wrong floor at the wrong moment. 'I'll take the stairs. Good for the figure.'

'Round the corner, by the flower shop,' she was directed. The woman looked after her and gave a little shrug. If she wanted to climb all that way, that was her business. She had an English accent; the English weren't normally health conscious, unlike the Americans, and they always took the lift.

Lucy skirted the kiosk overflowing with vases and baskets of flowers; the heady scents were sickening. A man came out with a big bouquet of Regale lilies, festooned with white ribbons. He looked miserable and anxious; he almost bumped into Lucy.

He said, 'Oh, scusi Signorina,' and walked towards the lift.

She hurried past him to the stairs. It was a longer climb than she expected. Nervousness made her breathless. She paused at the landing leading onto the third floor. Carefully she pushed the door open and looked left and right before stepping into the corridor. There were five consulting rooms, two waiting rooms, the lift doors and another door marked 'fire exit only'. The floors were carpeted, the lighting soft; flower prints in gilded frames hung between the doors. It reminded Lucy of a luxury hotel.

Then she stopped dead. There was a nurse's cubbyhole with a little desk behind a glass door. Someone was moving in there. She caught a glimpse of uniform and retreated behind the door on to the landing. She watched through a crack and at last a nurse came out of the tiny office and went to the lift.

Lucy could hear her humming as she waited. Then she was gone and the corridor was empty. The name was stencilled inside a brass frame on the fourth door along. *Dr I. Volkov.*

Lucy paused. She raised her hand to knock. If the secretary had come back early, and if she answered, Lucy had decided to go in and bluff it out. '*Doctor Volkov asked me to collect something from her office. Would you open the door please? She's in a terrible hurry.* It had sounded convincing when she rehearsed it. Quiet authority was the key. She mustn't hesitate. Just walk in, say the words, demand that the office be opened for her.

At that moment Lucy realized that no responsible employee in an ordinary office, let alone a hospital, would have admitted her without written instructions or a telephone call to confirm. She knocked. She knocked again. Nothing happened. She couldn't hear any movement from inside. She tried the handle. It turned and the door opened. She slipped in and closed it very carefully. A quarter to two. She had lost precious time waiting for the nurse to leave.

She crossed the room in a few quick strides, grasped the handle of the door set in the wall and pulled. It was locked. She couldn't help it. She gave a stifled cry of disappointment. Then she swung round to the empty desk. Word processor, internal and external phones, a tiny switchboard with dead lights, linking the office to who-knew-what departments.

The key was in the top drawer, neatly labelled. I. Volkov. She couldn't turn it at first; she fumbled and wrenched and then made herself try again, without forcing. At last she was inside the consulting room and the door was closed behind her. The blinds were half-drawn against the sunlight. She ran to the desk, bumping against a large armchair, not feeling the impact. She had the key out of her pocket and in her hand. She was trembling as she bent down and inserted it carefully into the left-hand drawer of the desk. She didn't hear the door open.

Irina slammed down the telephone. She had arranged to lunch with friends at the Lion d'Or at Cologny and call in to the clinic afterwards to see one or two patients. The Italian lady was being particularly troublesome, demanding that the baby be left alone with her. Irina refused to allow it; the mother was a danger to her child as well as to herself.

She gave the clinic the restaurant number. She always let them know where she could be reached in an emergency. They telephoned in the middle of the dessert. She came back to the table and excused herself. Both her friends were women. They were partners in an art gallery that specialized in avant-garde paintings by young artists. Irina accepted their lesbian relationship without feeling threatened herself. They were intelligent and amusing companions and soon she would be leaving them forever. Without even saying goodbye. She had invited them to lunch as a silent farewell.

'I'm so sorry,' she said. 'It's an emergency. One of my patients has gone missing. Damned woman!'

She drove fast towards the clinic, her mood angry. She had no sympathy for the rich, spoiled girl who'd walked out of her room and disappeared. Her frantic husband had gone to visit her and found the empty bed and her nightgown on the floor. Mercifully the new baby was in a special room with a maternity nurse. They were searching the clinic in case the mother was hiding somewhere. She hadn't been seen leaving the building.

Irina jerked her car to a stop in her reserved bay and hurried up the steps into the main hall. The receptionist called out to her as she went to the lift.

'Excuse me, Doctor. There's a package for you. Vera's not back from lunch, so I kept it at the desk.'

'Damn Vera,' Irina said under her breath. Taking extra time off because I wasn't in till late this afternoon. I'll have a word to say to her when she gets back. She took the envelope and stepped into the lift.

It was special delivery. She tore it open. Dimitri's passport was inside. She pressed the third-floor button to go to her office, and put the passport away before she went down to her patient's room and the distraught Italian husband. No Vera, she noted furiously, striding across the empty office, ignoring the fact that it wasn't even two o'clock. She felt like punishing someone because her lunch was interrupted. She saw the key in her door and lost her temper. Now that was inexcusable. To forget to lock her private office *and* leave the key in the lock.

'I'll sack her for that,' she said out loud. 'As soon as she comes back, I'll tell her she's sacked!'

She opened the door and froze. A woman was going through

her desk. Not her errant secretary; she was plump and dark. The intruder was blonde; her hair shone in a shaft of subdued sunlight from the slatted blind. She was bending down, absorbed in what she was doing.

Irina was startled, but she wasn't afraid. People didn't frighten her. She was used to controlling them. She stepped in to the room on the soft carpet and said loudly in French, 'What the hell do you think you're doing?'

Lucy jerked upright. She stood rooted staring at the woman. She didn't answer. The drawer held various Russian documents and certificates, Lucy had discovered Irinia's passport, but there was no sign of Volkov's.

'Who are you,' Irina demanded. 'What are you doing in my office?'

It must be a patient, she thought, wandering about and creeping in to steal something. The emergency button to summon help was by the desk, under the ledge. She moved closer to Lucy. Then she saw the drawer that was open and knew this was no ordinary thief. She made a quick lunge across the desk for the call button. Instinctively, Lucy grabbed at her wrist.

'You rotten little spy,' Irina hissed at her in Russian. 'You'll pay for this, whatever you're up to.'

She wrenched herself free, and aimed a blow at Lucy with all her weight behind it. It sent Lucy reeling backward. She stumbled and fell to her knees. Irina reached the button and pressed hard.

'We have people here,' Irina said, in French this time, 'who know how to deal with people like you.'

Blind terror washed over Lucy like a wave. And from that terror she drew unexpected strength. She propelled herself forward and grappled with Irina. For a moment or two she was the stronger, but not for long. The other woman had one hand on her throat and she was squeezing brutally. Any second now, the door would open and she'd be seized.

'You bitch,' Irina spat at her. 'I'll have you in a strait-jacket.'

There was a box on the desk, just within reach. Lucy grabbed for it; she was choking with the grip on her throat. She slammed it down as hard as she could on her opponent's head.

Cigarettes scattered everywhere. The fingers gripping her wind-

141

pipe slackened and Irina slumped backwards against the desk and slid to the ground. Her mouth was open and her eyes had rolled back.

Lucy was sobbing, getting her breath. She stumbled across the floor to the door and kicked something. She saw it lying at her feet, half out of the opened envelope. Dark background with a red hammer and sickle in the centre. She stooped and picked it up. Volkov's wife had dropped it in their struggle.

It was Dimitri's passport. Her heart was pounding and her head felt light; she thrust the passport into her blouse and closed the door behind her. The key was still in it. She locked it. *She is dead*, Lucy said to herself. *I hit her so hard I killed her.* She put the key in her pocket and walked into the corridor. She saw the bright-red arrow of the lift ascending. No time to use the stairs. She ran to the emergency exit door and pushed the bar to open it.

Outside she found herself at the top of a fire escape. The ground dipped and swayed beneath her; she felt dizzy and clung to the rails, forcing herself to go down, to keep looking up, away from the void below.

At last her feet touched the ground. She was at the rear of the clinic. Thank God she'd locked the door. They couldn't get in and find the dead woman until they got another key or broke the door down. She had time to get to her car, to make her escape.

The engine coughed and wouldn't start. She tried again; it sulked, spluttering. A third time. When she was about to abandon it, and get out and run, it fired. She put it in to gear and eased out of the space, willing herself not to rush, not to panic.

On the Quay Gustav Ador, she overshot two traffic lights; cars hooted furiously at her. Her throat was still painful where the other woman's fingers had dug in to her. She banished the horrible image from her mind; the contorted face, the eyes rolling back as Irina fell after the blow to her head. The cigarettes scattered all around the floor.

Nausea welled up in her; she fought it down, forcing herself to concentrate on the road, to hang on until she saw the street sign Chemin de la Tourelle. There was the apartment block. She was home. She was safe.

Dimitri opened the door and she fell into his arms. 'I've got your passport. Oh Dimitri, your wife found me in her office. We fought and I hit her . . .' Lucy burst into tears.

'You're crazy. How could you have taken such a risk? My darling, please stop shaking.'

Volkov held her close; marvelling at her selfless courage even as he reproached her.

'I killed her,' Lucy wept. 'I hit her so hard because she was choking me. Oh, darling, what have I done?'

'It doesn't matter,' he insisted. 'What terrifies me is what she would have done to you. You'd have been drugged, and locked up. God knows what lie she'd have made up to the staff, and they'd have believed her. I am so angry with you, Lucy, and I love you so much for doing it.'

Tears filled his eyes.

'What are we going to do?' she cried.

'The first thing is to find out what's happened,' he said gently.

'We've got to get away,' Lucy insisted. 'Pack a few things and get on a plane.' She held on to him. 'Where are you going?'

'To phone the clinic,' he said.

Lucy watched him. *He's wrong*, she thought. *He didn't see her face. The way she fell.* She heard him say, 'Doctor Volkova, please. It's her husband.' There was a pause, a long pause while he waited. 'What? But that's terrible! I'll come right over. How did it happen?' Lucy's heart gave a wild jump and started racing as she listened. 'Yes, of course. Thank God it wasn't worse. Thank you, thank you, doctor.' He hung up and turned to Lucy.

'She's not dead, my darling. But you did give her quite a blow. That was a doctor at the clinic. She's concussed and they're keeping her in overnight. She doesn't remember anything about what happened. Her secretary said some crank had tried to get an appointment and a woman came to the clinic pretending she knew the secretary. They think they're one and the same, and that she was responsible for the attack. Apparently, they've issued a description and it's in the hands of the police.'

Lucy said slowly, 'Thank God. I'm so relieved I only knocked her out.'

He put his arms around her. 'So am I,' he said. 'For your sake

143

rather than hers. But you're right, we have to leave at once. By the morning she'll remember. She'll be able to describe you properly. The receptionist was vague. We have to leave today, Lucy. Before Irina realizes that I've gone and my passport is missing.'

'We can fly to London,' she said. 'And then get a plane to Jersey.'

Volkov picked up the passport and flipped through it. He looked at her with a frown. 'No, we can't. Unfortunately. I didn't think. I told you, I've been moved around like a parcel. I have no visa. I can't get into England without one. I'd be stopped and deported. My wife's friends in the KGB would be happy to escort me home to Russia.'

'Oh, Volkov! It was all for nothing! Why didn't I think of it?' She sank back in despair. 'I thought all I had to do was get you a valid passport and we'd be safe.'

He said gently, 'I didn't think of it either. We're like children playing grown-up games. We don't even know the rules. Me with all that fine talk about liberating the Ukraine, and I can't even remember about a visa. It's my fault, not yours, sweetheart.'

He reached out for her hand. 'But we're not going to be beaten. We can't fly, but we can go by car. We can travel from Switzerland to France. It's all very casual these days at the frontier. Then we'll think of a way to get to Jersey. Come on, it's time to pack.'

Lucy got up. 'I love you,' she said. 'And you're wrong about us. We're not children and I'd say we're learning the rules pretty quickly. You may have noticed I'm not shaking any more!'

They packed her clothes and his few belongings, pyjamas, shaving kit, a change of shirt. His experience was useful. If you expect to be arrested, you clear out everything that might give a clue or be used to incriminate you. Volkov scoured the flat clean of their presence, down to the last crumb in the kitchen cupboard and a twist of make-up-stained tissue in the waste basket. No rent was owing. Lucy had paid in advance. She left cash for the telephone, erring in favour of overpayment, and put it in an envelope by the phone.

At last they had her suitcases strapped up and were ready to drive away from the little haven they had shared.

At the door, Lucy paused and looked back. 'We were so happy here,' she said. 'I'll never forget this place.'

'Maybe one day we'll come back,' Volkov said, taking her by the arm. 'No more time, darling. We must hurry.'

He threw the luggage into the boot of her hired car and helped her into the front seat. He bent and kissed her quickly.

'We'll be in France in about twenty minutes,' he said.

She looked up at him. 'You're sure we won't be stopped?'

'My wife used to go across regularly. She said they only look at the car's registration number. If it's Swiss or French they don't usually bother.'

The car started first time for Volkov. He put it in gear and they were on their way.

The Renault in front was halted at the French border. Lucy felt her heart leap, but they were waved through. Volkov smiled at her, squeezing her hand. It felt cold.

'Our luck is holding, my darling,' he said. 'I told you we'd be all right.'

He'd mapped out a route for them, and given it to her to follow. It would take two hours or more to reach the Auto-Route du Soleil on the long way to Paris. He hadn't thought further than that and he didn't want to worry Lucy more than he had to.

As they passed through the town of Issèrre, spots of rain spat on to the windscreen. The sky had darkened and thunder rolled in the west. They were on a main road, wide, well signposted. The rain came lashing down.

'Try and sleep,' he said. 'We've a very long way to go.'

She looked pale and tense. 'I'll try, but I don't think it'll work,' she said.

The conditions were horrible, the visibility poor, but the traffic was light. Which was why he noticed the Peugeot.

It didn't come close or overtake. It was a faster car than their small Renault. Volkov changed gear and increased his speed. He watched in the driving mirror. The Peugeot accelerated, its wipers flashing at double rate against the driving rain. He was being deliberately foolhardy. There was no reason for the driver of the Peugeot to copy him.

'We're learning the rules,' Lucy had said, before they set out.

But there were some rules he knew better than she ever would. And he hadn't forgotten them.

He might have forgotten about needing a visa because he'd developed the prisoner mentality, so common among people who were never permitted to travel. You didn't know what you would never need to know. But he remembered very clearly what it felt like to be followed. They'd followed him for years when he was politically active.

He looked up at the mirror once more and saw the car behind him, keeping the same distance, the rain spurting fanwise from its front wheels. For a moment the old fear ran through him, the fear associated with that word of infinite menace. *They*.

He'd been allowed to cross the border. Was there another car ahead, waiting to pull out and sandwich them with the Peugeot coming up behind? He knew the technique. A half-empty road, a forced halt. A quick struggle and it was over.

He had to make absolutely sure, but he didn't want to alarm Lucy.

He said, 'I'm going to pull in at the next layby. I want to check the rear tyre.'

He stopped the car, but left the temperamental engine idling. Lucy had told him about her desperate moment when the car refused to start outside the clinic. There was nothing wrong with any of the tyres. He walked round the back of the car and busied himself with the boot. The Peugeot drove past. He waited, seeing it well out of sight down the straight road. A few more cars sped by. He climbed back in.

Lucy said, 'Everything all right? Oh, darling, you're soaked. Here, take your jacket off.'

Ten minutes later they passed the Peugeot. Within fifteen minutes he spotted it again in his rearview mirror, lurking behind a large French container lorry. He laid a hand on Lucy's knee and said,

'We're being followed.'

He heard her gasp. 'I stopped to make sure. They passed us, waited for us to catch them up and they're behind us again.'

'Who is it? Oh, Volkov. Is it the police?'

146

'Not the police, no. We'd have been stopped long ago. There's a turn-off two miles further on. Sit tight. I'm going to lose them.'

He swung off the main road without signalling. The road ahead was narrow; a signpost flashed past them, too quickly for Lucy to read it. Behind them, the Peugeot veered into view, skidding slightly on the wet road.

A right-hand fork appeared suddenly; Volkov took it, the Renault's tyres screeching. A rapid gear change gave them speed on the corner and he sat bent over the wheel, concentrating fiercely on the road through the sheets of rain.

'For God's sake,' Lucy muttered.

'Shut your eyes if you're scared.'

She was clinging to the seat with both hands. A hill loomed ahead of them. They went up and down as if they were on a roller-coaster. An isolated house was on their right, guarded by dark gloomy barns. Without any warning, Volkov braked so hard she was thrown forward against her seatbelt.

'Sorry, darling,' he said. 'I only just saw it.'

It was a farm track, little more than a rough pathway across the fields. They bumped over the potholes and stones and then Volkov reversed the car, facing the way they'd come.

'We'll see them from here,' he said. 'They won't see us, it's nearly dark.'

She managed a shaky laugh. 'You didn't tell me you were a racing driver!'

He slipped his arm round her. 'I used to enjoy playing the fool in a car when I was young,' he said. 'Country roads like this, no traffic. It was an old car, but I had a friend who worked in an engineering factory and he fiddled with it till it could go quite fast. We saved up for it together. He hit a tree and that was the end of the car. He wasn't hurt, but I was a fully fledged professor before I could afford another. We've lost them. Nothing's passed.'

'If it wasn't the police, who were they?' Lucy asked.

'I assumed it was a KGB trap,' Volkov admitted. 'One following, one ahead. But they didn't know I was leaving. How could they? I don't think I would have got away from the KGB so easily. I don't know who it was, but I know we were being tailed. But now, we get back on the road. Let me look at the map and

147

see where we go to rejoin the main road to the auto-route. Do you mind driving through the night?'

'I don't mind anything so long as we're safe,' she said. 'When you're tired, I can take over.'

They reached the auto-route du Soleil and settled down to a steady ninety kilometres an hour. The little car had served them well, despite its temperamental starting mechanism, and he didn't want to stress the engine. Lucy slept after the first few hours, and woke with a start from a nightmare where she was being chased and her feet were weighed down with heavy, heavy shoes.

Volkov stopped at an all-night café. 'We can stretch our legs and have some coffee and something to eat, but we'd better keep going,' he said. 'Of course, I haven't any money. I'm so hopeless you should have left me behind!'

'I needed a driver,' she said, and managed to smile at him. 'I can change some Swiss francs.'

The coffee was strong and they were both hungry. It was self-service, presided over by a bored cashier. Three other late-night drivers were eating sandwiches and drinking beer. They glanced up without much interest at the couple who came in. Their lorries were parked outside.

Lucy paid for the coffee and the rolls full of ham and cheese. The cashier grumbled about changing Swiss money, but made a calculation that was to his advantage on the rate.

'I can drive,' she offered. She still looked pale, with deep shadows under her eyes.

Volkov shook his head. 'You sleep tonight and drive tomorrow. It's auto-route all the way to Paris. Now settle down and go to sleep. But kiss me first.'

She put her arms up and held him close to her. He kissed her slowly, with great tenderness, gently exploring her mouth.

'You're a wonderful girl, Lucy. You know that was a brand new passport? Issued from the Embassy. You know what you saved me from by that crazy thing you did today? They were going to take me back to Russia.'

She broke away and stared at him. 'They couldn't. You wouldn't have gone!'

'I wouldn't have had any choice,' he said slowly. 'They'd have left it to Irina to arrange that.' He silenced her with another kiss, and gathered her to him.

'Now put your head back and shut your eyes. No more excitement for tonight. I'll wake you and we'll stop somewhere for breakfast. Now sleep, my darling.'

Slowly Irina reached up and touched her head; the windows were shaded and the room was in semi-darkness. The headache was thunderous. She felt nauseous. There was a dressing over a large lump; when her fingertips made contact she winced. Gradually her eyes became accustomed to the dim light and to her surroundings. She was in bed in a private room in the clinic. In spite of the pounding in her head she tried to concentrate. The day before was a blur; it had been a complete blank. Concussion, she diagnosed. I've been concussed. I still am, that's why there's no light to hurt my eyes. I've had an accident. Hit my head. There should be a bell within reach to summon a nurse. With her other hand she groped and found the switch. She pressed. An accident. A fall. No, not a fall. The sudden movement as she started to remember caused an agonizing throb of pain and she froze. The door opened and a nurse came in to view.

'Doctor?'

Irina focused on her; her sight was clear now.

'I need painkillers,' she said. 'What happened to me?'

'Do you remember anything? Doctor Rodier said you weren't to try too hard, just let it come by itself.'

'I know how to treat concussion.' Irina croaked at her. She couldn't raise her voice. 'Just tell me what happened.'

The nurse hesitated. 'You were attacked,' she said at last. 'Someone broke into your office. They struck you on the head and left you locked inside. You don't remember any of it? I'll call Doctor Rodier.'

The nurse hurried out. She didn't want the responsibility. X-rays showed there was no serious damage to the skull, but Dr Volkov had remained unconscious for some time after the door had been finally broken down.

Attacked. *Yes*, Irina whispered inwardly. *Yes, that's what hap-*

pened. A woman. A woman stealing from my desk . . . Unconsciously one hand became a claw reaching for the other's throat.

The image came and went, but it was sharper, the fuzz was clearing round the edges. Blonde hair in the sunlit shaft coming through the blind. That's how she knew it wasn't Vera.

Vera who? Vera her secretary. She was struggling to reach the bell under her desk top. They were grappling, and she'd got her hand on the woman's windpipe, holding her off, squeezing.

Then nothing. Blackness, blankness.

'Good morning, Irina. How are you feeling?'

She opened her eyes and saw Rodier standing by the bed with the nurse hovering behind him.

'Terrible, thank you. How bad is it?'

'Not too bad. How's the memory?'

'I can remember finding a woman in my office. We struggled, then nothing.'

'She hit you with the cigarette box,' he explained. 'Very hard; I was worried about a hairline fracture, but luckily it was just a bad lump. We kept you sedated and put you to bed here. Can you describe the person who did it? We have a vague description, but if you saw her close up and could tell us, it would help the police. But only if it comes easily. You know you mustn't strain to remember.'

'I know,' she muttered. 'She was blonde, quite young. Thin, not heavy. She didn't speak. The blinds were partly drawn. It all happened so quickly.' And she had opened my locked drawer where I keep my private papers, but I'm not going to mention that. 'Was anything stolen?' she asked.

'Nothing that we know of,' the doctor answered. 'Your secretary checked and everything was there. Your passport, some money, a diary.'

Passport. The word danced behind her closed eyelids. Her passport. No, that wasn't taken. Why did passport mean something when it hadn't been stolen? The headache seemed to split her skull.

'You husband telephoned,' she heard the doctor say. 'He was very concerned. He said he was coming over.'

'I don't remember,' Irina said.

150

'He didn't show up,' the doctor said. 'We telephoned your apartment, but there was no reply. We thought he'd call in again or come over. I tried myself this morning, in case you were fit enough to go home, but still no answer.'

'He's drunk,' Irina mumbled. 'He'll be sleeping it off somewhere.'

'I'm sorry,' the young man said. 'I didn't know.'

'A shock would start him off,' she said, more to herself than to him. 'I knew it wouldn't be long before he went back to it. If only I could get some relief from this headache . . .'

'Nurse has got something for you. Sleep for a couple of hours and then see how you feel. You won't be going home, Irina, especially if your husband's not able to look after you. Just relax, take the tablets and don't worry. I'll come back and see you this afternoon.'

She managed to swallow the pills with sips of water. The nurse smoothed the bedcovers. Irina could have screamed at her to go away and stop fiddling, but it hurt even to whisper. Passport. The word was running through her consciousness like a tune without a title. Her passport. No, not hers. And then the answer came to her. It came as the drug took control and she began to slide away.

Ten minutes later the nurse checked on her. She was in a deep sleep. The hand reaching out for the bell had fallen slackly over the edge of the bed.

It was late afternoon and the nurse had gone off duty. When the bell rang again the new nursing sister hurried to answer it. She found Irina Volkova sitting up in bed, the bell switch gripped hard between her fingers.

'Have you seen the papers?'

'No,' Peter Müller said. 'I came straight from the shop. Why?'

Eloise Brückner handed him the Munich *Zeitung*, open at the second page. It was a small paragraph.

'That woman was attacked,' she said. 'Knocked out by someone who broke in to her office.'

'What woman?' he asked. He wasn't really interested. He was aware only of Eloise sitting next to him, with her legs crossed at the knee, one delicate ankle encircled by a thin gold chain. He couldn't stop glancing at it, and the foot in its black silk court shoe with the very high heel, swinging to and fro, making the erotic little chain glint.

'That doctor who treated Adolph,' Eloise said impatiently. Müller stopped thinking about the foot, the ankle, the long leg and what lay hidden out of sight under her skirt.

'Doctor Volkov?'

'Yes,' she said. There was triumph in her voice. 'Here, read it.'

He took the evening newspaper and skimmed quickly through the story. A woman intruder. That was unlikely. The doctor was knocked unconscious during a struggle. Even more suspicious.

People like Irina were trained to deal swiftly with a violent patient.

'Who could have done it?' he wondered.

'Perhaps one of her patients came back to give her a taste of her own vicious medicine,' Eloise snapped.

She had developed an implacable hatred for Adolph's doctor. Irina was judged and found guilty before she was tried, Müller thought. He was surprised by the depth of Eloise's vindictiveness. And excited by it, too. He titillated himself with thoughts of her applying that cruelty to him. He'd never tried that variation before. He had always dominated in bed, as he intended to dominate her. But a role reversal might be interesting to start off with.

He shrugged and passed the newspaper back. It sounded as if Irina was setting herself up for the planned return to Moscow, ahead of the Brückner lawyers. For medical treatment after the assault. It was an old ruse, but useful.

'It says she suffered a concussion, but nothing serious,' he remarked. 'The police are looking for the woman. Never mind about that, my dear. I've been looking forward to seeing you so much. You're looking so much better, you know.'

He leaned closer and lightly touched her hand. He let the contact lengthen; she didn't move away.

'I'm fine,' she said. 'Thanks to you, and all my friends. You know, Peter, everyone's been so good to me. I knew people thought so highly of Adolph. He was so clever, so successful, but I never realized they cared about me, too.'

He slipped his fingers round her palm and held it comfortingly. 'You underestimate yourself. You're beautiful, charming and intelligent. And warm. Adolph was admired – he was quite awe-inspiring, too. But you are loved.'

'The children have been very brave,' she said. She let him hold her hand. He was so kind, so steady. There was nothing sexual, she told herself. Just a warm hand holding hers.

'You're sure you won't let me take you out to dinner? It would do you good,' he suggested again.

'No, no.' She shook her head and the rich scent flowed towards him . . . But we can have a quiet dinner here, if you don't mind. If you won't be bored?'

It was a little flirtatious, she admitted that. But pleasing men was second nature to Eloise. She smiled and she lifted her eyelids at a man in a way that conveyed how attractive and interesting he was. It was a harmless habit and besides, she liked Peter Müller. He had beautiful, strong white teeth.

He squeezed her hand for a moment and then let it go. 'You know I'm never bored when I'm with you. Now why don't I pour us a drink?'

'Friedrich can do it,' she said.

'I think I can manage,' he said, getting up. He didn't want the Brückner's butler coming in and out. He wanted her mellow with wine before dinner, and then he would advance a few more steps. Good food – they kept a marvellous table – more wine, and perhaps a little brandy.

An arm along the back of the sofa that could lightly rest upon her shoulders, a casual pressure of his thigh against hers. Instant retreat if she signalled he was going too far. He wasn't going to rush this. Planning her seduction was an excitement in itself. He would be patient, stalk her carefully right up to the bedroom door.

He poured Moselle for her, brushed fingers as he handed her the glass and looked into her eyes. He drank Scotch whisky. She once said she liked the smell. She was the kind of woman who convinced herself that she liked all the rich smells associated with men. Brandy, cigars. She told men this, with the lift and flutter of the eyelashes that was her trademark.

She used it now as she said, 'It's so sweet of Susan to spare you tonight. I do hope she doesn't mind lending you for just one dinner. I've got so many problems at the moment.'

'Of course not,' Peter Müller said. 'She's gone to see some Polish art film. You know the kind of thing, all black shadows and gloom. She's gone with a friend who likes that stuff. I couldn't sit through it. I like to be entertained, to be happy. And *you* must be happy, my dear. Adolph wouldn't want you shutting yourself away. All right, we dine here tonight and I'll help with any problems you want, but next time we go to the Hofburg!' He named the best restaurant in Munich.

Eloise smiled. 'Just the three of us – that would be lovely.'

'Just the three of us,' he echoed. He didn't mind. He knew she didn't mean it.

Dinner was excellent, as he anticipated. Eloise was an accomplished hostess and Adolph had expected perfection in his home. Looking round at the elegant dining room, waited on by the unobtrusive Friedrich, Peter Müller wondered what it would be like to live on such a scale, with so much money to make life as smooth as silk.

He and Susan lived well; their two sons in America wanted for nothing, but this lifestyle was majestic by comparison. He put the fleeting temptation aside, surprised that it had even occurred to him. He loved his sons and was fond of his wife. His plans were laid for retirement. Money and a house in the Caribbean sunshine – more than most spies, however successful, could dream of achieving at the end of their careers.

He was going to take Adolph's place in bed, but not at the head of his table by marrying the widow. No, that was a foolish fantasy, impractical. He set out to be amusing; he had a fund of anecdotes, some about people Eloise knew well. They were funny without being malicious. She laughed and encouraged him. He thought she looked maddeningly attractive, and emboldened by the fine claret, pressed his knee against hers under the table. She let it rest for longer than she should have done and then moved slightly away.

'A wonderful dinner,' he declared as they left to take their coffee in her sitting room. 'As always; you spoil me, Eloise. Now

I want to spoil you in return. I want you to unload all your problems on me and let me take care of them. If I can.'

'That would be wonderful,' she said.

He followed his plan, eased himself down beside her on the cushioned sofa and slid his arm along the back behind her. Her hair was drawn back, skilfully arranged to fall in loose waves from a gold clasp. It brushed the back of his hand.

'My real problem is dear Adolph's collection,' she said.

He smiled at her. 'Which collection? His pictures? The porcelain? There's so much, such priceless things.'

'I know,' she sighed. 'It'll take months and months to settle the estate. He was even richer than I thought. No, I shall keep the house exactly as it was; he'd want me to do that. What worries me is his Russian collection. It worries the lawyers, and the insurance company were always fussing about keeping it in a private house. The burglar-alarm system is a nightmare, just because of them. All those boxes and objects, and the early jewellery. Apart from the desk set. As you know, Peter, that's unique. Not another like it in the world!'

'I do know,' he said. 'Clocks and calendars, but not a matching set with the Imperial provenance.'

He had stopped thinking lewd thoughts; his mind was concentrated on what might be a perfect opportunity to obey Viktor Rakovsky's order.

'They say,' Eloise went on, 'that the value of the Russian works of art could make quite a difference to the total outcome, after taxes. And I must admit, I find the restrictions very boring. They're suggesting that I have a permanent security guard on duty, day and night, apart from an alarm system that would be more suitable to the Bundesbank than a private house! They wouldn't have dared lay down conditions like that to Adolph.'

'You mustn't let them take advantage of you,' he said.

The steel flashed behind the velvety eyes. 'Don't worry, I won't! They're not going to dictate to me just because Adolph's dead. In fact, the lawyers suggested something and I'm beginning to think it's a solution. It would put the insurers in their place as well. I want to ask you what you think of it.' She turned and looked at him. 'Why don't I give the Russian collection to the

Munich Museum of Fine Arts in Adolph's memory? The Adolph Brückner Bequest. Don't you think it sounds rather nice? Wouldn't he like that?'

Müller's expression of concern was only too genuine.

'My dear Eloise – I don't know. Let me think a moment.' It was worth trying, but he didn't have high hopes. 'From the moral point of view,' he said slowly. 'There is an alternative. Everything Adolph bought was effectively stolen.'

'Peter! You're not suggesting? . . .' She flushed with indignation.

'No. No, my dear, of course I'm not linking Adolph with what I've just said. Let me explain what I mean. All those treasures were part of Russia's heritage. They were bartered for Western currency, sold by families desperate for money to buy food. Looted, smuggled out. It's one of the ugliest stories in the art world. I remember an old friend saying it was the rape of Russia's heritage.'

'But you dealt in those things yourself,' she protested. 'Two of our gold boxes came from you. The one from Catherine the Great to Potiemkin and the other one, the Orlov snuff box!'

'I know,' he said gravely. 'I was no better than anyone else. But I have thought about it ever since my old friend said that. Eloise, why don't you do something remarkable in Adolph's memory?'

'What?' she said coldly.

'Give the whole collection back to the people of Russia. It would cause a sensation. And set a great precedent.'

She didn't hesitate. She stared at him and he knew what the answer was going to be.

'I wouldn't dream of it,' she said. 'Adolph hated the Communists. Certainly *not*, Peter.'

No easy solution to his problem, he thought. He forgot about sex; he was angry instead. Nothing showed on his face.

'If that's how Adolph felt, you're right, of course,' he said. 'But don't be rushed in to giving such a priceless collection away till you've had plenty of time to think about it. The museum will accept it, no doubt about that. They'll jump at such an offer! I'm just wondering whether there's any connection between your lawyers and the museum itself? They don't act for the governing body, by any chance?'

'I don't know,' Eloise frowned. It was a point Adolph would have made. He checked out everything. Check first and trust afterwards, he used to say to her.

Müller pressed the advantage. 'It might be wise to find out,' he said. 'Would you like me to make some enquiries?'

'Yes,' she said. 'Yes, if you can, that would be most helpful. If they are trying to use me to get something for the museum, then I shall think of something else. It doesn't have to be Munich.'

'You know, I haven't had a look at the things for a long time,' Müller remarked. 'I'd like to see everything again, refresh my memory. Then maybe I can advise you better. That's if we're not going to set off the alarm system!'

Eloise's mood had lifted. She laughed.

'We'd have half the police force here in a few minutes if we did,' she said. 'It's connected to all major stations throughout the city.'

Steal it if you have to. Müller wished Viktor Rakovsky to a special place in hell. Let Moscow Centre try and organize a burglary and see what happened.

'All right,' she said, 'Let's look at it together. I haven't been into the room since Adolph died. I just went through the catalogues with those damned lawyers. He was so methodical, he kept everything documented and photographed. I wonder whether they *weren't* trying to get it for the museum. They have a lot of government work.'

Müller had sowed the dragon's teeth of doubt. Munich Museum of Fine Arts was unlikely to benefit now. Suspicion was inherent in the super rich. He followed Eloise out of the sitting room – she called it her boudoir, which he thought an affectation – and along the wide corridor towards the big first-floor room where the Brückners held their parties and the guests were able to admire his Russian art collection.

In the corridor, Eloise paused by a console table; a superb bluejohn vase with Louis XVI ormolu mounts was in the centre. An identical table and matching vase was a few yards further on.

'This is the first switch,' she said. 'There are three on this floor, just for the ballroom.'

She stopped by the table and pressed a carved and gilded flower head. It depressed a fraction.

'That turns the first part of the system off,' she explained.

'How clever,' Müller remarked. He had noted the flower head carefully. Third on the left of a larger floral carving. 'Very ingenious.'

'Adolph's idea,' she smiled at him. 'He was so inventive. Now, it's the same here, only on the other side.'

She pressed another carved and gilded flower head on the second table. Third on the right of the larger flower group this time. He followed her as they approached the green-and-gold-painted double doors leading to the ballroom.

Eloise paused and said, 'This is the last; it clears the system completely so we can open the door.'

Müller stopped. He said, 'My dear, I don't think you should let anyone know what it is. Even me. I'll turn my back.'

'Oh Peter, don't be so silly!' She was herself again, fluttering the melting look at him. 'It's so brilliant I want you to see it. You know that's one of the reasons I loved Adolph so much. He had the most amazing brain. Look!'

It was a bronze elephant clock, complete with gilded howdah, and the clockface on its back. Eloise opened the glass case and adjusted the minute hand until both golden hands were on the twelve numeral. The clock chimed the hour.

'Isn't that genius?' she demanded. 'There's no clock mechanism in there, just the final switch for the ballroom system.'

'Supposing someone moved the bronze?' Müller asked.

'They couldn't,' she said. 'it's bolted to the table and the table is secured to the floor. Now we can open the doors and go in.'

He remembered the first time he had come there, his first coveted invitation to the home of one of the richest men in West Germany. A client of enormous potential if he managed to hook him.

Eloise switched on the lights. The room was flooded with a soft illumination, cleverly directed at the Gobelin tapestries that lined one wall. He glanced up.

'Ah,' he said, and meant it. 'How beautiful that is!'

Brückner had bought the painted ceiling from Italy and had it fitted. Tiepolo no less, before the artist had commanded the fortune of the present day, but still a great deal of money, even twenty years ago, when Brückner renovated the old mansion and started filling it with treasures.

Together they walked across the carpet; a splendid Second Empire Aubusson which was always rolled up for the parties. At the far end, specially lit, Adolph Brückner's collection of Russian works of art sparkled in a glass display case. It always excited Müller to see them.

'They are lovely,' Eloise murmured beside him as they stood and admired. 'Perhaps I should keep them. Adolph left it up to me to decide what to do with everything.'

There were the two gold and jewelled boxes Müller had sold him at a staggering profit, considering he had bought them from someone facing criminal charges, and desperate for cash. The early Byzantine pendants and a necklace that had graced some medieval nobleman's wife. Two fifteenth-century icons set in beaten silver, studded with amythest and quartz. Rarity was what Brückner valued more than gems and gold. A pair of rock crystal goblets engraved with the cipher of Peter the Great. Boxes, portrait miniatures and then in a section of its own in the centre of the display, the works of Carl Fabergé in the high days of Tsarist glory.

'I think he's my favourite,' Eloise said, one slim finger directed at a toad made of nephrite, its bulging eyes two big ruby cabochons, surrounded by a ring of diamonds. Diamonds formed the wide mouth so that the little creature seemed to grin with light.

'He's got such a naughty look,' she said.

Müller smiled. He thought that if he'd had the choice, it wouldn't be the toad snuff box, but the marvellous box in yellow and white opal enamel, with the unhappy Nicholas II's cipher and crown, and the Imperial eagles in diamonds and black enamel.

By comparison, the desk set was almost modest. It had the place of honour because, as he'd said earlier, it was unique. Designed and made as a present from the emperor for his niece.

A Christmas gift, since the Easter feast was celebrated by the exchange of eggs and was more important in the orthodox calendar. They gleamed watery green, with the diamonds like frost, sparkling under the light.

He stood for a moment in silence. In his imagination he saw Brückner stuffing them in to his pockets, wrapped in the clothing of the woman he had raped, while his companion murdered her.

God knows how she had got hold of them, he thought. Or how the greatest treasure of all, St Vladimir's Holy Cross, came to be hidden in a humble farmhouse in the Ukraine. For all those years Adolph Brückner had guarded his bloody loot and built his reputation as an art lover around it. The Grand Duchess Elizabeth, owner of the clock and the calendar, had been murdered by the Bolsheviks, like her uncle the Tsar. Like the woman in the house by the woods. In the end they had driven Brückner to near madness and death. It was no more than he deserved.

Müller caught Eloise by the elbow.

'Don't give anything to anyone, my dear,' he said. 'I was wrong to suggest what I did. Keep them; I'm sure that's what Adolph would have wanted. Let's go back, shall we?'

Outside in the corridor she said, 'I must reset the alarm. You see what I mean about it being a nightmare? And this is just one room!'

It worked in reverse. The elephant clock was set to twelve-thirty. Third gilded flower on the left of the first console table going the opposite way, third flower on the right of the second table. A light touch and not even a mouse could have scuttled through that ballroom without setting off the alarm all over the house – and the city.

'A brandy before you go?' Eloise offered.

Müller decided to abstain. 'It's late,' he said. 'Susan will be home by now.'

He thought he detected a flicker of disappointment on her face. No harm in that. He came close and took her hand in both of his. He kissed it and then lightly touched her cheek with his lips.

'I've had a wonderful evening. And, next week we are going to the Hofburg. I'll call you tomorrow. And you know, anything I can do for you – just ask. Give my love to the children.'

She crossed and rang the bell.

'Friedrich will show you out,' she said. 'Thank you for being such a dear friend. I look forward to our dinner.'

He drove home slowly, thinking. The sight of the desk set had emptied him of all desire. He was reminded of his priorities. He had to get it. His reward, as Viktor promised, would be commensurate. The Volkovs would soon be back in Russia. That part of his operation was closing down.

As he drew up outside his own apartment, he shut off the engine and sat there, thinking through to the future. He'd boasted to Irina that politicians come and go, but spies go on forever. He was in his early fifties. He had a thriving business, a good life by any standard. But his secret life was contracting as East/West tensions slackened. There would be less and less for him to do without the outlet at the Amtel clinic. And, therefore, less reason to go on, to take the occasional risk.

He didn't want to play the game part time. The risks were still there and the satisfaction alone wouldn't justify them. He would get Rakovsky the desk set, then retire before they retired him. It was a bonus that he could do it by way of Eloise Brückner's bed.

He drove the car into the garage reserved for residents and went up to his apartment. Susan was waiting. She hadn't gone to any cinema and she hated art films with subtitles. He had explained that he was going to see Eloise, in the hope she might be willing to sell him something. She came and kissed him in her brisk way.

'Any luck, darling?'

'I might get the two boxes back,' he lied. 'The Orlov one anyway. It's worth three times what he gave me for it.'

'She won't give you any bargain,' his wife said. 'That lady knows about money.'

Müller couldn't argue with that. 'So do I,' he said. 'Leave it to me. I'll get it out of her.'

They sat hand in hand and watched a late-night television movie. They were very companionable. The next morning the Swiss detective agency called to say that Dimitri Volkov and his companion had crossed over to France. Regrettably, their surveillance team had lost them.

4

The Soviet consul came to see her. He brought an assistant and it was the assistant who did all the talking. The consul introduced him.

'This is Vladimir Turin from the trade department,' he said.

Irina shook hands with him briefly.

'Please sit down,' she said.

She didn't offer them a drink. It wasn't a social visit. She had discharged herself from the clinic as soon as she heard about the empty envelope lying on her office floor and that Dimitri's passport had not been found. That, she concluded, must have been what the intruder was looking for. The implications were too serious to be concealed. She got back to her apartment and, with a vicious headache, managed to search through the cupboards. Nothing belonging to him was missing.

But the emptiness had a special quality she recognized. Real emptiness, not absence. There was a difference. He wasn't out, he was gone. She had felt so weak and sick that she was tempted to delay. To go to bed and sleep on it before she called the embassy. But that was failing in her duty. She had never failed. Except, she thought bitterly, when she fell in love with Dimitri Volkov.

The consular official was very understanding. This surprised her. He didn't express shock at what she told him. Later, with time to collect herself, Irina realized he knew already. She must rest, he insisted. Everything was in hand and he would come and see her the next day.

She wasn't surprised to see two of them when she opened the door.

'How are you feeling?' the young man called Turin asked her. She looked ghastly, with a dressing taped on top of her head.

'Better,' she said to the consul. 'Thank you for not coming last night. I'm much clearer this morning. Is there any news of my husband?'

Turin answered. 'He was heading for the border into France two nights ago,' he said. 'Unfortunately the surveillance team lost him.'

'Surveillance?' Irina looked up sharply. 'You were watching him? Why wasn't I told?'

'Not our people,' Turin corrected. 'Swiss private detectives. If it had been our operation, he wouldn't have got away.'

She put a hand to her head; she felt dizzy for a moment.

'Swiss detectives? I don't understand.'

'It was a routine precaution. Your husband was involved with a woman and Moscow wanted a low-key investigation. A private firm was chosen to do it.'

'A woman? You say he was involved with a woman?' She stared at them in turn. Two bright patches of colour blazed in her cheeks. The consul thought she looked very ill.

Turin proceeded without mercy. 'He'd been having an affair with her for some time. Meeting in secret, sleeping overnight in her apartment. She was with him when he escaped. A blonde woman, in her twenties.' He referred to a note he'd taken out of his pocket. He had flat brown eyes, deep-set like stones in his face. 'A similar description to the one you gave of your attacker,' he said.

'Yes,' Irina managed to speak.

'Obviously they planned to leave Switzerland and they had to get a passport for him. He couldn't travel through Europe without that. Did you mention returning to the Soviet Union to him at any time, Comrade Doctor?'

'No,' Irina made an effort to control herself. 'No, of course I didn't. He wouldn't have come. I'd planned another way of getting him there.'

Turin smiled. 'A sudden illness?'

'It's been done before,' she retorted. 'I had it all worked out. Excuse me for a moment.'

She left them and made her way to the bathroom. A woman. Sleeping with her, staying together overnight. She retched into the basin. She drank some water, splashed her face and dried it. Her reflection stared back at her, ashen, sunken-eyed, the mouth caught in a rictus of pain. Years of lying beside him, hungry for the love he couldn't give her. Bearing the taunts, the drunken emptiness. He had betrayed her with someone else. Slept with her. Made love as they used to make love long ago when they first met. Stolen afternoons, long nights when the dawn came before they tired.

Five years of living in exile, the price she'd offered to pay to save his life and win his freedom from the Gulag. She forced herself to stand up straight. She turned from that sorry sight in the glass and went back to the two men.

'Tell me about the woman,' she said curtly.

'I have no authority to go into details,' Turin sounded apologetic. 'Except to say that you are not being held responsible for what has happened. I can assure you of that. In fact,' he repeated the message received from his superiors that morning, 'in fact, the official view is very sympathetic to you, Comrade. Also,' he looked at his notes again. 'A reservation has been made for the Aeroflot flight out tomorrow morning at eleven o'clock. You'll go direct to Moscow.'

A scheduled flight, not a special plane. She understood the significance of that. She was going home, but not in disgrace.

'Will you let my family know?'

'Your father will be at Sheremetov to meet you and take you home,' Turin answered. 'Is there anything else we can do?' He turned, including the consul this time. 'You seem to be still groggy. We can send someone round to pack up for you.'

'That would be a help,' she said. 'I'm recovering every day. You know, I very nearly had her? I had my hand on her throat – a few seconds more and she'd have passed out. I'd got the carotid artery under my thumb.' She stopped.

Neither of the men spoke. The consul looked at his fingernails. Turin nodded to him and they stood up. They each shook hands.

'I'll collect you in the morning,' Turin said. 'We'll issue a short statement to the Press saying you are going home for a rest after your ordeal. It would be as well if you confirm this to the clinic director yourself.'

'I'll speak to him,' Irina promised. 'Let yourselves out, please.'

She lit a cigarette and put it out after a few puffs. She couldn't smoke. It tasted vile. The room was very quiet. Peaceful. She looked round it. Home for the last five years. It had never been home to her. She would leave it behind without a pang. She felt no attachment to the clinic or to the patients there any more. To her they all seemed to assume the identity of that damned Italian whose antics had dragged her from her lunch that day – into the office to find her husband's lover rifling through her private papers.

Her mouth filled with a bitter taste; the bile of jealousy almost choked her. He'd stopped drinking for that other woman. She'd noticed the change and had been too blind to guess the reason. How, where had he met her? On one of his endless, aimless walks, trying to kill time between drinks?

She closed her eyes to shut out the torture of imagining them together. Younger than she by at least ten years; surely she'd glimpsed bright blue eyes in that surge of violence between them?

'If he were here now,' she said out loud, 'I'd kill him.'

She started to cry and let the tears spill out and run down her face. So many tears she'd shed for him. When he was arrested, and she'd rushed from friend to friend, begging them to help, to use their influence. Her father, trying to comfort her and reproaching her at the same time: *I told you not to marry him. I warned you he was no good for you.*

The terrible anguish of seeing him in prison, hearing the rough consumptive cough and knowing that unless she did something, he would disappear into the Siberian wasteland and die. And the silent tears during the time they had lived together in that flat.

Seeing him turn from her, degrading himself by trying to escape in drink. Losing the man she had loved because Peter Müller had betrayed the deal she'd made to get him out of Russia.

Müller! Müller with his arrogance and his contempt for her husband. Opening his loud mouth as if the man sitting close by was no more sentient than a waxwork dummy. Dummy is what he'd called him to her once. Müller! She heaved herself up and sat by the telephone. She dialled the Munich number of his shop.

'Irina? How are you? I read about what happened.'

'I'm all right,' She kept her voice steady. 'Can you talk to me?'

'Yes, the place is empty at the moment. Anything urgent?'

She paused, masking the mouthpiece for a few seconds with her hand. Does he know? Is he pretending? Was he part of this surveillance without telling me? Her instinct urged her to attack, to tear down his defence.

'Volkov's disappeared,' she said.

He'd been prepared since he got the apologetic call from his detectives saying they'd lost the trail. He'd sent the news post-haste to Moscow Centre. Just twenty-four hours after his dinner with Eloise Brückner.

'My God,' he said.

'He had a woman, Peter,' she cut in on him. 'You knew about it, didn't you? Don't lie to me. You knew!'

He thought very quickly. Why should she guess? Viktor must have broken confidence and told her.

'Yes, I did know. I saw them in the street together. Viktor didn't want you upset. He told me to say nothing. Find out about her. But keep it low key. I got a Swiss firm to keep a watch on them.'

She cleared her constricted throat. 'Tell me about her.'

'Listen Irina, I know you're blaming me. I'd have told you, but Viktor wouldn't allow it. He said you are too valuable to be upset. His own words.'

'They were together for how long? Weeks, months? She's the one who broke in to my office and knocked me out. She stole Volkov's passport. It had just been renewed. We were summoned back to Moscow. I was to bring him with me. Like it or not, Peter. You understand?'

'Christ, yes,' he said.

He'd dismissed the story as a cover to get her out of Geneva before Eloise could bring a legal action, but it was true. The woman called Lucy Warren had gone to Irina's office, bashed her over the head and made off with Volkov's passport. He'd been right to alert Moscow when he discovered she was the daughter of a Ukrainian *emigré*, founder of an anti-Soviet organization that had international affiliations. They'd set off by car the afternoon of the attack on Irina. And lost the experienced Swiss tail after a hair-raising drive in the rain and darkness. He couldn't believe it when he heard that it was Volkov at the wheel.

'We'll find them, don't worry,' he said. 'We have the number of the car. They'll be tracked down. He can't get far without a visa.'

'No,' Irina said. 'He can't. If you'd told me instead of going to Viktor behind my back, I could have stopped it. I'm going to point that out when I get home. They don't hold me responsible. They've been very helpful, very sympathetic. You let him cheat on me and kept it to yourself. You kept it as a titbit to feed Viktor, didn't you? Getting yourself well in. Just wait till I get home! My father has some extremely influential friends.'

Müller said what he'd been longing to say to her for years.

'Why don't you go fuck yourself, Irina? No one else wants to.' He hung up on her.

She sat beside the telephone for some time. The headache was becoming less painful. She tried another cigarette; her hand trembled. The taste was still disgusting. No alcohol, she knew that. Stay quiet, rest. Apart from a mild concussion there's the element of shock. She went in to the kitchen and made herself a glass of tea. She concentrated upon being calm. She lay down on the bed and forced herself to breathe deeply, keep her eyes closed. She took her pulse at intervals. It steadied. At five o'clock the buzzer sounded from the street entrance.

A girl came up and said shyly that she'd been sent from the embassy to help her pack. She could, if the Comrade Doctor liked, make supper for her and stay the night. She was young and pleasant; she said she worked as a secretary. She wasn't KGB. Irina could scent them, however cleverly disguised.

167

Suddenly she was glad of the girl's company. She didn't want to be alone. Why not be looked after for a change? Have someone to talk to if she felt like it.

'You can stay, if it's no trouble,' she said.

'I'd be glad to. You must be feeling awful. What would you like me to do first?'

Her name was Elena and she said it was her first overseas posting. Irina tried to smile. No, not left alone in the flat on that last night. Someone to take care of her. To deal with the packing up of her life for the last five years.

'You could make us both some tea,' she said.

As they sipped it together, the girl said, 'You must be looking forward to going home. There's nowhere like it, is there?'

'No, there isn't,' Irina agreed. 'Russians aren't happy outside Russia.'

The girl looked away in embarrassment as the doctor's eyes filled with tears.

Colonel Leon Gusev was feeding the jig-saw pieces into his private computer. Names, dates, locations, questions, suppositions, possible answers and conclusions.

Yuri Warienski had been traced to the early records kept in the Ukraine, when all births and deaths were registered and lodged in a central filing system in Kiev, with duplicates for the state security in Moscow. Born in January 1930. Parents worked on a collective farm. The area was overrun by the German army in the attack on Smolensk. The civilians who had not escaped into the countryside were rounded up, the adults shot and the children sent back to Germany as slave labour. Warienski, Yuri, aged sixteen, was on the list of Ukrainian nationals rounded up at the camp at Spittal in 1945. No Ukrainians had been forcibly repatriated from that camp, except specific war criminals and members of the Ukrainian arm of the SS. A hundred and fifty out of ten thousand troops, and thousands of civilians. The Allies, with the Pope's connivance and the pleas of their Polish brothers, had snatched the rest from Soviet vengeance.

He ran through the notes on the criminals. A lot of information had been extracted from those who'd been returned. Their interrogations, the sentences; death by shooting on arrival, or deportation to the labour camps in the Arctic.

The name Yuri Warienski came up in the brief report on one man, Boris Malik, known to have served in the Einzatz commando, the SS death squads. One of his compatriots, hoping to save his own skin from the machine-gunners, accused him of being a homosexual, and cited his friendship with a young boy (Yuri) in the camp. Fifty years later the man's bellow of contempt rang in Gusev's ears. 'I buggered women, not boys! He was just a hungry kid!'

He had been condemned to death, along with his accuser. The name Warienski appeared on the Red Cross list of displaced persons in a camp in Rimini. Two years later, it appeared he had been issued with a set of papers and was allowed to settle in England under the guarantee of a Major Richard Hope. The same name as the officer in charge of selecting the war criminals at Spittal. Gusev found the pieces fitting, only to leave tantalizing gaps in the electronic puzzle he was putting together.

The murderous Boris Malik had befriended the boy. So had the English army officer, who got him to England and gave him a job. An interesting youth, this Warienski, to have attracted such diverse patrons. Perhaps the turncoat's charge of homosexuality was true.

The computer rejected this. No record of misdemeanour either at Spittal, in the DP camp at Rimini, or thereafter in England. He had been thoroughly investigated as an active anti-Soviet in the hope of finding something that could be used to discredit him. There was nothing. He married, had a daughter, Lucy Eileen, and remained on such good terms with his benefactor that Richard Hope left him his manufacturing business when he died. The computer flooded him with pieces for his puzzle after that.

Warienski, naturalized and known as Warren, had sold the business after a heart attack and moved to the Channel Islands to avoid punitive taxation in Socialist Britain. He had devoted the rest of his life to making trouble for his native country.

A founder of the Free Ukrainian movement in the British Isles; in close communication with other anti-Soviet organizations throughout the world. A tireless worker in the exposure of the Yalta Agreement and the fate of the Cossacks. He had organized a worldwide protest at the arrest and imprisonment of the dissident Dimitri Volkov in 1983. A large piece of the picture slotted into place.

Within a few days of his death, his daughter had gone to Geneva and made contact with the exile. That contact had become a liaison. All his careful conclusions were being proved right. There was a political conspiracy, as he told Viktor Rakovsky. Times had made such a move possible. There was unrest, instability, opposing factions fighting a last battle for the way Holy Russia should proceed. It was permissable to call it that, even applauded.

He rested. The computer screen was blank. He'd proved all the connections necessary, but he hadn't justified the extra time it had taken. By now they had pinpointed the venue for the anti-Soviet activists' meeting. The Makoff Galleries were run by the grandson of a Tsarist *emigré* who specialized in pre-Revolutionary art. The coming exhibition had alerted the London Embassy, and a man well known to them, Mischa Czernov, had visited the Makoff and asked for the use of the proprietor's flat above, during the reception. A rival gallery, specializing in Soviet art and on good terms with the embassy had obtained a copy of the guest list for the Makoff private view. There were some very interesting names there . . .

But it wasn't enough. He hadn't answered his own niggling doubt. His conclusion lacked the strength and depth to have real political significance. Volkov was Ukrainian, a dissident who'd suffered for his views. But he'd spent five years in idleness in Switzerland. He'd dropped out of the protest movement as effectively as if he were in the Gulag. More so, since many of those imprisoned there had continued to smuggle out messages and make their commitment known to the outside world.

It fitted, but it didn't fit tightly enough to satisfy him. He sighed. He couldn't go further. He decided to compile the information in a concise report and put it in front of his chief. Omitting nothing. Not a name, a date or an observation. He knew Rakovsky liked to analyze in depth for himself. He didn't appreciate synopses. Gusev's report was on Viktor's desk by the next afternoon.

It was followed within the hour by Peter Müller's urgent message sent via the Russian Embassy in Berlin, that Dimitri Volkov had left Geneva and vanished. His wife, Irina, was on her way back to Moscow.

Leon Gusev was there to meet her when the Aeroflot jet landed at Sheremetov Airport.

Lucy saw the signpost *Auberge des Brumes*, and slowed down. She had taken over from Volkov despite his protests and he had slept for the last four hours of their journey. It was monotonous driving, endless miles of auto-route at a steady cruising speed. It was very hot and dusty. She looked at him asleep in the seat beside her. The dark hair fell over his forehead and he had slipped down to lean against her.

She would never forget that feat of driving. He hadn't been afraid; he'd been exhilarated, full of daring. They were going to spirit him back to Russia. Pumped full of drugs, suffering from some 'illness' that his wife would certify, and flown home. Thinking of Irina Volkova made Lucy swallow, as if that steely grip was round her throat, the thumb seeking a pressure point while she choked for breath. If she'd faltered, not found the heavy box with her groping hand . . . she shivered.

A strait-jacket, Irina had threatened in Russian, not realizing she would be understood. Lucy would have been restrained, locked away as a violent patient who'd attacked the doctor. She would have been ignored when she protested. She would have been helpless, at the other woman's mercy.

And Volkov wouldn't have known what had happened. He'd thought she was going out to buy a new dress. He'd have waited, worrying, wondering and finally gone back to his apartment where his wife would have been ready for him. It was worse than the worst nightmare dredged up during the night. She felt cold with horror at what might have been.

It was almost six o'clock. She'd been at the wheel for so long she felt stiff. Auberge des Brumes. She slowed and followed the exit sign. It might be a motel. It might be shut, it might be anything, but she liked the name. The Inn of Mists. They were near the river.

They'd skirted Paris to the west and got on to the auto-route l'Oceane. They were aiming for the Normandy coast because they dared not risk trying to get through customs and immigration at Jersey airport. Their best hope was a sea crossing. It was vague enough and no details had been worked out. Fugitives don't plan, she realized. They run, as we are running, and trust their luck will hold.

Volkov stirred beside her, yawned and woke up.

'Where are we? What time is it? I've been asleep for hours.'

'You needed it,' she said. 'I've turned off the main road. We're going to have a soft bed to sleep in and something to eat. And a bath. Darling, that's the first thing I want – a hot bath!'

The hotel was small and heavily beamed, with an overhanging medieval upper storey, and it sat in a garden full of flowers.

'We can hide here for ever.' He kissed her cheek. 'We're husband and wife?'

'Mr and Mrs Warren,' she said. 'I'll fill out the registration cards. That's if they have a room.'

They had two vacancies the *propriétaire* said. She was tall and thin, quite the wrong type to appear in the dark little hallway as they went in. But she smiled and said they were lucky, not the best rooms, but she had one with single beds and one with the *matrimoniale*. . . . Both on the upper floor, one with a river view, the other looking down on to the garden.

Volkov spoke first. 'We will take the *matrimoniale*, Madame. The view is not important. And we'll have dinner later. Come on, darling. It's been a tiring day. We've driven all the way from Paris and it's so hot,' he explained.

The *propriétaire* smiled at him. She thought he looked a most interesting man, rather romantic. They got a lot of stodgy English and even stodgier Germans coming in off the auto-route.

'If you'll fill out the registration cards,' she said.

'I'll do that. You take the bags,' Lucy volunteered quickly.

'Upstairs and the fourth door on the left. Number seven. It's a nice room; you'll be comfortable. How many nights? It's not booked.'

Volkov paused with the suitcases, one foot on the stairs.

'Two nights, Madame. We're not in any hurry.'

The room was low, dark-beamed, with leaded windows that looked out over the deep flowing river. Volkov stretched out on the bed. The *matrimoniale* was not very wide.

'French people must be very small or they like lying very close together,' he remarked.

'Two nights?' Lucy shook her head. 'We can't.'

'Why not?' He locked his hands behind his head. 'Nobody knows we're here. Now go and have your bath. Then we'll make love before dinner!'

Afterwards, lying side by side in the little room, listening to the cry of seagulls swooping outside, he said to her, 'I feel so free. I can't explain it. You wouldn't understand, Lucy, my sweetheart, because you've never lived in a country where nobody is really free. I was in prison in Geneva, too; I'd made my own Gulag and sentenced myself to life. Till you came along. Now I'm so happy that I could die here tonight and not care, just because I've discovered what it feels like to be with you and to be a free man for the first time. So let me be a bit reckless? Don't scold me.'

'Only as long as you don't talk about dying. I wouldn't scold you about anything, my love. I want you to be happy, as happy as you can possibly be.'

She held his face in both hands and bent down to kiss him. His arms locked around her.

He murmured, 'I love your skin. Only witches have skin like yours.'

'We'll be late for dinner,' Lucy whispered in his ear.

'Yes,' he whispered back. 'We will.'

Madame gave them a table which looked out over the river. She had taken a liking to them. They were obviously in love. She smiled on them benignly as they held hands and gazed at each other. Outside, the ferry passed across their window, its lights dancing on the dark surface of the river.

The food was delicious in the simple way of good French provincial cooking. Lucy refused wine.

'Just mineral water,' she said to the young waiter.

'Not because of me?' Volkov asked her.

'No, darling,' she said gently. 'I'd fall asleep at the table if I drank anything. I can't believe it's real. We got away just in time. You may think it's nonsense, but I believe God was on our side.'

'Somebody was,' he admitted. 'We're not going to talk about it tonight. We're going to pretend that we're on holiday and we can stay here as long as we like. Till your money runs out,' he teased her. 'Beware of a Russian when he's happy. He's capable of anything.'

'I know,' she said. 'But tomorrow we've got to come down to earth.'

They fell asleep in each other's arms and woke late the next morning to a glorious day. As they walked along the riverbank after their breakfast, Lucy turned to him and said, 'I've been thinking, darling, and I know how we're going to do it.'

'Do what?' he asked.

'Get you into Jersey without anyone even knowing you're there.'

It was there, staring at him in the middle of Gusev's painstaking report. Viktor Rakovsky sprang up from his desk. He jammed a finger on the intercom and snapped at his secretary.

'Get Colonel Gusev up here. Immediately!'

The name had struck him like a punch to the heart. Boris Malik. His mother's murderer. Malik had befriended Yuri Warienski in the camp. Gusev had even repeated the dreadful retort to the accusation of homosexuality. The words mumbled by Adolph Brückner to Irina's tape machine echoed in his head. Her question, in that cool voice, '*How many times was she raped?*'

'*Boris did it twice . . . He turned her over.*' Malik had stolen the Holy Relic. Malik had given it to the boy at Spittal when he knew he was being repatriated. And it was Yuri Warienski who had offered it for sale to the jeweller in Paris. Yuri Warienski who'd sent his daughter to find Volkov because she had the Relic. And with the Relic, Volkov could set the whole of the Ukraine alight in bloody revolt against the Soviet government.

When his secretary buzzed through to say Colonel Gusev was in the outer office, Viktor composed himself. He put his private feelings aside. He came towards Gusev. He gripped him hard by the shoulders.

'You've done it, Leon! Your instinct was right – there *was* another factor in the Volkov scenario. And I've just found it. I've been investigating something else and the two themes have come together. I know why Volkov was singled out. Sit down. Have you ever head of St Vladimir's Cross?'

They were shut up together for a long time; no one was permitted to disturb them. At the end of the session, Viktor said, 'Give the search for Volkov and the Warren woman top priority. Put "stringers" on the French ports and airports. Circulate descriptions of Volkov and photofit of the woman.'

Gusev said, 'We have the hire car number – those Swiss idiots managed to get that before they lost them! And, comrade, one other thing.' He hesitated.

'What?' Victor encouraged him.

'It can't be coincidence that the woman took such a risk to get his passport. His wife must have let something slip and that set them running. I'd like to talk to her again. Somebody must be held accountable for his escape. I know you're on friendly terms with her.'

'She may even have warned him,' Viktor said slowly. 'We'll both go and see her at home. Make it a friendly visit. I'll arrange that now. If she did warn him in some way, she'll be regretting it enough to admit it by now. She didn't know he had a mistress.'

He had asked Gusev to leave them alone. Irina was on her feet, walking up and down, her hands twisting in front of her. She had been crying at one stage.

'I didn't tell him,' she said. 'I didn't tell him anything! Why won't you believe me, Viktor?'

'It's not what I believe that matters,' he said. 'Leon is a good interrogator. He's reasonable and he's calm. He doesn't believe you. Our superiors won't either. If you can't convince them . . .' He let the sentence die away.

She swung round to face him. 'How could you think I'd be such a fool? Why would I want to warn him?'

'Because you loved him,' he suggested. 'And you weren't sure what we had in mind for him when he came home. After all, you loved him enough to go in to exile and to work for us for all that time. You did very good work, but if we don't get the cross back, it won't help you.'

'Love him!' She almost spat the words out. 'I gave up everything for him. Do you know what my life was like for those five years? He hated me. He taunted and abused me for what I was doing. He never touched me in all that time. Not once. He hated me so much I made him impotent! You think I wanted him to run away? I wanted him back in Russia with me! I still hoped we might get back together. I told myself that if he was at home, among his own people, he'd change, he'd understand and we could try again.'

She turned her back to him, fighting down the surge of bitter grief.

'And all the time he was with another woman. Making love to her. Lying to me about where he was while he was with *her*. Planning to leave me and go off with her.' She turned back and faced him. 'I had something prepared to give him. It simulates a mild fit. I'd have been able to sedate him and fly him home.'

After a measured silence, Viktor said, 'I believe you, Irina. But whatever happens you will be censured. I can't guarantee what form it'll take. You may be suspended from practice. You'll certainly lose your old job at the Lenin Institute.'

She said in a harsh voice, 'You mean I'll be sent to some provincial hospital to work? Dealing with common lunatics in some God-forsaken hole?'

'That might be the outcome. I'll do my best for you, but I can't promise anything. It all depends upon finding him and getting our hands on the Relic.'

'My life is ruined,' she said slowly. 'Now my career is finished. Viktor, what are you going to do when you find them?'

'Kill them both. Bring the cross back to Russia,' he said.

'Let me do it.'

He stared at her. 'You're crazy. That's impossible.'

'I've been thinking about it,' she said slowly. 'Ever since I got home, I've been thinking of finding Dimitri and that woman. You want them dead and you want the cross. Let me suggest something to you. Why not let your Colonel Gusev hear it. A witness is always a good thing.'

They sat facing her. She was very calm now, her eyes hard and bright. Gusev thought she was the most dangerous sight he'd seen in a very long association with trained killers. But she wasn't trained, that was the stumbling block. She was a doctor with a little basic training in handling unpredictable patients, but she had no other skills. Except her knowledge of drugs. He leaned a little forward, paying more attention as she talked.

'It's got to be an accident,' Irina said. 'A murder would be attributed to the KGB. That's not our image any more. Isn't that so? That's why a lot of people have got away with things we'd have crushed them flat for a few years ago?'

'Yes,' Viktor admitted.

'So why not let someone handle it who isn't a professional?'

'You weren't very successful in dealing with the Warren woman,' Gusev pointed out. 'How would you cope with two of them?'

'I wouldn't,' Irina said. She reached for the cigarettes on the table, lit one and inhaled deeply. 'I couldn't even smoke for a time. It was misery. I wouldn't do anything myself. I'd take someone with me for that. I told you, I've been thinking about it. I have a man who would do exactly what was needed. Exactly what I told him to do . . . and enjoy it.'

'Tell us,' Viktor said. 'Who is this man?'

'The only survivor of "Spartacus".' She glanced at Viktor then to the impassive colonel who'd done nothing but put obstacles in her way. 'Ten years ago,' she said. 'We ran a series of experiments at the institute. We selected certain criminal types with a history of psychopathic violence and a talent for survival in the worst of the labour camps, and exposed them to re-education and programming. My professor thought of the project and called it Spartacus. The Romans used to choose gladiators from the most rebellious of their slaves, like Spartacus. My professor was a great authority on ancient Rome. He wanted to see if we could harness their anti-social tendencies to the service of the State. I believe Andropov supported the idea.'

'And it worked?' Gusev enquired. 'I never heard of it.'

'Only in some cases,' Irina admitted. 'Most of them went insane and had to be destroyed. About twenty responded satisfactorily.

Some were sent back to the camps where they disposed of anyone encouraging resistance. Others were given special tasks. A few were allowed a limited freedom afterwards. One of them is still available.'

'And you could trust yourself with him?' Viktor asked. He had never heard of the Spartacus programme. But he'd never been involved with the most sinister branch of the security services.

'I helped train him,' Irina explained. 'He was the most remarkable example. He did very good work till the scheme was abandoned. He would do anything I told him.'

'Sounds like science fiction to me,' Gusev said. 'I couldn't support it.'

Viktor ignored him. 'Why do you want to do this Irina? Personal reasons?'

'No,' she said coldly. 'Professional. If I solve the problem satisfactorily, my career won't suffer. I'll resume my post at the institute. That would be the deal.'

'If you succeed,' Viktor said. 'I'll recommend you for a professorship.'

On the way back to Dzerjhinsky Square, Gusev said, 'You're going to authorize it?'

'Yes,' Rakovsky answered. 'I am. I believe she'll do it. She and her tame monster. She didn't warn Volkov; I'm sure of that. I'm going to give her the chance. I want you to help her any way she wants.'

Gusev felt it his duty to make one more objection. He admired Rakovsky but he was anxious on his own behalf. He was sorry he'd been dragged in to what seemed a high-risk, low-probability solution to something requiring a team of skilled professionals.

He said, 'Comrade, have you thought of the risk you are taking? The personal risk if this goes wrong? You could be charged with treason if Volkov escapes us. I have to point this out.' He coughed awkwardly. 'And I'm an accessory,' he added.

Viktor shook his head. 'You don't think I'd let Irina go without back-up? We'll have our experts in place the moment we know where Volkov and Warren are hiding. Ready to deal with them if Irina fails. And to deal with her if she succeeds.'

Gusev drew a sharp breath. Viktor went on, gazing calmly out of the window as they drove fast down the reserved central lane into Red Square.

'A jealous wife who kills her unfaithful husband and his mistress. And then kills herself. She'll be the perfect alibi for us. Our team will dispose of her Frankenstein monster, whoever he is, and bring back the cross. A crime of passion with a Soviet dissident and his lover as the victims. The Western media will love it.'

'It is a masterpiece of forward planning.' Leon Gusev apologized. 'I was being very stupid. I thought she was a friend of yours . . .'

'I have known Irina for a long time, but I have no friends, Leon, when it comes to the safety of my country. Remember that.'

The car drew up outside the entrance to the Lubianka. They went up in the lift together.

'I'll come to your office,' Viktor said. 'I want to ask your computer some questions.'

'Well, Leon, there we have it. All the pieces fit the puzzle. As we suspected, there's the heart of the conspiracy. That's why the anti-Soviets are gathering from all over the world. Volkov appears and produces the Holy Relic! Think of it! The Press conferences, the propaganda machine shifting into gear in the Ukraine itself. And the hero, Volkov, returns to Russia with the whole Western media at his heels and St Vladimir's Cross in his hand! Fifty million Ukrainians would take to the streets!'

Gusev said, 'It would be chaos. Under the present conditions, I think the State would collapse. And you think that's where we'd find them?'

'I'm sure of it, even without your electronic toy,' Rakovsky answered. 'Varienski had kept the cross hidden. His daughter would never have risked bringing it to Geneva. She and Volkov are making for that island to get the cross so he can declare

179

himself in public. Concentrate your people there. As soon as they're sighted, we must be ready.'

'He has no visa,' Gusev pointed out. 'He can't get into the UK without one.'

Rakovsky smiled sourly. 'He can if he goes by sea,' he said. 'That's how I'd do it. Let them get there, Leon. Watch the airports, but do nothing, even if they're identified. Have our team waiting for them at the girl's house. Our first objective is to get that cross. In our hands, it could *unite* the Soviet State under one leader.'

A car met Irina at Sverdlovsk airport and drove the short distance from the big Siberian city to the village on the western side of the Bashkir River. It was a poor place, a huddle of rough one-storey buildings connected by tracks that were frozen solid in winter and choking with dust the rest of the year. The inhabitants scratched a meagre living from the land, growing a sparse crop of cereal, keeping the mangey hens that roamed scavanging for food in the yellow earth, cutting wood to keep warm against the savage winters. It was isolated, primitive and an earthly paradise for anyone released from the Gulag and allowed to live there.

She had christened him Remus, because he might well have been suckled by a wolf. He had no name, only the number that proved he existed. When she saw him first he had forgotten his name. He was as wary as a wild animal, cunning, vicious in his determination to survive.

She hadn't seen him for ten years. She told the driver to wait and covered her nose with a handkerchief against the acrid smell of human waste. There was no drainage system. The people living there dug holes in the ground.

It was the nearest of the little wooden buildings; a woman in the long skirt and shawl of the region directed her with a wave. The *Irtusky*, the foreigner, lived over there.

He was eating when Irina came through the door. A woman, the one he'd chosen to live with him, was serving him from a bowl, standing beside him while he ate. The plate was clean; the earth floor swept, pine table scrubbed white.

'Remus?' she said, and he stopped with the spoon to his mouth, squinting at her. 'How are you?' she said and came towards him.

He put the plate down, scrambled to his feet, knocking the stool over. The woman shrank back, receding in to the background.

'*Matiushka! Matiushka*, is it you?'

Little Mother. By the time Irina had finished with him, that was what he called her. He peered closer and his mouth split wide open in a delighted grin. She noticed that he had lost several teeth.

'It *is* you!'

He stood towering over her, still so tall and built like a great tree in spite of his age. He bowed down from the waist. She held out her hand, smiling at him.

'You look well, Remus,' she said. 'Have you been well?'

'Well enough. She looks after me. I beat her if she doesn't!' He laughed like a bear grunting, deep in his throat. He turned and said to her in the dialect, 'Get the lady some goats' milk to drink, you lazy bitch!' To Irina he said, 'Sit down, please. I have a nice chair. I made it myself. She'll bring something for you after your journey.'

He hadn't changed, she decided. His response to her was the same mixture of respect and humble obedience. For such a brute he had become doglike in his dependence. She sat down in his chair. There was a big sofa cushion, covered in the bright regional embroidery.

'Bring me the stool,' he shouted over his shoulder, and the woman scurried forward, setting it for him to sit on.

'Does she understand?' Irinia asked him.

He shook his grizzled head. 'She speaks only dialect,' he said. 'This is an honour, *Matiushka*. A great honour.' He beamed his broken smile at her.

She took the cup of goats' milk; the smell revolted her. She had always been a goddess figure who must be revered and obeyed and never made angry. She put the cup down and said, 'Are you happy here, Remus?'

'Very happy,' he said eagerly. 'I have food, a warm stove and the woman. She's a good woman. I don't have to beat her often.'

His records said they'd had two children. She saw no sign of them.

She said, 'How are your children, Remus?'

'They got sick and they died,' he said flatly. There wasn't a gleam of emotion in the deep set eyes. 'Last year. There was a lot of sickness here. She won't have any more. She's too old.'

'I'm sorry,' Irina said. 'But you didn't catch the sickness?'

'No. I'm strong. I've always been strong,' he said.

Irina nodded. 'Yes. I remember how strong you were. Would you like a younger woman? If this one is too old?'

He looked over his shoulder at the swaddled figure, standing mute against the wall. Irina missed the expression on his face. It would have surprised her.

'No,' he said after a moment. 'I don't want a new one. She's a good woman.'

'Well, then, would you like to move to a new place?'

His brow furrowed. He shrank into himself. He looked an old man.

'What have I done wrong, *Matiushka*?'

'Nothing, nothing,' she soothed. 'I'm very pleased with you. You did good service, Remus. That's why I've come to see you. I'd like to put you to work again. Just once more. Then you can move away from here to somewhere not so isolated. Wouldn't you like that?'

'I'm content,' he insisted. 'But – yes. Yes, I'd be glad to live nearer my own people. This is a dead and alive hole. What do you want me to do?'

'Come on a long journey with me,' she said quietly. 'Forget about your life here. Speak Russian again. Dress like a Russian. And punish two people who are enemies of the State. You'll be rewarded. I'll send you to a nice village a thousand miles south. No more winters here, Remus. What do you say?'

He looked up at her. 'Just show me the traitors, *Matiushka*,' he said.

'Good,' Irina stood up. He was on his feet immediately, waiting respectfully. 'Now you're coming back with me. You won't need anything. Say nothing to the woman.'

He pointed to the cup of milk. 'She can take this away and drink it herself. It's all right when you get used to it.'

He spoke briefly in dialect and the woman did as she was told. He followed Irinia in to the dusty heat. His Siberian wife lurked by the window out of sight. He had told her he was going into the city and would bring her back a necklace. She watched impassively as the car started up, its wheels churning more dust, and disappeared out of sight.

They landed at Sheremetov airport. Irina had bought him a suit of clothes in Sverdlovsk and had him shaved by a barber. He sat like a rock in the plane throughout the long flight down. No nerves, only a mild curiosity. He ate the in-flight food ravenously. She allowed him to drink vodka. Alcohol had never disturbed him.

He said, 'I'm very happy *Matiushka*. When I've done what's needed, can I have the woman in my new village?'

For a moment Irina hesitated. He had no emotional attachments. He hadn't blinked when he talked of the death of his children. He had never loved anything or anyone. That had made him so receptive to the programming.

'Why do you want her?' she asked. 'There are other women.'

'She suits me,' he said.

Irina nodded. He was over seventy. At that age he wouldn't want to be bothered by a change of companion. He had his slave. Let him keep her.

He was lodged in a house on the outskirts of Moscow. Irina briefed him. She was in charge of him.

'You are a Pole, Remus. Your home is in Kraków and you have a Polish passport and an entry visa into England. Your name is Stanislaus Szpiganovitch. You are visiting friends. I will speak for you,' she said. 'But you must have the right answers ready if an official asks you. And you understand Polish, don't you?' The Ukrainian dialect was very similar to the Polish language. 'And I am your daughter,' she went on. 'I am Polish, too. My name is Marie Szpiganovitch and I am keeping you company on the journey. We are a simple Polish father and daughter from Kraków.'

He laughed in his throat, growling at the joke of it all.

'*Matiuskha*,' he rumbled. 'How can my little mother be my daughter?'

'Because I say so, Remus,' she reminded him and he agreed at once.

'Yes, yes. As you say.'

He didn't make any more jokes. He looked hunted and confused because she wasn't pleased with him. It was a marvellous experiment, Irina thought. A pity it had only been effective with so few of the intake. After ten years it only needed a look and a change of tone to bring him to instant obedience.

'This is Remus,' Irina said.

He got up and bowed. Viktor nodded to him. He was standing at attention, like a soldier or a long-term prisoner. He was fit and tough for his age. He hadn't gone to seed in his sojourn in the Siberian village. The eyes were guarded, Viktor noticed. Whatever he thought or felt was carefully blanked out. And he followed Irina's every movement.

'You're going on a journey,' he said.

'Yes, Comrade Excellency.'

Viktor raised his eyebrows in surprise at the form of address.

'That's how we addressed all persons in authority,' she explained. 'Didn't we, Remus? It impressed them with the difference in their status and ours, you see. Remus has been one of our best pupils. Tell Comrade Excellency about what you did in Bashkir.'

He actually grinned at them. 'I got rid of a wasps' nest,' he said.

'Muslims who were stirring up trouble,' Irina explained. 'It was the start of the fundamentalist movement; Iran had been taken over and we had copycat movements here.'

'I remember,' Viktor said. 'I remember there was trouble in Bashkir and Azerbaijan.'

'Tell him about the wasps' nest,' Irina prompted.

'There was a mosque,' Remus said. He rubbed his nose with a thick forefinger. 'At Birsk, I think that was the name of the place.

184

They were all meeting there, the men in one part and the women upstairs. They're made of wood, those mosques.

'It was quite easy. I jammed the main doors shut. Lucky I'm strong. It was a heavy wedge more like a tree trunk. Then I just threw a couple of molotovs through the window. Like we did in the war with enemy tanks. It's the only way to get rid of wasps. Smoke them out.'

Viktor heard him chuckle.

'Remus eliminated the leadership that night,' she said. 'We were very pleased with him.'

'Killing doesn't trouble you?' Viktor asked.

'I kill enemies of the State,' he said. 'That's good.'

'Yes,' Viktor agreed after a pause. 'Yes, it is good. Irina, could we speak for a moment? I wish you luck,' he said. He couldn't bring himself to offer a hand to the man. He remembered that fire at Birsk. Over two hundred people had been burnt to death. It was attributed to a rival Muslim faction, and the fundamentalist movement in Bashkir collapsed.

Outside the room he said to her, 'And that is the product of your experiment? He is a monster.'

'He was born one,' she said. 'We merely made use of the material. As you are doing now.' Her tone was sharp.

'This is your idea,' he corrected her. 'After this is over, I want him eliminated.'

Irina shrugged. 'I didn't think you were so sensitive, Viktor. You knew what we were doing at the Lenin Institute. You didn't object to my work at the Amtel. You certainly won't object if Remus kills Volkov and Warren and I come back with your precious cross.'

'I shall be the first to congratulate you,' Viktor said and forced himself to smile. 'I didn't mean to criticize, Irina. It was my first encounter with a mass murderer. Now, I've approved the cover story and the plan. Gusev's done an excellent job.'

Stanislaus and Marie Szpiganovitch travelling from Kraków in Poland to pay their respects to the daughter of his old friend, Yuri Warren. With the strong religious and ethnic ties between Poland and the Ukraine, it was entirely credible. The papers were perfection: passports, visas, the best products of the forgery section.

Remus carried no weapons. It appeared he could use his hands better than most marksmen could use a gun. He knew exactly what was expected of him.

The wasps' nest at Bashkir was the climax of his service. He had committed half a dozen individual murders in the brief time he was on special duties. She didn't mention that to Rakovsky. His squeamishness irritated her.

'All we're waiting for now,' she said, 'is news.'

'We expect it any moment,' he answered. 'Warren's house on the island is being watched. You and Remus will leave for Warsaw tonight. As soon as we hear they've arrived on the island, you fly direct to Paris and by charter plane to Jersey. It's been organized down to the last detail.'

And the trail has been laid both ways, he thought, saying good-bye to her and setting out for his office. All those years ago, his father had taken the same route through the Moscow streets, with Ivan driving, carrying the Holy Relic as a bargaining counter for his family's life. He, as a little child, had seen it, glowing red and gold on the white counterpane of his mother's bed. And sketched it secretly.

He had made a pilgrimage to the place where his mother and his brother, Stefan, were buried. A quiet spot under the trees near the old house, long destroyed. He had marked their grave with a simple stone obelisk, engraved with their names. From that house of death, the cross had travelled with their murderer, all the way to the camp at Spittal and to an orphaned boy who'd been given it by a condemned man.

Nearly full circle. He drove up to the steps of the imposing building just as his father Alexei had done, to plead with Lepkin.

The Cross of St Vladimir would come back to Russia when Russia needed it most. To unify, not divide, as he had said. He dismissed his car and went inside. He had enough work to keep him in his office until late that evening. A lesser, personal matter came to mind.

Müller. What progress was he making with Brückner's widow

about the Fabergé desk set? He dictated a short memo reminding him.

'No,' Volkov protested. 'I can't let you do that. It's too dangerous. We'll think of another way.'

'There isn't one,' Lucy insisted. 'If we fly you'll be stopped and you know what that means. Immigration is terribly strict with people coming from the Continent. We wouldn't get away with it on the ferry because all foot passengers have to produce their passports. If I had a Jersey-registered car, I'd chance it, but not otherwise. There's nothing to worry about – I've made the crossing dozens of times.'

'With your father, not on your own,' he said. 'No, Lucy. What happens if something does go wrong? If there's a storm?'

'Darling,' she said gently. 'You don't know the first thing about sailing or the sea. I've been handling a boat since I was a child. I'll make the crossing back in a few hours. All you've got to do is wait for me in St Malo. Daddy and I sailed over once or twice a month. I could do it blindfolded!'

They'd been arguing for most of the morning. She couldn't convince him that she was an experienced sailor and that the trip from St Catherine's Bay to St Malo was not a dangerous crossing which would put her life in jeopardy.

'You'll see how easy it is when we sail back – I love the sea. There's nothing to be frightened of. Now let's go back to our hotel and have some lunch. This is supposed to be a holiday, so let's not spoil it by arguing.'

In the end he gave way, but he was unhappy and kept referring to it. Supposing the engine failed on the boat? It wouldn't, and anyway it had a sail, she explained patiently. What happened if she hit a rock and started to sink. Then she'd drown, she agreed, except there weren't any rocks in the English Channel, so would he please stop being silly about it.

The next morning, they set off again. Saying goodbye to the *propriétaire*, suddenly Lucy's mood clouded with the old fear so far kept at bay. She'd been too anxious and too busy making plans to feel afraid, but now the plans were made. As they drove

187

the long miles past the lovely city of Chartres, towards Rennes, she felt increasingly uneasy. It was still very hot. Volkov was subdued; he couldn't come to terms with what she was going to do and it depressed him. They didn't talk much on the journey to St Malo.

The charming port was full of boats: sailing yachts, motor cruisers, ferry boats plying across to the Channel Islands. She made him walk along the quayside, pointing out the different types of craft, trying to reassure him.

'That's like our boat,' she said, showing him a smart little single master. 'She's lovely, so easy to handle. Now, let's find a *pension* where we can stay the night, and then I'll take you somewhere for a marvellous cheap dinner. The fish soup round here is wonderful.'

'I'm not hungry,' he said. 'I can't eat when I'm worried.'

'You and my father,' she said. 'You'd have got on so well. You're just as bad as he was. I said to him once, why do Russians cry when they're happy? And he said because we enjoy it more than laughing! Please trust me, darling. I know what I'm doing.'

He cheered up over dinner. He held her hand and admitted that he'd never even learned to swim, so naturally he thought the sea was dangerous. And she was right, the fish soup was delicious. He'd been ungrateful and ungracious, but then he loved her *so* much. They made love that night in the stuffy *pension* bedroom as if they were facing a long separation.

Lucy caught the early morning hydrofoil to St Hélier. She had given Volkov money and told him to buy shorts and a sweatshirt in one of the tourist shops, and to wait for her on the quayside. He could amuse himself walking round the town till about four o'clock. She expected to reach the harbour at about that time, given a smooth crossing. And it would be smooth. There wasn't a ruffle of breeze on the water.

She paid the *pension* before she left and posted the keys of the rented car back to the Geneva hire firm. They had left it in a public car park. He insisted on coming to see her off. At the last moment, when the sailing was announced, he tried again.

'Why don't I come with you. I'm sure I could slip through.'

'No,' Lucy said. 'You promised last night, Dimitri. Go ashore.'

188

Reluctantly he left her. She saw him watching intently as the hydrofoil began to move out of the harbour.

It was a simple plan. She would go back home, pick up her boat at St Catherine, and sail over to St Malo. Volkov would sail back with her. Anyone seeing them on board together would assume that she'd gone out for a sail with a friend. Fleets of private craft cruised round the island and sailed across to Guernsey or Sark for a day out. Lucy was well known among the yachting enthusiasts. She could come and go without anybody suspecting anything.

At St Hélier she hurried to be among the first off; was waved through on a brief passport inspection and greeted by one customs officer who was a friend.

'Hi, Lucy. Had a good holiday?'

'Yes thanks, Bob.' She smiled at him.

'Sorry to hear about your father,' he said. 'I'll give you a call – maybe we could have dinner.'

'That'd be nice,' she said and slipped away.

She took a taxi home. The island looked so welcoming and green, with its abundance of lush flowers and the immense hydrangea bushes that grew everywhere, nodding their pink heads like friends welcoming her back. I've missed it so much, she thought. Dear God, it's so wonderful to feel safe, not to look over my shoulder any more. Just let me get him here and we can shut the door on the outside world at St Catherine's tonight.

The watcher camped on the hill above the house saw movement and focused his binoculars. They honed in on the car arriving and the girl getting out, paying and unlocking her front door. The watcher carried a short-wave transmitter. He signalled across to his contact at Carteret on the French mainland. It was the closest shoreline to the island.

'Target One has arrived. No sign of Target Two. Will report at 0300 hours.'

Lucy opened the windows to rid the ground floor of a faint musty smell. Dead flowers wilted in a stale vase. She threw them out. She went upstairs to her father's room and opened the shutters and the windows wide to let in the sunshine and the fresh sea air. Volkov would sleep there with her tonight.

She changed into shorts, shirt and a visored yachting cap, slipped rubber-soled plimsoles on her feet. She filled a Thermos with coffee and another with water, and took some food from the deep-freeze for their evening meal, leaving the dishes to defrost. The preparations had a calming influence; it was real to prepare supper, more real than taking a boat out to France and bringing back a fugitive Russian. I'm not afraid, she told herself. The trip is nothing. It's Volkov fussing and fretting over me that's made me nervous for the first time in my life at going out alone.

She packed the two Thermoses in a canvas bag, and looked round once more at the house where she had grown up and been so happy. Then she locked the door behind her and headed for the grassy slope which led to the shingle beach, with its outcrops of massive rocks and the cluster of small boats swinging gently at anchor by the jetty.

The watcher saw her ease the single-mast motor yacht out of its berth. The boat was engine-powered, its sail furled. It left a thin line of white foam as it headed out to sea. He ducked back inside his tent and sent another radio message.

It was a windless, sunny morning, without a ripple on the surface of the sea. A perfect day for motoring, giving her a good chance to reach her rendezvous at the time she had given Dimitri. Lucy had never sailed the sloop alone for any distance, but she knew the waters and, before setting out, she had determined a navigation plan to take account of wind, distances and landfall. She and her father had followed the routine so many times over the years. She felt confident. They were well equipped with IMRAY's folding charts, instruments giving water depth, speed and distance.

At mid-morning, the west and then south-easterly tides would help to carry them round the terrifying Minquier Plateau. At a steady speed and with favourable weather, she would reach St Malo by early evening, and slip in unnoticed, mingling with the flotilla of French and foreign boats returning for the night. No yellow Q flag would fly from the mast on this trip.

Lucy climbed down to the neat little cabin, opened the sea cock under the port quarter berth to pass cooling water through the engine, turned the battery isolator switch, returned to the cockpit, and pressed the starter button.

The engine was not really intended to make passage, but in the flat, calm water there was no choice. It was a tough little engine, and it would cruise at a steady six knots until a breeze picked up.

Lucy had decided to take the Violet Channel to round the south-east tip of Jersey, rock-strewn and hazardous. At last the Conchiere beacon was safely astern and she set her course.

It was a glorious day. She felt safe and confident in her boat, and no thought of danger occurred to her as the landmarks of the island blurred. The engine thumped away, and Lucy detected some catspaws' wind starting to shimmer across the water. An onshore breeze was coming up, drawn to the warming mass of the French mainland.

Lucy drank some coffee. Fortune, like the sun overhead, was shining on her. The hours passed, and she set a new southerly course for the St Malo approaches. She thought of Dimitri waiting. The mental picture made her smile. In so many ways he was an innocent, in spite of his intellectual brilliance. It made her love him even more. One day, she promised herself, I'll teach him to sail.

As she skirted the rocks there was a sudden change in the engine note. It began to cough and stutter.

'Oh God,' she exclaimed, 'Don't you dare die on me . . .'

But there were more coughs, a final wheeze, then nothing. Silence. Just the slip slap of wavelets on the hull. Not a whiff of breeze.

'Get to know your engine,' her father had always insisted. 'You can't rely on wind if anything goes wrong.' She cranked the engine on the starter. Nothing. It wasn't overheating; she'd checked the fuel before setting off. There was plenty in hand for the trip. 'Stay calm,' she told herself. 'Go down and see if you can find the fault.'

In the engine compartment her worst fear was proved right. Pinkish froth and air bubbles swirled in the glass bowl of the fuel filter.

There was a loose joint in the fuel line. Even if she bled the line and restarted the engine, it would die on her in a few minutes.

She climbed up to the cockpit, and immediately forgot about

the engine. The east-flowing tide was dragging her towards the rocks, and on the horizon a low bank of thick sea fog was looming.

Whatever she did, this was no place to linger. Better to keep starting the engine and pray that it lasted long enough to take her near a saving breeze.

She bled the fuel system, started up, and the little sloop began to move. The rocks receded. The engine stopped again. She repeated the routine. A little progress, another half mile or so. Then a westerly wind came up across her starboard quarter.

'Thank God, thank God,' Lucy prayed aloud.

As the engine spluttered into silence, once more, she managed to raise enough of the mainsail to swing the boat into the wind. She had to heave it to the top of the mast before a freshening gust laid her abeam. Lucy thought of Dimitri, waiting helplessly at St Malo, watching for her. She would find the strength to succeed. She pulled with all her strength, her heart bursting with the effort. But the main sheet had snagged and the boom couldn't run out freely. In desperation, Lucy tried to make fast the halyard round a cleat, but the rope slipped in her grasp and ran free. Her sharp cry was caught by the wind and swept away. The rope-to-wire slice ripped across her palms. Tears blinded her. But she *had* to get the mainsail up. At least high enough to make the halyard fast round a cleat.

Once more Lucy exerted all her strength, willing herself to ignore the agony in her hands. It was done. She swayed, sick with pain and shock.

Then she grabbed the tiller, held the boat head to wind and managed to unfurl the genoa, holding the boat motionless. She stumbled below to find antiseptic ointment and bandages for her hands. They were raw and bleeding. She was shaking as she dressed them awkwardly, wincing as the bandages made contact with the ruptured skin. Her right hand was the worst. She could only use the left with difficulty. Lucy found some pain killers and swallowed two, and then went back on deck.

Volkov had been pacing up and down the quayside since half-past four. He didn't know exactly what to look for; a single mast – a small boat. She'd promised to wave when she sailed in, as close to the rendezvous point as she could manage. Half a dozen times Volkov had started up at the sight of some small craft, thinking it must be hers.

But there was no familiar figure among those who sailed into the harbour and soon there were no boats arriving. She was three hours late. He sat on the damp jetty in his new shorts and the only sweatshirt he could find that didn't shriek St Malo across the chest in fluorescent colours. The smell of oil, sea water and refuse stung his nostrils. A skinny cat with hungry eyes stared hopefully at him from under a seat. He had nothing to give it. He felt sick.

His instincts had been correct. She hadn't made the crossing back. He stared out across the forest of masts, listening to the transistor music blaring across the water and the noise of people on board, laughing in the warm evening, drinking on deck, preparing to go ashore and eat.

A Brittany ferry loomed to his left, preparing to disembark. Lights gleamed along her sides. It was dusk now. Soon it would be dark. A group of small children scurried towards him, kicking a ball. They saw the cat and clustered round the seat. The animal crouched down, ears flattened. One boy found a pebble and threw it. Volkov leapt up and shouted at them in Russian to leave it alone. They stared at him, pulled faces and ran away. He sat down and resumed his hopeless watch out to sea. In the end he couldn't bear it any longer. He went back to the café where he'd spent the afternoon swallowing cups of coffee.

After five years in Geneva he spoke fluent French; he didn't even think about his accent.

'Don't talk to people, darling,' Lucy had warned him. 'You're such an obvious Russian, they'll look for the snow on your boots.' They had to keep a low profile, blend in with all the other holiday-makers and tourists. He forgot about being careful. He caught hold of one of the waiters.

'Can you tell me,' he said. 'I'm expecting a friend. She's terribly late – in a boat – do you know if there has been a storm?'

'Not that I've heard. I've been too busy to ask about the weather.' He pulled away impatiently. He was tired and fed up with serving a bunch of idlers on holiday, and cursed Volkov under his breath.

Volkov walked back to the jetty, and stopped by one of the large cabin cruisers. A man and woman were sitting in deck chairs, sipping champagne. He shouted down to them.

'Excuse me. Can you help me, please?'

The man looked up with the wariness of the wealthy. The boat was flying a Dutch flag.

'What do you want?'

'My friend was coming over in her boat and she's hours late. Something must have happened to her.'

The man heaved himself up from his deckchair and came to the side.

'Have you notified the coast guard?'

'No. What is the coast guard? Where do I find it?'

His wife said quickly, 'The poor man's been walking up and down for ages. I noticed him earlier. He looks quite desperate. Derk, hadn't you better go and help him?'

'Wait a minute,' Volkov heard him say. 'I'll come ashore. You'd better report it. I'll show you where to go.'

He put down his glass and clambered onto the jetty.

'What sort of boat is she in? How long is she overdue?'

'I don't know,' Volkov said. 'I know nothing about damned boats. She said she'd be here at four o'clock. It's after eight.'

He wiped his hand across his face.

'Where are you both from?' the Dutchman asked.

'Geneva,' Volkov answered.

'She may have been delayed. You can't tell. Does she have a radio?'

'I don't know,' Volkov said desperately. 'It has an engine and a sail. That's all I know.'

'Come on then, we'd better put in a report and see if anyone's picked her up. It's probably engine failure and she's just drifting with the tide. It's crazy not to have a radio.'

Seeing the look in Volkov's eyes, he clapped him on the shoulder.

'Don't worry; I'm sure she's all right. Just sitting out there cursing. The sea's like a millpond and the forecast is fine. Don't worry.'

But Volkov wasn't listening. He had turned for one last look. A small boat, its sail bellied out in a light breeze had entered the harbour. There was a woman at the helm.

'That's a single master,' the Dutchman said. 'Could be your friend?'

Volkov sprinted down the jetty. The Dutchman followed at a more leisurely pace. Now the figure guiding the craft slowly and skilfully among the anchored yachts was waving, and the crazy fellow was waving back and shouting. He was jumping up and down, both arms in the air.

'Lucy! Lucy!'

'All's well, then,' the Dutchman said. He smiled and shook his head. They might come from Geneva, but that lunatic certainly wasn't Swiss. 'You'd better come and join us for a drink to cele-brate,' he said. 'She's a good sailor, your friend. She's handling that little craft very well with all this traffic round her. I'm glad everything's OK. See you in a few minutes.'

'Thank you, thank you,' Volkov said.

When the Dutchman climbed back on board his yacht he told his wife that the man had had tears in his eyes.

'What a drama,' he said. 'God knows what the coast guard would have made of him. There they are. Hey, come and have a glass of champagne with us!'

He reached up and helped the girl down on to the deck. Her companion was not at all sure-footed.

His wife came forward. 'I'm Beta, and this is Derk. Come and sit down and tell us all about it. Your poor boyfriend was con-vinced you'd been drowned! Here, drink this.' She handed Lucy a glass of champagne.

Volkov kept his arm round her. She was trembling with fatigue.

'My engine conked out,' she explained. 'I couldn't get the bloody thing to go for more than a few minutes at a time. I tried everything. I just sat there drifting. Then the wind did come up.'

Derk shook his head. 'Putting up sail is tough enough for a man,' he said. 'How the hell did you manage on your own?' Noticing that Lucy's hands were heavily bandaged, he added,

'Beta, I think we need the first aid kit. You'd better let my wife have a look at your hands. What happened?'

'I let go the halyard,' she explained. 'I'm all right. Really.'

He didn't think she looked it.

'Where have you come from?' he asked her.

Lucy decided there was no point in lying. They seemed kind, friendly people. All sailors had danger in common, from the owner of the largest ocean-going yacht to the smallest dinghy.

'From Jersey,' she said. 'I haven't been out for a while. I didn't check the engine. I'd plenty of petrol and that's all I looked at. We were supposed to sail back today.' She turned and laid her head on Volkov's shoulder. 'I'm so sorry, darling.'

'Come below,' Beta said firmly, 'and let me take a look at those hands. Rope burn can be very nasty. Our crewman will look at the engine first thing in the morning. We can't offer you a bunk, the boat only sleeps three, but we can feed you. I hope you'll have some dinner with us.' She spoke to Volkov. 'Please, help yourself to a glass. The bottle's right there.'

'I don't drink,' he said. 'But thank you. Thank you for your kindness, but I think we've been enough trouble already.'

'No trouble,' was the answer. 'You're staying.'

The Dutch couple walked back to the little boat with them. They were a curious pair, impossible to place. But it was nice, they agreed afterwards, to see people so much in love. They said goodnight promising to send the crewman up to look at the engine. There was no way the girl could sail back, even with help, with her hands in that state.

Volkov and Lucy bunked down in the bottom of the boat. There was a spare tarpaulin in the locker. It wasn't particularly comfortable, but they were oblivious. Volkov held her in his arms, her head resting on his shoulder.

'I thought I'd lost you,' he said. 'Your poor hands!'

'I've gone soft living in Geneva, that's the trouble,' Lucy said. 'It's just blisters, they'll heal up very quickly.' She closed her eyes; she was numb with exhaustion. 'I kept thinking you must be going crazy, imagining something's happened. I was terrified you'd start

196

talking to people and give yourself away! That's what gave me the strength to sail her on my own. I held on to those bloody ropes because I had to get back to you. I knelt down in that bloody boat and prayed, my darling. I prayed for a wind. And thank God, it came.'

He heard her sigh and knew she'd fallen asleep. He smoothed a strand of hair back from her face. At last, lulled by the gentle movement of the boat and the slap of little waves against the sides, he fell asleep beside her.

They took their seats on the flight from Warsaw to Paris. It was a long journey. Irina didn't talk to him. There was nothing to say. He soon nodded off, and, even when they hit turbulence and the airliner lost height, he didn't wake.

She let her thoughts roam ahead. They'd hire a car when they landed in Jersey. They'd been booked in to a modest bed and breakfast hotel in St Hélier. She'd been shown the Warren house on a map of the island. It was secluded, on a hilltop overlooking the sea, in four acres of grounds. The woman had been spotted by their watcher. The last report said she'd taken a boat out. That had been the signal for Irina and Remus to set off for Paris. Viktor had been right. The woman was going to smuggle Volkov in from France by sea.

She tried to imagine his reaction when she surprised them. His face wouldn't come into focus. She tried to relish the scene when the man beside her put them out of action, and Volkov watched helplessly while he tortured the woman to make her give up the cross. She could see that in her mind's eye. But not the sequel. Not the moment when she gave the order. *Kill them, Remus.*

Would she be proof against him, even now? Was her love completely dead or paralyzed by hurt and jealousy? She couldn't answer that. She had staked everything on her promise to Viktor and the greater authority he represented.

I won't know if I can do it, she thought. *I won't be sure until I see him. Till the moment comes.*

They landed at Charles de Gaulle airport at two in the afternoon. By five-thirty the charter flight taxied to a halt on the runway at St Peter's, Jersey. Irina signed for and took possession of the Ford Fiesta.

'Get in the back,' she directed. He smiled and muttered, 'Yes, *Matiushka.*'

He smelled acridly of sweat and she didn't want him close to her. She watched him in the driving mirror, as he looked out of the window.

'It's nice here,' he said. 'Lots of trees and grass.'

'It's just a little island where the rich come to escape paying taxes,' she said sharply.

He didn't speak for the rest of the drive. The bed and breakfast hotel was in a side street. There was a sign outside: St Margaret. It was a modern two-storey house with a fine garden. Even Irina couldn't help admiring the profusion of flowers and shrubs.

The air smelt salty from a breeze coming in off the sea. It reminded her of the Crimea, where she and Volkov used to take holidays when they first married. The same warm climate, the lush growth, the tang of the ocean. She registered and they were shown to their rooms.

'Where's the bathroom?' she asked.

The proprietress pointed down the corridor.

'Second door on the left, It's marked. Toilet is next to it.'

'Thank you,' Irina said.

She spoke to him in Russian.

'Go and bath yourself, Remus. Then wait for me in your room.'

Irina went downstairs.

'Is it possible to get something to eat for my father?' she asked the proprietress. 'He's tired after the journey. Just bread and cheese would do.'

The Jersey woman smiled. 'Of course, dear. I'll find something. Come a long way, have you?'

'From Poland,' Irina said.

'On holiday, are you?'

'We have friends who spent their holiday here. They recommended it. My father wanted to come. He's never travelled abroad before. I thought we'd do it properly and go on to England.'

'I suppose you weren't allowed to go anywhere, were you, while those Communists were in charge. Don't worry, I'll bring a bite of supper up to him. Would he like a drink? I've got some lager in the fridge.'

Irina managed a chilly smile. 'I'm sure he would. That's very kind of you. He doesn't speak a word of English, I'm afraid.'

'We'll manage. But you speak very well.'

'Languages were compulsory in our State schools,' Irina said. 'We all learned English and one other European language. Otherwise we weren't considered fit for higher education . . . I'll be back later.'

She drove into the centre of St Hélier, and stopped at a small fish restaurant just beyond the port, called the Lobster Pot.

The woman's remarks had needled her. Ignorant, prejudiced little bourgeois. It soothed Irina's irritation to imagine her fussing round Remus. Little did she know! She parked the car and went into the restaurant. It was dim and cool, festooned with nets and hideous plastic lobsters dangling from the roof. She couldn't bear the idea of eating with him, sharing a table. Mistress and slave didn't take food together.

She asked for a table and then said, looking round, 'I was supposed to meet someone here.'

The waitress said, 'There was a gentleman, but he said he couldn't wait. Are you Mrs Spigo? Sorry, I'm not sure how you pronounce it.'

'Yes, I am,' Irina said quickly.

'He left a message for you. If you'd like to have a look at the menu I'll go and get it. The crayfish are very good tonight.'

Irina tore open the envelope, and took out a scrap of grubby paper. The message was scribbled in pencil. 'Do nothing till I contact you at the hotel. I'll leave a message from Rudi if they're in the house.'

'Everything all right?' the waitress asked.

Irina crumpled the paper and put it in her bag. 'Yes, thank you. I'll have the crayfish. And a bottle of Moselle.'

The girl smiled in apology.

'I don't know if we've got any,' she said. 'I'll get the list for you. I hope you enjoy your meal.'

*

'She goes sweet now,' the Dutch boy said. He wiped the grime and engine oil from his hands with an even dirtier rag. He grinned at Lucy and shook his blond head.

'Broken fuel line joint. Must have come loose on the way.' he said. 'No surprise she won't go for you. Next time, don't ask too much of her, eh?'

'Next time,' Lucy promised. 'Thank you so much, Jan. I'm sorry it's taken you so long.'

'Thank you,' Volkov echoed. He wasn't sure what a fuel line joint was but he did know that the engine was working now. It had taken the Dutch couple's crewman most of the morning to fix it.

'No trouble,' he said. He spoke to Volkov. 'You a good sailor?'

'I've never been in a boat.'

'It's fun. Not so great in a storm, but today – beautiful. OK? Have a good trip!' He shook Volkov's hand briefly and jumped ashore. 'Mr and Mrs de Groot say good luck and goodbye,' he called out. 'They gone to buy provisions. If the boat don't start, they say come back to us. I tell them, she starts. I make sure of that!'

'Say thank you again from us, won't you?' Lucy called out.

He waved and hurried back down the jetty. She turned and hugged Volkov.

'We're all right, darling. We can cast off and start for home. Now, you undo the tow rope and wind up the anchor. Here, you just do this.'

He was clumsy and unsure, but he wouldn't let her use her bandaged hands. Everything had turned out extraordinarily well. They'd breakfasted with the hospitable Dutch couple and spent the morning watching the boy working on the engine.

Lucy knew by the steady throb that it was perfectly tuned. The sky was cloudless and a hot sun blazed down upon them. She went to the controls, leaving Volkov in the stern, and carefully eased the boat out through the other craft moored close by.

They began to rock, and a swell built up behind them as they cleared the congestion and approached the harbour mouth.

'Are you all right, darling?' Lucy glanced over her shoulder at him.

He was sitting rigidly in the stern, holding the sides with both hands. Suddenly he smiled.

'I'm more than all right,' He laughed. 'I like it! When are you going to show me how to sail?'

'When we're out at sea,' she said. 'Don't worry, it's not hurting me. We'll keep to this speed. That boy certainly knew what he was doing. She's going like a bird!'

He said, 'They were so kind, those people!'

'They were wonderful,' Lucy agreed. 'I took their address. I'll write and thank them properly.'

'I was thinking last night while you were asleep,' he said, 'how brave you are.'

She looked up at him and smiled. 'Not as brave as you' she said.

Late that afternoon, long after they had left St Malo, Lucy pointed to a land mass on the horizon.

'Look, you'll see Gorey Castle soon. We're home!'

The Relic

5

The watcher had set up a little tripod, with his binoculars fixed to it, trained on the bay below. He was eating out of a tin, hidden under a camouflaged sun shield. He had his equipment laid out ready. The automatic weapon was quite small, less deadly than the Armalite he preferred, but it fitted easily into the struts of his backpack, the firing mechanism and ammunition sealed up in cans of food.

He was a big man, fit and well-muscled. He'd trained with the French paras and been dismissed after serving a four-year gaol sentence for robbery. He hadn't hesitated when the offer of this kind of job came along. He had no political loyalties or prejudices. He had skills to offer which the French army had provided and he didn't care who paid him.

He had a bicycle hidden under more camouflaged sheeting outside. He had made one excursion in to St Hélier to leave the message for the woman at the restaurant. His instructions were to stay on watch and out of sight. He had spied out a little delicatessen in the village a mile down towards the bay. When he had to make the coded call to the hotel, he could use the phone he'd seen at the back of the shop. He had his story ready.

It was sweltering under the canvas. The sweat ran down into

202

his eyes. He spooned up the last of his cold meal, tossed the empty can aside and swigged from a bottle of beer. It was tepid. He swore; he was impatient to get the job over, slip back to France and collect his money.

His instructions were clear. He was to monitor what happened at the house when the Russian woman and her goon arrived. Their job was to kill the girl he'd seen take out the boat, and her companion, after forcing them to hand over a cross. From this, he judged it better not to intervene if he heard screaming. When the Russians emerged, he was to eliminate them both, the woman with a shot to the head that could be seen as self-inflicted. Her body was to be disposed of among the other corpses, with a handgun left beside her. That had come in in pieces, in his saddlebag behind the bike. The body of the man she'd brought with her could be buried or thrown into the sea.

A single radio call to Carteret would bring a contact to the same restaurant in St Hélier, where he would hand over the cross and get himself on to the next ferry to St Malo.

He wiped his mouth and his sweating face and peered through the binoculars. He saw the small boat, its sail furled, cutting through the slight swell into the bay. Adjusting the focus, he was able to see the girl quite clearly. Blond, blue shirt, shorts. A man with her. He watched the boat slow, inch into its berth at the jetty and drop anchor. He remained absolutely still, concentrating like an animal stalking its prey.

The man helped the girl out, and put his arm round her. They walked up from the sparkling sand to the pathway among the rocks. Up to the little road that ran along the coast, and out of sight until they came into view again, climbing up the steep, grassy incline to the lower reaches of the garden, then through the wooden gate, and up a brick path among the flower borders.

He tightened the focus, bringing them into close-up. She was a goodlooking piece. The man looked like a Slav of some kind. She unlocked the front door and they went inside.

The watcher unscrewed his binoculars and folded down the tripod. He sent the radio signal to Carteret first. 'Targets One and Two in place. Operation activated.'

He crept out, keeping low and hauled the bike from under its cover. A few minutes later he was pedalling towards the village and the delicatessen. It was pleasantly cool inside and he wiped his face with his forearm. The woman behind the counter said, 'Good afternoon. Hot, isn't it?'

He smiled at her. He had strong white teeth and he was not bad looking, in a coarse way. She smiled back.

'You have any Orangina on ice? And I need to make a telephone call, Mademoiselle. Can you help me? I'm meeting a friend in St Hélier and I'm going to be very late.'

'There's a phone through there,' she said. 'You're French? On holiday?'

'Only a week unfortunately,' he shrugged. 'I like to do a bit of walking, biking round the island and swimming. I'm going home tomorrow. I'll take three Oranginas; I'm gasping. Can I use the phone?'

'Just give me twenty-five pence for the call,' she said. 'I'll get the drinks. Bottles or cans?'

'Bottles'll do fine.'

He grinned at her and made for the telephone. He dialled the number.

A voice said, 'St Margaret's'.

He spoke as softly as he could.

'Can I speak to Miss Szpiganovitch . . .'

He added a choc ice to his purchases and ate it outside the shop quickly before it melted. He went back the way he'd come and slipped under his shelter to watch the house. He guessed the Russian woman wouldn't waste time coming after them.

'I can't believe we're home and safe,' Lucy said.

He picked up a photograph in a silver frame. 'This is your father and mother with you? She was very pretty.'

'She had lovely colouring,' Lucy said. 'It doesn't show up there. It's very good of my father.'

'I wish I had met them,' Volkov set the photograph down. He came to her and put both hands on her shoulders.

'It's time to show me the Relic,' he said.

*

The shutters were fastened in her father's study. Volkov had to open them. Her hands were painful and very stiff. Sunshine poured in, lighting a million dust motes in its beam.

Everything was as he'd left it. The desk with his selection of pens, the shabby blotter he wouldn't replace because it was a Christmas present from his benefactor, Major Hope, the calendar with the date long past.

She said, 'Move the desk out and pull up the rug.'

Volkov pushed it aside and rolled up the bright Persian rug. The surface of the parquet glowed dark in comparison with the sun-bleached floor. Lucy stepped forward and pressed the fourth square on the left. The flap rose up.

'Can you get the box?' she said.

He knelt down to lift out the plain wooden box, and put it on the desk.

'This is what my father dreamed of,' she said. 'This very moment.'

The catch was simple, it slipped up and the lid rose. Slowly, reverently Volkov lifted out the gold cross. Red lights danced and flashed as he examined it; the frame was the honey colour of pure gold.

'A thousand years of our history,' he said. 'I don't know what to say.'

'It belongs to you, now,' Lucy spoke quietly. 'It will give you the power to free millions of our people. It's the proof that Communism didn't win.'

He held it between both outstretched palms. 'It makes me afraid.' He looked up at her. 'Am I strong enough, Lucy? Can I really go home and offer myself as a leader?'

'You must,' she answered. 'You have the Holy Relic. You've got no choice. You've been chosen.'

'I could look at it forever,' he said. 'I could just sit here and look at it.'

She came close and said softly, 'I'll leave you alone for a while. I felt the same when my father showed it to me. Don't ever doubt yourself, my love. You were born for this. I truly believe that.'

She slipped out of the room.

It weighed very little. The workmanship was as delicate as lace.

Evelyn Anthony

The big central stone was rounded and roughly polished so that its facets caught the light.

A bloodthirsty tyrant had commissioned it as a proof that he was converted to the Christian faith and would bring peace to the land and mercy to its people. There had been little peace and no mercy from the moment it disappeared from its shrine. Millions starved to death, were deported and murdered. Millions more were slain in Russia's most terrible war.

With the sun shining on him, Volkov's hands looked as if they were dipped in blood. He had never uttered even a mental prayer in his life. He didn't do so then. Lucy saw the hand of God. He felt the touch of history. Destiny had chosen him. She was right. He had no choice.

He laid the Relic back in its box, replaced it in the cunning floor cavity and pressed the section of the wood down. It fitted into the parquet, invisible in the design. The rug was laid on top, the desk manoeuvred back into place. A dead man had guarded his treasure well.

Lucy came to meet him when he left the room. He looked very pale. She put her arms round him and they held each other. They didn't speak.

'Remus!'

She didn't knock. She opened the door and saw him lying on the bed, his shoes kicked off, his mouth agape, dozing.

His eyes opened and he jerked upright. '*Matiushka!*'

'Get ready,' Irina commanded. 'You've got work to do. I'll be downstairs. Hurry.'

She went down to the hallway. 'Rudi' had telephoned and rung off without leaving any message. She'd turned her back on the woman's curiosity and gone upstairs to fetch him.

They were on the island together. Celebrating their escape. Touching each other. She allowed herself a few seconds of mental torture before blotting out the image of Volkov with his hand on the woman, his mouth closing on hers. She was trembling.

Remus came downstairs. He moved very lightly for such a heavy man. Like a dog, he followed her outside.

'Get in the back,' she ordered. It would take twenty minutes or so to negotiate the narrow country roads to St Catherine's Bay. 'You know what to do?'

He nodded.

'Don't be too hard,' she reminded him. 'I only want him stunned. Just long enough to tie him up.'

'Just a tap on the neck,' he promised.

'They must give me the treasure they stole.'

She saw his reflection in the driving mirror. His eyes were bright and he had wet his lips. He had always reacted like that; violence excited him.

'You'll torture the woman,' Irina instructed. 'To make him tell us. If that doesn't work, then we'll make her watch while you work on him. One of them will break. Probably him.'

She bit her lip. She hoped so. She couldn't imagine sweeter music than the screams of Lucy Warren. But to see Dimitri suffer . . .

'Men give in quickly when their women squeal,' Remus grunted.

Irina drove as fast as she dared on the twisting roads. Twice they met an oncoming car, had to pull to the side to let the other pass. She didn't want to lose the light. It was better to rush the house in daylight. The back-up was close by, she knew that. But he wouldn't be needed. Remus was at the right pitch of controlled brutality. She could feel the energy emanating from him in the confines of the car. He was like a coiled spring.

She slowed down and took a right turning off the road, which twisted and wound its way through green countryside and little wooded hills. There, just ahead of them, was the driveway leading to the house. On her left Irina could see the blue sparkle of the sea in the bay below, with its little marina and the few boats bobbing up and down on the evening tide.

She stopped the car under some trees. She could see the white painted façade up ahead. They wouldn't be visible.

He was so quiet she didn't hear him close the rear door. And then he was beside her. 'You're serving the State, Remus,' she said. 'You will punish our enemies.'

The watcher grunted. He'd seen the car and guessed where it was going. There wasn't another house in sight. He was right.

207

They hadn't wasted any time. He bent low, watching the woman and the man begin to circle round the house to the back. He decided it was time for him to move in closer. He took his weapon and began to run, bent double, down the gentle rise to the level of the distant garden. As soon as he was out of sight of any passing car on the road above, he straightened and broke in to a fast loping stride that brought him to the shrubbery a hundred yards from the house. He waited. He heard a sharp scream that was cut short. He grinned. They were inside.

Irina saw them through the french windows. They were slightly open to admit a light breeze; the sun was sinking and it was suddenly cooler.

She heard her husband say, 'My darling, I want you to rest. I'll go and get us something to eat.'

And, for the first time, Lucy Warren, speaking in Russian. A melodious voice, a little deep. It would find a new pitch very soon, Irina promised.

'I'll come with you. You don't know where things are kept.'

'I'll find them. You sit down.'

'Now!' she hissed at Remus.

He launched himself with the speed and lightness of a great predator. He was through the door and into the room before she could even start to follow. She saw Lucy Warren jump and heard the brief cry, choked at its source as Remus swept her to the ground. She lay dazed, without moving as Irina stepped into the room. Remus put a finger to his lips. They heard Volkov running from the kitchen.

The door was flung open and he shouted, 'Lucy! What . . .' when Remus snapped the ridge of his right hand up and across, striking Volkov on the side of the neck. He collapsed, instantly unconscious as the blood supply from the carotid artery was halted by the blow. Remus left him there, while he hauled the girl onto the sofa.

Irina came close. He slipped a luggage strap out of his pocket. He buckled her arms tight to her sides, rolled his handkerchief in to a ball, then forced her mouth open, and thrust it inside.

'She'll give no trouble, *Matiushka*,' he growled. 'Now I'll fix him.'

Irina stood looking down at them. He'd used two straps to secure Volkov by the hands and feet and pushed him into an armchair facing the girl. She was lying where he'd thrown her, her eyes wide open, her mouth distorted by the crude gag. Irina turned away from her; one hand instinctively touching her head.

'He's coming round,' she said.

Volkov was moving, wrestling with the straps. She saw his horrified expression and heard him gasp her name as he saw her.

'Yes,' she said softly. 'It's me. Look over there, Dimitri. My friend is going to amuse himself with your whore. Let her scream, Remus. Nobody can hear her.'

They were giving the girl a hard time. The watcher wondered what that old bastard was doing to her.

Volkov was begging. 'Irina, stop him, stop him. Oh, Holy Christ!'

He writhed and jerked in helpless agony, when the man tore the bandages off Lucy's hands and gouged his fingers into the raw skin. The sobs of pain drove him to a frenzy. He was shouting, pleading with his wife. Irina didn't answer. She just watched. She heard him curse her, beg her, cry out in horror as Lucy's shirt was torn from her and his wife's lighter flickered into flame in the man's hand and hover before her breast.

'Wait!' Irina commanded. She turned to Volkov. 'Where's the cross, Dimitri?'

'Don't . . . Don't tell them!' Lucy cried out.

She swung round, and snapped. 'Shut her up! Tell me where you've hidden the cross,' she said. 'Otherwise he'll burn off the nipple!'

Volkov didn't hesitate. He shouted, hoarse with anguish.

'I'll get it! I'll give it to you. Tell him to leave her alone. Don't hurt her any more.'

'You tell me and I'll get it,' Irina said.

He loved her. He loved her more than Irina imagined he could love anyone. His cries of agony and pleading rang in her ears.

He said now, 'You can't. You won't be able to work the mechanism. Send him with me.'

Irina shook her head. 'Oh, no. You'd try something. I know you would. He stays with her and I wait here. Remus, I'm going to untie him. If he tries anything kill her.'

He took his hand away from Lucy's mouth, hooked his forearm under her chin.

'You do what you're told,' he said to Volkov. 'Or I'll break her neck.'

Irina unbuckled the belts. For a second she thought Volkov was going to lose control and throw himself at her. She saw him resist the temptation. *How much he must love that girl.*

'If I give it to you, will you let Lucy go? I'll come back to Russia with you.'

She said coldly, 'Bring me the cross or I'll tell him to burn her.'

He stumbled out. She took a cigarette from her bag, and snapped her fingers.

'I'll have my lighter, Remus.' He handed it to her. 'Don't choke the girl yet,' she said. 'I want him to see it.'

Lucy closed her eyes. Her hands were on fire. His arm was like a band of iron on her throat. She didn't want to see the woman's face. It was a mask, the eyes glittering, in exultation at her victims' agony. Lucy's death was in those eyes. She shut them out and prayed for unconsciousness.

Volkov threw open the door to Yuri Warienski's study. He heaved the desk out of the way and threw the rug aside. He was trembling, blinded by helpless rage and fear for Lucy. He might plead, he might bargain, but it wouldn't save her. As soon as he handed over the Relic, he knew that they would both be killed. He stamped on the floor and the cavity opened.

Volkov forced himself to kneel, and lift out the wooden box. He had no thought or fear for himself. He looked desperately round the room. There must be something, something he could use. He wrenched open the desk drawers. Nothing. Then he saw it. It had fallen to the ground when he pushed the heavy desk aside.

A silver paper knife. A thin, sharp blade with a chased handle. He picked it up, felt the tip with his finger. With enough force it would penetrate a human body. Volkov stuck it in the waistband of his trousers, out of sight. He carried the box in both hands and walked back down the passage to the sitting room. He couldn't hear anything. Silence. One chance in a million. He was going to take it.

Irina drew on her cigarette. Her hand was steady. She felt calm and drained. There was no dilemma about Volkov now. No doubt, no hope left. He belonged to the other woman. He would die with her.

Remus said, 'He's taking a long time, *Matiushka*. You want me to look for him?'

'No,' Irina said. 'He hasn't run away. He wouldn't leave her.'

As the door opened she turned slowly. She ground out her half-smoked cigarette on the carpet, and held out both hands when she saw the wooden box.

The point of the silver knife pricked Volkov's back.

'Let her go, Irina,' he begged. 'Don't punish her for what I've done.'

There was a smile on her lips. 'The cross,' she said. 'Give it to me.'

Volkov lifted the lid and plunged his hand inside. He brought the cross out into the light. It flashed red fire. He stepped close and put it into her outstretched hand. As she grasped it, he sprang at her. The cross fell to the ground. He had her arms pinned down and the knife point was aimed at her throat.

'Tell him to untie her,' he said. He crushed her hard with his left arm. 'Go on, tell him to let her go! Or by the Holy Christ I'll kill you.'

He was gripping the handle of the knife so hard his knuckles were bone white under the skin; she felt the muscles holding her go taut. He raised the knife to strike. His strength was manic; she could hardly get her breath. She opened her mouth and found strength of her own.

'Kill her, Remus!'

But the arm had fallen away from Lucy's throat. Remus had left her. He was staring at the cross. Volkov held the knife suspended. The man bent down and picked it up.

'My cross!' he said. 'That's my cross!'

'Remus,' Irina screamed at him. 'You heard me. Kill her!'

He didn't move. He was staring at the Relic. 'Gold and fucking jewels,' he said and a grin spread over his face. 'I'll be rich!'

'You'll be punished,' Irina hissed at him. 'You'll go back to the Gulag. Do as you're ordered!'

He glanced at her. The little eyes were bloodshot and gleamed with cunning.

'You made a dog out of me. You made me lick your feet. Now you want to steal my cross.' His voice rose to an infuriated roar. 'You don't give me orders any more, you bitch! You're not stealing my cross!'

He lunged at her and Volkov dropped his knife. The man struck with lightning speed at Irina's windpipe. It shattered and she fell.

'Not Remus!' the man cried. 'Boris!'

The watcher heard the shouting. It was time for him to act. He came up to the windows at a run, his weapon at the ready.

Volkov rushed over to Lucy. He unfastened the straps and urged her to make a run for it.

But it was useless. She was in a state of shock, unable to move.

Boris stood in the middle of the room, Irina dead at his feet, holding the cross up to the light. He looked a them and smiled. It was a terrifying sight. He looked like a happy child.

'I gave it to the kid. I gave it to Yuri. I thought they'd shoot me. But there was a bastard of an officer – he said, "Not this one – he's strong! We'll work him till he drops dead in his own shit." But I fooled them, I didn't die.' He glared round him, and his voice rose in fury. 'I did their dirty work. They scrambled my brains and I did what *she* told me . . .' he turned and kicked Irina's body.

'They sent me to a stinking hole as a reward – no doctor, no medicine, just a stinking dusty hole. I saw my kids die. My woman cried . . . But now, I've got my cross back. My cross!' The rage died in him; he gurgled with laughter. 'It's going to make me rich!'

The watcher took in the scene in seconds. The woman dead, the targets still alive, the goon gloating over something red and gold. He moved nearer.

Boris heard the sudden movement, and sensed an attacker.

The burst of close range shots caught him in the chest. He spun and staggered under the impact. The cross slipped out of his hand. He gave a terrible roar of rage and anguish. With a burst of superhuman strength he threw himself on the watcher before he could fire again. His hands found the man's throat and locked around it in his death throes.

The two men crashed to the ground. Boris lay, a dead weight, upon the watcher's body.

He had managed to break his neck before he died.

There was no report of any crime. The network in France had no information for Moscow. Since the last radio message to Carteret, Jersey had gone silent. The Warren house was closed up. Volkov and Lucy had disappeared. So had Irina's team.

Leon Gusev was very nervous. He didn't sleep. His work suffered. He considered himself a ruined man for having agreed to Rakovsky's plan. Now it seemed as insane as it appeared brilliant at the time. He fretted and wondered whether he might help his case by confessing his part in the failure before he was actually arrested. It meant denouncing Viktor, but even so – Viktor understood his feelings.

Viktor sent for him three days before the Makoff Galleries private view. He offered him whisky. Gusev refused it. He didn't have to pander to him now. Besides he hated the taste of the stuff. Viktor had been drinking a lot of it lately.

'Well, Leon, you'll be out of your misery soon.'

'How?' Gusev asked him.

'The reception is on Thursday. If Volkov's going to make an entrance, that's where he'll do it. Our embassy has a man in place there. On the catering staff.'

He actually laughed. Gusev felt his stomach heave.

'Volkov will come out of hiding,' Viktor went on. 'He'll appear among the faithful like Jesus, walking through the walls into the upper room – with the Holy Relic to prove he's risen from the dead.'

He finished his drink.

'With the connivance of the British, of course. They must have been waiting for us in Jersey. My guess is our three are dead. They wouldn't have been taken alive.'

Gusev saw a faint hope.

He said, 'The British will not want to foment trouble for us. They may be holding him so he can't come out in to the open. They don't want to see bloody revolution here!'

'We've already sounded them out.' Viktor retorted.

Gusev looked up frowning.

'I didn't know.'

'I reported the whole business as soon as it went wrong,' Viktor said calmly. 'Before you had a chance to make up your mind to do it. We're not living in the old days. We wouldn't be shot or sent to the Arctic circle. Just retired and disgraced for failing in our duty. You can be honest with our President. So whatever happens, we're prepared. No, the British didn't respond. If they wanted to avoid trouble for us, he could have been quietly deported. They said nothing. They knew nothing. Which means they have him. He's in England and by Thursday he'll be in London. Don't worry, Leon. I emphasized your resistance to the plan. You won't get promoted, but you won't be posted to Armenia either.'

He stood up. 'What worries me is how did the British know? Our security was absolute.'

'Müller?' Leon Gusev suggested.

'No,' Viktor dismissed it. 'He only knew Volkov had left Switzerland. How could he know about Jersey?'

'He knew about St Vladimir's Cross,' Gusev pointed out. 'If he tipped off the British, they'd expect Volkov and Warren to end up there to collect it.'

Rakovsky sat down again, and stared at the brightly polished toe cap of his shoe. He was a fastidious dresser.

'You think he's turned double?'

'You've run him for years. You know him. Do you think it's possible?'

'In the beginning he worked for a political ideal,' Viktor said slowly. 'But for a long time I've felt he was working for money. He's greedy. I think you could be right, Leon. We'll look into it. He has one little job left to do for me. After that . . .'

He gave Gusev a cold smile. 'I'll find a way to retire him.'

He had introduced himself as Ian Freemantle. He was representing the Foreign Office. His companion, James Harper, was from the Home Office. The head of the Jersey police force brought them in his car.

Volkov saw them come up the steps of the old manor house, two tall men in lightweight suits, with briefcases in their hands. He recognized officialdom at a high level.

The police had made him and Lucy very comfortable. She'd been treated for shock and the injury to her hands, and she was recovering well. They weren't under arrest, but it was accepted that they wouldn't leave the house.

'You realize, Mr Volkov, that you've put Her Majesty's Government in a very awkward position?' Freemantle said.

'I know,' Volkov agreed.

'You have asked for political asylum at a most sensitive time in our relations with the Soviet government.'

'I know that, too,' he answered. 'I'm sorry. But they did try to murder us.'

Freemantle had been shown the photographs of the dead Soviet agents, and the equipment and weaponry found at the watcher's hidden campsite. A serious KGB operation within British territory. That was very awkward, too. The Jersey police had given him graphic details of the ordeal suffered by Lucy Warren, a British subject. Their attitude had been aggressively sympathetic to the Russian and the girl.

'You are also an illegal immigrant. Miss Warren has committed a serious offence in that respect.'

He saw Volkov flush angrily.

'She was trying to save my life. Is that a crime in your country?'

Freemantle glanced at his companion.

'No charges will be brought, Mr Volkov,' Harper said. 'My colleague was just making a point.'

Volkov looked at them with contempt.

'There have been enquiries from the Soviet authorities, un-officially, of course, and we have denied all knowledge of you up

till now.' Harper continued. 'We have been considering what line
to take, if we do decide to grant your request and admit you to
the United Kingdom as a political refugee. It poses a number of
problems. You'll attract a lot of media attention.'

Volkov remained silent.

'Worldwide, in view of your past political activities.'

'I spent a year in prison,' Volkov pointed out. 'It wasn't just
making speeches.'

'And five years in exile,' Freemantle remarked.

There was instant antagonism between him and the Russian.
He objected to the man's attitude. Britain owed him nothing. He
had the government's decision in his briefcase, but he was going
to drive a hard bargain.

'We would need assurances from you, Mr Volkov, that you
would not engage in anti-Soviet activities.'

Harper played the emollient role again.

'That means you refuse interviews and media coverage and
avoid criticism of the present Soviet regime. In other words, Mr
Volkov, we would offer you a temporary entry visa, but play
down any suggestion that you were seeking political asylum. If all
went well that visa could be extended and a request for residency
would have sympathetic consideration from the Home Office.'

'So it's your Foreign Office who's objecting to me?' Volkov
asked Freemantle.

'Legally we could have deported you. That's still an option.'

'Then you *would* get all the media attention,' the Jerseyman
spoke up. 'I don't think it would look good for any of us. And I
don't believe that the States here would sanction any action of
that sort, sir.' He made the last word sound an insult. 'We have
kept the facts of the case *sub judice* as you asked, but I don't
think I could guarantee that, if any force was used against Mr
Volkov.'

'There's no question of force,' Harper interposed. It was clear
that he was the senior of the two, and Freemantle was obliged to
retract. 'Is there, Ian? I think you meant it hypothetically, didn't
you?'

'It didn't sound like that to me,' the Jerseyman said.

'Then I expressed it badly,' Freemantle capitulated. 'I felt Mr

Volkov's attitude was provocative. There is no question of him being deported.' He looked disdainful. 'What my department is anxious to avoid is embarrassment to the Soviet President at the present time. There are a number of anti-Soviet activists making a nuisance of themselves already.'

James Harper stood up. 'Perhaps you'd like time to think about it?' he said to Volkov. 'Your country has made remarkable progress in the last few years. People are enjoying a degree of freedom that was unthinkable before Mikhail Gorbachev. Surely the last thing to do is destabilize the situation and give the hardliners their chance to put the clock back. If you could see this attempt to silence you in that perspective, Mr Volkov, you might take a different view. I understand that one of the participants was your wife. There must have been a personal element in the attack on you and Miss Warren. Why not consider the wider implications? We're at Government House until tomorrow morning. We can call back later.'

Volkov didn't answer. Then he said, 'You'll give me a visa if I promise to say nothing to call attention to myself. In other words to stay quietly in the background. Is that what you mean?'

'Yes. That is exactly what we mean. Please give it careful thought.'

Volkov didn't leave his chair to shake hands with them. He waited till the room was empty before he got to his feet. He watched them out of the window, the Establishment personified, getting into the official car, driving away to their rendezvous with the governor of the island.

Then he went upstairs to Lucy's bedroom.

'Have they gone?'

She came towards him. He'd wanted her to be present, but that was not allowed.

He nodded.

She looked so pale and frail after that terrible experience.

'What did they say?' she asked.

He was tempted to lie. But he had never lied to her.

'They'll give me a temporary visa – with conditions. One of them threatened me with deportation,' He silenced her anxious gasp, 'No, no my darling, it was only a threat. Our friend, the

217

commissioner, soon stopped that. He's a real friend. They can't send me back, but they can keep me here until after the meeting in London. It's the day after tomorrow.'

Lucy looked up at him. He was over-protective. She insisted she was strong, and recovered mentally as well as physically.

'What conditions?'

'No publicity. No statements. Nothing critical of the Russian regime. I can stay in England as a private individual so long as I keep quiet.'

'You can't do that,' she said. 'You have the Relic, you can't accept those terms! It would be Geneva all over again!'

'We could make a life together,' he said slowly. 'There'd be another opportunity – later, when you're recovered properly. My darling, I can't involve you in any more. I can't stop thinking of what happened – and it was my fault. I brought you into danger. I'm not going to do it again.'

'Volkov,' Lucy said, 'Listen to me. I went looking for you. I started this – I put *your* life on the line. And we're going to see it through together. You've got to attend that meeting. When they come back, say you've decided on a quiet life. Agree to everything so long as they fly us out tomorrow and we get to London in time. If you don't you'll have betrayed yourself and everything you believe in. And what that brute did to me will be for nothing.'

He drew her close and kissed her.

'We're together,' she reminded him. 'That's what we promised after that dreadful day. Promise me. No going back.'

'I promise. In my heart I hoped you'd say that. I'll lie in my teeth to the "gentlemen" from London. I'll go to the meeting.'

'And when you get there,' Lucy asked him, 'what are you going to do?'

'There are a lot of things I want to say. It won't be the speech I wrote in Geneva. The Ukraine doesn't need a rabble rouser, or a martyr. The people want statesmen, politicians who can get the better of Moscow. That's what I'm going to tell Mischa and the rest of them.'

*

218

Freemantle and Harper caught the morning plane back to Heathrow.

'I never thought he'd give in so tamely,' Harper said, settling into his seat after take-off.

'I'm not so sure he has,' Freemantle countered. 'The girl's father was a bloody nuisance even before Perestroika. All these *emigrés* are the same. They love to sabre-rattle, while we have to cope with the mess afterwards. We'll have to keep a sharp eye on them.'

Harper opened his newspaper.

'There's not a lot we can do about it if he does,' he said.

'He's really got up your nose, hasn't he Ian? Forget about it. We've got the undertaking signed; we've done our bit.'

They'd been booked in to a hotel in South Kensington. Special Branch reported that they'd done a little shopping and spent their first evening quietly at the hotel. At six the following evening, they left in a taxi and were followed to the Makoff Galleries in St James's Street. There was a private view of pre-Revolutionary photographs and memorabilia.

At ten minutes past eight, the Press and the first television crews gathered outside the galleries. Ian Freemantle was on his way home to Sussex, listening to the car radio when he heard the news. He changed gears with such force that they screeched in protest.

'The bastard!' he said. 'I knew we couldn't trust him!'

It happened after they'd been to the theatre and to supper. Peter Müller had chosen a new play and booked a table at an intimate little nightspot where a pianist played sentimental music and couples could inch their way round a tiny square of dance floor. The play was witty and frankly erotic. He noticed how often Eloise laughed, turning to smile at him.

At one moment he bent close and whispered, 'I'm sorry. I didn't realize it was going to be so naughty.'

'It's delicious,' she murmured.

219

Müller's wife was involved with a charity meeting and couldn't come with them. Their dinner at the Hofburg had been a great success, but instinctively Müller knew Eloise wasn't ready. She was still conscious of her widowhood, still loyal to Adolph's memory. But he could feel the sexual restlessness in her, and the constant moistening of her lips with the tip of her tongue made him sweat with desire.

He was going to have her that night, he knew it. He thought she probably knew it, too. The play set the mood for the slow piano music and the body contact as they circled, hardly moving, their cheeks close together, his pelvis pushed forward till their groins were touching. She must feel him through her thin dress.

At her door he asked her softly, making his voice very low, 'May I come in?'

He discovered that she wanted him to be strong and insistent, to take command of her. Once only, as he abandoned her wet mouth for her throat and neck, did Eloise protest.

'We shouldn't,' she murmured.

'Adolph wouldn't mind,' Müller said. 'He'd want you to be happy.'

It was better than he'd imagined. He lay in Adolph's bed and made love to her until he was drained and slack. But he didn't sleep. When she dozed off he woke her with powerful caresses, demanding that she service him. She was imaginative. She surprised and delighted him. She filled him with fresh energy and at last he exhausted her.

There was no sham about her when she slept. She lay back with her mouth open and snored. Müller whispered to her. He stroked her. She didn't move. The rhythmic ugly breathing didn't check even for a second. She slept as if she was drugged. Carefully he got out of bed. He drew on his trousers and slipped on surgical gloves. He paused by the bedroom door and waited, listening. She was not going to wake till the morning.

He had made this journey in his imagination many times. The long corridor leading to the ballroom. He had brought a pencil torch with him; the tiny spotlight was enough. He moved on, barefoot without a sound.

There was the first consul table, the bluejohn vase, its ormolu mounts gleaming in the beam of light. The third gilded flower head on the left of the larger carving. He pressed it cautiously and it moved under his finger. The second consul table, its vase, its carved flowers. To the right this time. Again the slight depression as he touched the flower.

One more to go. And there it was. The bronze elephant clock, its trunk rising lewdly in the torch light, its clockface in the centre of the gilded howdah. He had steady hands, but they were sticky with sweat in the tight gloves. With a tentative finger he moved the minute hand. The clock chimed. He jumped back. He'd forgotten the chime. It sounded so loud in the heavy silence. He shone his torch on the ballroom door and turned the handle. It opened. He closed it behind him. He didn't dare switch on the lighting system. There was a security guard on patrol outside the house. The insurance company had won that battle.

He followed the spot of light until he was in front of the cabinet and the treasures inside it sparkled as the beam played over them. It was never locked, because Brückner liked to open it at will and handle his possessions. He loved the feel of the Fabergé animals. He was fond of saying so to Müller.

He lifted out the clock and the calendar. They fitted into each of his pockets. He took a deep breath. Now, everything in reverse. The clock set to twelve-thirty. Another nerve-tingling chime, but this time he was prepared for it. Third gilded flower on the left of the consul table going back, third flower on the right of the next one.

The room was alarmed again. The theft wouldn't be discovered until someone went into the ballroom. That could be weeks. He crept back to the bedroom, peeled off the gloves, transferred the little objects to his jacket. She hadn't moved. He stepped out of his trousers and joined her in the bed.

He couldn't leave the house before she woke: he wanted it to be a memorable leave-taking.

'I'm going to fly to Kiev and meet him,' Viktor Rakovsky said. 'I'm to welcome him home. That's the official line.'

No action had been taken against Viktor. Not even a rebuke.

Dimitri Volkov, followed by a planeload of media from all over the world was on his way back to the capital of the Ukraine. Viktor was clever, but not as clever as the master tactician who was directing him. Volkov must be walking in to a subtle trap, a political embrace that would eventually crush him.

Leon Gusev said, 'Why didn't he produce the Relic? What's he planning? So far we've heard him saying the same thing to everyone. I'm going home to offer myself in the service of my fellow Ukrainians. If they'll accept me. All good humble stuff and the West are loving it. He's the biggest hero since Solzhenitsyn. The nationalists are planning a big demonstration. He's just what Rykhoh wanted.'

'What Rykhoh doesn't want is for the government to upstage them, and that is what we're going to do. I'm leading a group of Politburo members and we'll be there to shake his hand as he steps off the plane. We're not going to make a martyr of him, whatever he does. We had our chance and we bungled it. Thanks to Müller's treachery.'

It was the accepted view that their agent, Peter Müller, had warned British Intelligence of the attack planned in Jersey. It had mitigated the official anger at the failure of Viktor's department.

'And if he preaches sedition, with the Relic as a rallying point? Are we going to kiss and hug him because of what the West thinks? I can't see it working. I can only see disaster.'

'That's what I said to the President,' Viktor admitted.

'*Then I am relying on you, Viktor Alexzandrovich, to see it doesn't happen.*' That was the response. He hadn't repeated it to Leon. Leon was still young and inclined to be nervous. He suffered from the legacy of the past.

'I'm leaving in half an hour,' Viktor said. 'You can watch it all on television.'

He waited alone for the official car to take him to Sheremetov airport. They were catching the internal flight to Kiev, scheduled to arrive an hour before the Illuyshin jet came in from London. Volkov had made a point of refusing Western air transport. 'I'm a Russian. I shall go home on a Russian aircraft.'

He'd said that during a final interview. Bringing his wife. He had married Yuri Varienski's daughter in a Catholic ceremony in

London. That closed the file on Irina. It was significant to Rakovsky that none of the activists who'd been present at the Makoff Galleries when he called the Press and television, was coming to the Ukraine with him. None had asked for entry visas. Whatever Volkov was planning, he was doing it alone.

Only the Relic could have given him this new authority, the steadfast sense of purpose that came across in every interview. Volkov was no longer the firebrand who'd talked himself into arrest and persecution. Viktor had monitored every appearance before the television cameras and studied every word. This was a man with a mission and the maturity to accomplish it.

He'd noted his wife, too; she had dignity and a quiet beauty. They were a disturbing pair. She must be an unusual woman, Viktor judged, to have rescued the lost soul in Geneva and inspired him to escape and take up the challenge. She looked as if she'd suffered some baptism of fire. He recognized the marks it left; he'd borne them himself all his life.

Müller had sent the desk set back to Moscow via the embassy. For a few hours it had stood on Viktor's desk in the same room in the Lubiyanka where Lepkin had wound the clock and changed the calendar every day, until he brought them home to the house in the woods and gave them to Viktor's mother. He remembered his mother putting the clock and the calendar on the shelf above the stove. His brother, Stefan, had been forbidden to handle them. He himself was content to draw the exquisite trifles and admire them from a distance.

He found he couldn't bear to look at them. By the evening he had formally presented the Fabergé set to the State and it was put on display in the Hermitage Museum in Leningrad. It was out of the reach of human greed.

It was time to leave. He went down in the lift and out on to the square, where his car was waiting. At the intersection he joined the cavalcade of officials on their way to the airport. The Illuyshin had left London on time and would touch down on schedule.

*

Susan Müller picked up the telephone.

'Hello?'

'This is Eloise Brückner.'

She wasn't really concentrating.

'Hello, how are you? I'm just watching this Russian arrive on television. Isn't it fascinating?'

'I want to speak to Peter. I've been robbed!'

'How terrible!' Susan Müller exclaimed, still eyeing the screen. The jet had landed and was taxiing along the runway. A group of men were gathering on the tarmac.

'Look, Eloise, could I call you back?'

'No.' The voice was shrill. 'Just tell Peter I know he did it. I'm going to the police.'

Susan immediately forgot about the scene at Borispol airport.

'Peter? You've got a goddamned nerve. You must be crazy!'

'I showed him how the alarm worked.' Eloise's voice was rising hysterically. 'He's the only person who could have done it. He stole the desk set! The first night he slept with me! Just tell him, he's not going to get away with it!'

The line went dead. Slowly Müller's wife put the phone down. *'The first night he slept with me.'* Her husband had told her he'd bought back the gold boxes and sold them immediately for a huge profit. He had assured her that when he stayed the night it was only to comfort a nervous woman. She believed him when he said that it was always innocent. She wanted to believe him. And he had stopped seeing Eloise Brückner. She was becoming too demanding, he explained. It was time to phase out.

'Oh, Peter,' she said. 'You shit. Just for business!'

She switched the set off. After a few minutes she calmed down. She was a practical woman. Anyway, if he had screwed the bitch, he'd soon dropped her. That's why she was accusing him. He would never be involved in anything like theft.

She rang Müller at the shop and told him what had happened.

'I can explain,' he said. 'Don't worry. I'll talk to her.'

He sent the prints round to the Brückner house by special courier. He put a note inside the envelope: *'My dear, I thought you might like to have these as a memento of our wonderful first night together. I treasure my set. Peter.'*

When they woke that first morning he had persuaded her to pose for him. She had been excited by the idea. 'We can look at them together,' he'd suggested. She had adopted every erotic pose he suggested and then photographed him naked in turn. She had supplied the camera from one of Adolph's collection. They'd joked about it. A little different from his holiday snaps. She wouldn't put *them* in the album. Best of all, since Adolph was such an enthusiast, it was possible to take photographs by remote control. Müller had staged a series of unusual couplings, which the camera recorded. Eloise Brückner wouldn't go to the police and risk these photographs being produced as evidence. He wasn't in the least alarmed by her threat.

In their apartment overlooking the Bremner Canal, the Dutch couple were also watching television.

'Isn't it amazing, Derk,' she turned to him. They were side by side watching the replay on Amsterdam television. 'Just think, we helped that man get out of France!'

'I know,' he said. 'It makes you feel part of history. Nobody'd believe us if we told them.'

His wife smiled broadly.

'I've told everyone!' she announced. 'Your sister says I should write about it for the newspapers.'

'No, Beta, you mustn't do anything like that! We don't want a lot of journalists asking us questions. We were just doing a kindness. We leave it at that, eh?'

'All right, but it's amazing all the same. They're coming out of the plane now. Look at all those people!'

'Ssssh,' he admonished. 'Beta, listen to the commentary.'

She had a bad habit of talking through a programme, if she got excited.

'I'm nervous,' Lucy whispered to him as the plane door opened and the stewardess beckoned them forward.

'Me too,' he admitted. 'It's so long since I've been home. Last time I left in handcuffs.'

The sunlight was blinding as they came down the steps and on to the tarmac at Borispol. They saw the flashing cameras and the television crews behind a simple barrier. He breathed in the earthy sun of his country, the whiff of dust and pine trees borne on a hot breeze, and suddenly his heart lifted and he was happy. He caught her hand and walked towards the group of dignitaries: the President of the Ukrainian parliament and his deputy; bureaucrats, one high-ranking army officer, and another smaller group ahead of them all. The representatives of Central Government in Moscow, making his welcome official. There were handshakes, warm smiles. The media captured every moment of it. Viktor Rakovsky was almost the last to greet him.

'Welcome back,' he said. 'I represent our Foreign Ministry. There's a reception and a Press conference arranged for you. I hope you had a smooth flight?'

'Very smooth,' Volkov said. He brought Lucy forward. 'My wife,' he said.

Viktor shook her hand. He wondered how Irina had died.

'Welcome to the Soviet Union, Comrade Volkova.'

She answered him in Russian. 'Thank you.'

It had all been arranged beforehand.

Viktor said, 'Before we go in to meet the Press, I'd like to speak to you in private. Just a few minutes.'

'I thought you'd suggest something like that. What ministry are you representing?' Volkov looked at him coldly. 'I believe you were a friend of my late wife's father.'

'I've known all the family for a long time,' Viktor answered. There was a dark hatred in Volkov's gaze. His task was not going to be easy. 'This way.'

He ushered them ahead of him; his manner was friendly, even deferential. They were VIPs and they entered the exclusive lounge reserved for the highest Party members when they used the airport.

'A drink?' he enquired. 'What would you like? We have excellent Russian champagne or vodka.'

'I don't drink,' Volkov said.

Lucy shook her head.

226

'Then I'll have to toast to your homecoming on my own,' Viktor said.

He poured a measure of vodka into a glass and raised it to them.

'What do you want from me?' Volkov cut the pantomine short.

'I want your assurance that you haven't come back to cause civil unrest in the Ukraine.'

Viktor had dropped the pose. He stood taller than Dimitri Volkov. He was a man of years and hard authority facing an adversary.

'I bring you a message from the President himself. We welcome you back. We apologize for the harsh way you were treated in the past. We hope you will forgive and forget, and agree to work towards a Russia where such things can never happen again. If your intention is to stir up unrest, then we are not going to stop you. That's the measure of the changes Mikhail Gorbachev has made. You speak a lot about democracy and justice, Comrade Volkov. You always did, when there was no hope of either under the old system. That is being swept away. But we need peace to do it. Peace and stability. Any other way means bloodshed and misery. Are you prepared for that?'

To his surprise it was Lucy who answered. 'Dimitri would never want that!'

Viktor said quietly, 'Have you brought the Relic with you?'

'I think it's time for the Press conference,' Volkov replied.

'One more question, Comrade Volkov. What happened to your activist friends in London? They've left you to lead their crusade on your own.'

Volkov took Lucy by the hand.

'They didn't like my speech.'

Viktor opened the door for them and stood aside. He watched as Volkov took his place before the journalists and television crews. He looked very slight standing there with the lights beating down on him. Viktor moved closer to the woman who was responsible for it all. She was watching Volkov; she didn't seem to notice him standing beside her.

'I've heard his broadcasts from London,' he remarked. 'He's a fine speaker.'

'Yes,' Lucy answered. 'He speaks as he thinks.'

'You know what he's going to say?'

'We wrote it together.'

'With help from your friends in British Intelligence?'

'They're no friends of ours!'

Her vehemence surprised Viktor. For a moment, they turned their attention to the Ukrainian President, who was paying tribute to Volkov's stand against tyranny.

'We understood they saved his life in Jersey,' said Viktor.

She stared at him. 'It was the cross that saved us. They came when it was all over. We owe them nothing!'

He believed her. Perhaps Müller hadn't betrayed them after all.

'I don't want to talk about it,' she said. 'My husband is going to speak now.'

Volkov glanced briefly at his sheaf of notes and put them away in his pocket. He adjusted the microphone, and looked out over the expectant faces, the TV cameras, the journalists, with their notebooks ready.

A slight flush appeared on his cheeks; he brushed his hair back from his forehead. In the audience Lucy tensed, knowing the gesture so well. Then he spoke, and his voice was clear and resonant.

'My friends. Thank you for your kind words and your welcome. I would never have believed I'd live to see this day.' He paused, and took the notes out of his pocket again. 'I wrote all this when I knew I was coming home. With help from my wife, who's here with me. But I don't need any notes. I can speak from my heart. When you've been silent for five long years, you can't imagine you'll ever stand up, face an audience and talk openly again.

'I left this country in handcuffs.

'But I was luckier than many of my friends who weren't sent into exile. Some are still in prison. Most of them are dead.

'Times have changed, they told me. Russia has changed. I have to accept that because I'm here. But as long as one man or woman is in prison because of their beliefs, then nothing has really changed.

'The President has spoken about what happened to me. He talked about injustice and suffering. But for seventy years we have all been in chains. My country, the Ukraine, was perhaps the worst victim of oppression. Our culture, our religion, our land were all taken from us. Millions died. Stalin built upon their bones. But our people refused to abandon hope, held on to their faith that one day they would be free.

'I suffered, but I survived. I've witnessed cruelty and wickedness, but I've also seen courage, nobility, and love.' He paused and sought out Lucy in the crowd. Her blue eyes were fixed upon him. He raised his voice.

'In Europe the people have torn down the prison walls and cast off their chains. Just as we must do now.'

Volkov felt the silence. No one moved. They had gambled and lost.

'My experience is living proof of the folly of violence. Violence achieves nothing. It degrades us, if we have any part in it. It is self-defeating because the human spirit cannot be crushed for ever.

'For myself I forgive the past. I want to serve my people, if they'll have me. I want to devote my life to the cause of liberty, of every man's right to speak his mind and to live without fear. I have no political ambitions. I belong to no organization. I have no supporters. Only my wife, to help me. I am home and I look with hope to the future. But first, I have brought something with me that belongs to the Ukraine.'

If only I had a gun, Viktor Rakovsky thought, I'd kill him now . . .

He heard Volkov clear his throat, and give a little cough.

'But what I have brought home doesn't just belong to the Ukraine. It belongs to Russia and to all the Russian people.' He looked straight at Viktor. 'If the President of our Parliament will escort us we'd like to go now to the Cathedral of St Sophia.'

Someone started to clap. Soon they were all applauding. Rakovsky came face to face with him for a moment. 'I misjudged you, Volkov,' he said to himself. 'You are a patriot.' Then he stepped back into the crowd and walked away.

It was over. The media had departed. The demonstration organized by the Ukrainian nationalist party had dispersed with a feeling of anti-climax. St Sophia's Cathedral had emptied, the arc lights were dismantled, the commentators were gone; the Patriarch had made a speech and announced plans for a Mass of thanksgiving.

The Volkovs had retreated to a hotel suite provided for them. They refused all invitations for the evening.

St Vladimir's Cross glowed red inside its shrine above the high altar. People of all ages started coming in little groups to stare up at it.

Many stayed to pray.